CW00405594

Gorleston

Gorleston

HENRY SUTTON

SCEPTR

Lyrics from 'Crazy', by Willie Nelson ©, by permission of Sony Music Publishing UK

First published in 1995 by Hodder and Stoughton
A division of Hodder Headline PLC
A Sceptre Book

10 9 8 7 6 5 4 3 2 1

British Library Cataloguing in Publication Data

Sutton, Henry
Gorleston
I. Title
823 [F]

ISBN 0 340 64986 0

Typeset by Palimpsest Book Production Limited, Polmont, Stirlingshire
Printed and bound in Great Britain by Mackays of Chatham PLC, Chatham, Kent

Hodder and Stoughton
A division of Hodder Headline PLC
338 Euston Road
London NW1 3BH

To my grandmother, my mother,
my sister and my wife

AUTHOR'S NOTE

While Gorleston is real enough, not all the historical references in this novel should be taken as fact. Nevertheless, I am indebted to R.H. Teasdel, F.H. Emms and, more recently, A.W. Ecclestone for their fine histories, stories and notes of Gorleston, as well as to Gorleston Library and the library at Eastern Counties Newspapers. From all of these I built up my idea of the town's long past, and its short future.

Gorleston was Gorleston ere Yarmouth begun,
And will be Gorleston when Yarmouth is gone.
Anon

1

Marine Parade ran along the low Gorleston cliff top. The large detached houses, some with balconies, some with bay windows, looked out over a strip of grass which was once a crazy-golf course, and the North Sea. At the end of Marine Parade, at the end of Gorleston-on-Sea, the strip of grass turned into a carpark. A long, thin carpark that edged the cliff top.

Some people left their motors running, for the heat. Percy didn't. He found the noise distracting. He had sat in his car for over an hour. He had fallen asleep a few times, disturbed now and then by other cars parking nearby. At last he pushed himself up in his seat and looked around. Nothing much had changed. There were just a few more cars. It was morning, though Percy had given up all hope of the sun breaking through. It didn't very often. It was late November, hardly day. There wasn't a sky. The air was thick and grey and still. Below, the sea was as still and grey. There was no horizon. Just a vast greyness. Even the seagulls looked grey. And they looked tired as they circled slowly, almost silently overhead. It was as if they didn't have the energy to squawk. As if they had been stifled by the greyness. Percy had sat in his car, in this very spot, his spot, almost daily for the last year, since his wife had died, since he had little will and nothing to do any more. He liked to just sit here, on the cliff edge, looking, looking at the North Sea. She had loved the sea.

Something caught Percy's eye. He saw it again. And again. An orange blur. He could taste the salt in the wet air as he opened the car door. Stiffly he got out and walked across to the small paved upper esplanade that lined the very edge of the cliff. He peered down over the edge. He saw nothing for a while. His glasses began to mist up. He took them off, wiped them on his scarf and replaced them. Suddenly he saw a head of orange hair spring from behind a beach hut on the lower esplanade. It then shot behind another and another, weaving in and out of the faded huts. There was a man some way behind. He was struggling to keep up as the orange head moved quickly along the esplanade towards the model yacht pond, towards the beginning of Gorleston Pier.

The yacht pond was empty, baring salt-stained, cracked concrete. Percy could not now remember whether the pond had been filled the last summer. Maybe, he thought, it had been drained years ago. It looked totally forgotten. An image then came to him, of children playing on trampolines on the beach near the pond. Years and years ago. He had enjoyed watching them as much as they had enjoyed themselves. Laughing and screaming. He tried to remember when it could have been, and as he thought harder he began to wonder whether it was Gorleston after all. He wondered whether he might be confusing Gorleston with another seaside town. The children playing on trampolines elsewhere, in another time. For children played here no longer.

Percy had only been to Gorleston a few times before he and his wife moved here. He had never much cared for the place. But for a long time he had known he would end up here. End his life here, he supposed. His wife wanted to move here. Elizabeth had loved Gorleston. And he would have followed her anywhere.

The person with orange hair, whom Percy had decided was a young girl, was now making her way along Gorleston Pier. She was skipping. The man, her father perhaps, was still some way behind. He watched until they had both passed the harbour-master's look-out and sat down together on a capstan at the end of the pier, before he walked back to his car. It was the way the small girl with orange hair moved that struck him. So sure-footed, so quick. But something was not quite right. He felt unsure.

Though troubled he shortly fell asleep again, secure in the bright velour of the driver's seat. He didn't dream, but when he woke he didn't know where he was for a few moments. He sat up and waited for his eyes to get used to the greyness. Then he remembered the girl with orange hair, and feeling unsure. He looked out, far into the greyness, trying to find the end of Gorleston Pier. It seemed she had gone. The pier was deserted. The North Sea was deserted. There was not a trawler or ship in sight. Just a cold, damp ache. Percy wanted it to rain. He wanted the sky to open up. It all seemed so heavy.

He started the Vauxhall Cavalier and manoeuvred out of the carpark, past other cars he had come to recognise. He didn't wave or nod at the occupants, even though he knew every wrinkle on their empty faces. Nobody ever did. Everybody just stared at those arriving and departing and then resumed their watch over the North Sea, over nothingness. He pulled into Marine Parade and drove through the quietness towards the town centre. He saw two old women, wrapped-up and waiting by a bus stop. And he noticed pink paint peeling off the gate posts of a house about halfway along Marine Parade, just before the Links Hotel. The same paint was also peeling off the window frames and balcony railings. The house was dirty white and two thick lines had been painted across the front just below the flat roof. The lines were light blue, and they were wavy. He slowed the car to a crawl. There was something sad and desolate, something sunken about the house. He had driven along Marine Parade countless times over the last two years, but until now he had never noticed it. He wondered who, if anybody, still lived here. He wondered about who had lived here.

Wondering, he drove on. In the thick half light Marine Parade was almost eerie. There's nobody here, there's nobody here, he sung to himself. Though he spotted signs of life past the Links Hotel, signs of neat human lives. And his spirits lifted. Some houses had pink, or blue, paint that wasn't peeling off gate posts or window frames or balcony rails. Some houses had cars parked outside in driveways and forecourts, and some had windows with people peering out, peering out to sea. Some houses weren't sad at all.

Then he saw it again, the orange blur, the orange hair. Right in front of him, in the centre of the road. It was coming towards him. Fast in a dark car. He couldn't take his eyes off the colour, the brightness, his Cavalier happily continuing its course. The dark car then swerved out of his way and sped past, Percy's eyes following it all the way. Driving was the young girl. Only, she didn't look so young. This close she looked old, quite old. Sitting next to her was an elderly man, the father? Percy recognised the collar on his coat, large and upturned. But he couldn't have been her father. He couldn't. She was laughing. He saw her face, all wrinkles. She was laughing and she was smoking. Smoke plumed out of the corners of her mouth. The car was filled with smoke. He watched the dark car through his rearview mirror swerve its way into the gloomy distance. It could have been following the wavy lines on the sunken house.

It amused Percy, the way the men would talk amongst

themselves and the women would talk amongst themselves, however they were all seated. Stretching and shouting, waving, they'd communicate somehow with their own sex. Though every now and then an eyelid would flutter, someone would stammer. Someone would try to attract an old boyfriend, an old girlfriend, an old lover. Though maybe it was all imagined, or all hoped for. Tired voices searching for a sparkle. Married couples just didn't talk on their own. But they would talk to couples on other tables. And those really on their own, those widowed, would just talk, regardless of who they were sitting near, regardless of whether anyone was listening. They would talk of forgetting things and remembering things, of losing things and finding things. Objects and memories drifting in the steamy air.

'I lost my glasses three days ago,' someone would say, John Conway in fact. John was red-faced and had a loud voice he liked to use. No mistaking John. 'I wouldn't know what to do without my help Karen. She comes on Wednesdays. She's a gorgeous girl. She always finds them, my glasses. Often they're in the most unlikely places. Ha, ha.'

'I had a lovely girl working for me once,' someone else would pop in. 'She did everything. She came from a proper family. In building.'

'I see more bungalows are going over. Just breaking up and crumbling onto the beach,' yet someone else would add.

'I hated her, slovenly bitch,' someone might mumble into his food or her drink.

'And would you believe it, sure as rain, she found them this morning.' John would smile and take his glasses off and lovingly polish the lenses.

Nobody paid much attention, even those who could hear. Yet on they would talk, about television and bridge. About the weather and bingo. There was never much talk of families or pensions or politics. For here, Percy often thought, we have been forgotten, totally forgotten.

St Edmunds Hotel, at the other end of Marine Parade to the carpark and next to the Gables Nursing Home, was where everybody went for lunch. It was where Percy went for lunch since his wife no longer cooked it for him. Since he could no longer sit across the kitchen table from her. Like the Gables the outside was covered with wood beams, black with paint, that crisscrossed the cream-coloured walls in a plethora of patterns. Inside there were more patterns, on the floor and on the walls. More colours too, dark reds and shiny browns, all glowing and synthetic and sticky. And inside the Mascot Suite dining room, the very centre of Gorleston social life where lunch was variously consumed, it smelt slightly sweet. It smelt slightly of urine.

Percy picked a table by the window. He had never had a table he thought of as his, not like the others who were all most particular. He normally sat as far away from people as possible, but today he didn't care. Today, most importantly, he wanted to look out of the window. He couldn't get the old woman with orange hair out of his mind. He wondered whether he might see her again. Whether she might drive past. Perhaps with the elderly man, her husband? Perhaps she would be zigzagging down the road. He even contemplated her coming in for lunch. But it was unlikely. He had never seen her in St Edmunds before. He would have remembered. Rachel took his order. He knew her name because the other men all called her by it. 'Rachel, Rachel, over here, love,' they would shout and claw the air. She was young and pretty and popular. But Percy couldn't quite bring himself to call her Rachel. It didn't seem right.

'I'm looking for a woman with bright orange hair,' Percy cleared his throat. 'Have you ever seen her?' Rachel paused for a second before walking back to the kitchen. He presumed she hadn't heard him. Beyond ordering he never spoke to her.

'I think Karen is going to leave me.' Percy could hear John, his voice, strained, rising above the coughing and clatter. 'I know she'll be out of here before too long. She's too young to hang around in Gorleston.'

'You'll have to get another one then,' someone else said. Though Percy wasn't sure whether it was in reply, whether some sort of rapport had actually been struck up, or whether it was just another remark adrift in the dining room.

Percy's food came and he sat staring out of the window until it was quite cold and solid. He didn't feel like eating. Occasionally a blue bus passed by, the odd person staring back at him. Staring through the salty space. 'I'm looking for a woman with bright orange hair. Has anyone ever seen her?' he suddenly said, louder this time, much louder, and to no one in particular. The foursome sitting on the table immediately to his right stopped what they were doing, their loaded forks wavering in mid-air, and all looked at him. A number of other people turned Percy's way too, including John. 'An old woman with bright orange hair,' Percy added, looking up and smiling. Often people would shout out at lunchtime, they would shout all manner of things, but Percy never normally spoke. He was not surprised that people were looking at him. He wanted their attention. The room fell quite quiet as more people turned to look at him. A few mouths fell open, not all were empty. 'She drives a dark car. Rather fast and rather badly.' In the quietness again he could hear breathing, gravelly, difficult breathing, heaving really.

'I know who she is,' John said. Everyone turned to look at John, who had half risen from his chair. 'I know who she is. She's Toots Wharton's sister. But I don't think they speak.'

Percy knew who Toots Wharton was. Everybody did. He

had seen her in the dining room having lunch with her husband Charlie. He had seen Toots and Charlie Wharton at the Links Hotel. He had never spoken to them but he had seen John talking to them. And once he had seen them arrive at the Links in a sky blue Mercedes. Charlie, he remembered, was large but not fat, with lots of white hair. Toots was large too, and she piled her mauve hair on top of her head which made her look even taller. She always seemed to be talking. Her voice was vast and she accentuated her vowels. Even from the other end of the bar Percy would hear her, the unmistakable sound of her voice drawing out words. Her loud and desperate attempt to sound posh.

'The Wharton bungalow will be next down the cliff,' John said, standing proudly now. 'And I reckon the rest of Cliff Lane will follow shortly. Those cliffs are giving way so fast there's nothing that can stop them now. Not even Toots.'

'She's crazy,' a faint female voice offered. Percy looked around, but he had no idea who spoke. Or who was crazy.

Percy felt a companionship, solidarity even, with his car, the Vauxhall Cavalier. It was neither flashy nor fast. He didn't want a big Mercedes, bright blue, like Toots and Charlie had. Indeed, he was quite proud of the way his car was so unassuming, so conforming. The way it fitted in so easily. It was mustard yellow and always started. It had been his company car and it had retired with him. His wife hadn't been so proud of it, though. Elizabeth would have been happier with something a little special. She could be stern and difficult but she liked colour, she liked extravagant touches, gestures. Still, he had managed to resist her pleas to change it. He didn't see the point. He didn't like change.

Percy intended to pull into the carpark as usual. To stare at the numbing sea, and nod off. The day wasn't as grey as it had been for days, for weeks even. The thickness had lifted. The air was clearer, crisper. He could see further. As he drove along Marine Parade the North Sea appeared, patched in shade, rippling out towards Holland. He could see the horizon. There was a ship, its towering bridge topped by a funnel, seemingly motionless in the middle. He wondered where it had come from, Rotterdam, Hamburg, Gdansk maybe. He knew where it was going. If he parked and waited long enough he would see it glide into Great Yarmouth harbour. But he was feeling impatient. He passed the carpark and the great line of cars, all of which he recognised, at the end of Marine Parade and he turned inland into Yallop Avenue. He had to.

As Yallop Avenue retreated from the sea the houses became more confident, crazy chimneys ran up outside walls, glazed-in frosted porches hid front doors, miniature windmills and rockeries decorated front gardens. And then, as Yallop Avenue swung round so it ran parallel to the sea, the bungalows started. Neat and compact. The only flourishes were gaily painted window frames and garden ornaments carefully arranged in the small front gardens, all chained off from the outside world. Percy pulled over and stopped the car by a small lane on his left. Cliff Lane was the end of Gorleston. Many people regarded it as the beginning of Hopton. It ran straight down to the crumbling cliff edge. He felt like walking. The air was not too damp and on days like this his arthritis seemed to abate. He was not in pain. It was late morning, lunchtime. Interior lights gleamed. The bungalows at the beginning of Cliff Lane were chalets really, with wooden porches and pebble-dash walls. They had old rose gardens and grown-over lawns. Once, Percy thought, they must have been holiday homes. He tried to imagine the charm of a summer day in Gorleston a long time ago. Children playing in the lane. The children he and his wife never had. He often thought of children when he thought of summer. He reminded himself it was autumn.

A post van sat halfway down the lane, but the postman was nowhere to be seen. Beyond the van the bungalows began to expand, spreading far and low, seemingly in defiance of the advancing North Sea. Many of these great bungalows had satellite dishes planted in the gardens or forecourts, while some dishes were attached to garage roofs and chimneys. Percy saw the bungalow from a distance. It appeared to stretch to the end of the lane, to the cliff edge. As he walked nearer he saw the sky blue Mercedes parked in the drive, which looped round a very trim lawn and out of another gate. Now he was here he wasn't sure what to do, whether he wanted to be seen or not. There was a breeze. It was growing stronger. The end of the lane widened and was shaped in a semicircle for cars to turn around in. A wall followed the kerb, though Percy thought he could see a gap in the wall, a path perhaps. He aimed for that. Pale-green Venetian blinds were half pulled down all the windows which ran along the facade of Toots and Charlie's bungalow, and as he passed he saw the middle section of a woman walk across the window. It was Toots and he thought of a peacock. He hurried to the gap in the wall. The path was short and narrow, enclosed by a fence and a garden wall. At the end there was a wooden platform and some rickety steps that led down to the sea. He stood on the platform and suddenly felt very exposed. He clasped the rail for support, for security. From here the sea was endless.

Percy turned round. To his right he could see the side of Toots and Charlie's bungalow that faced the sea. It had French windows, a small patio and a lawn that just stopped in a ragged line some ten to fifteen yards away. He peered over the cliff edge and saw the rest of the garden down below in a dirty, grassy, sandy heap. And he thought it wouldn't indeed be too long before the bungalow started to break up and drop off, the rest of the lane rushing after it.

He walked back up the path and almost bumped into

Toots as he stepped onto Cliff Lane. Hello, he mouthed and nodded. He watched as she looked him over. Her eyes travelling from his head to his feet, then lingering in the middle. He was wearing an old overcoat and brown suede shoes. She had on a thick woollen skirt and tight fitting jumper. A pearl necklace hung over her large bosom. Her hair was a much brighter mauve than Percy had remembered, all wound up in a massive mound.

'Good afternoon,' she boomed at last. 'Afternoon,' she then added more quietly, in a strangely resonant way.

Her perfume lingered with Percy as he started to walk quickly away. It was strong and sickly. He thought of stewed violets. By the abandoned post van he looked back. She was still standing there, at the end of Cliff Lane, staring at him.

Percy was feeling flustered and hot and slightly sweaty when he got back to his car. He felt like a peep who had been caught. His heart was pounding. So he thought he was seeing things when he saw the dark coloured car that the woman with orange hair, Toots's sister, had been driving, outside a bungalow on Yallop Avenue.

There is no doubt Gorleston, on the west bank of the River Yare, was begun before Great Yarmouth. Evidence suggests Gorleston, or the ground on which Gorleston was built, was populated in palaeolithic times. Yarmouth is situated on land which did not rise out of the sea until after Christ was born, and it was not populated until the 11th century.

Sadly Gorleston will not be Gorleston when Yarmouth is gone, for Gorleston will be gone first. The North Sea, which created Yarmouth, is taking Gorleston away. Gorleston is crumbling into the North Sea. Indeed, one only has to take a walk along Cliff Lane to witness the destruction already taking place.

This is the story of Gorleston, a great town nearing the end of its life.

* * *

So she's called Queenie. Queenie, Percy said to himself. Queenie. He took a deep breath and Toots' perfume stung the back of his throat. It was the same brand, stewed violets.

'She must be back then,' Toots continued. 'And it looks as if she's got a new friend.' She raised her eyebrows at Percy, who had told Toots he thought he had seen her sister, the one with orange hair who drove a dark coloured car, a Mini Metro.

'She's a bit old for that sort of thing,' Charlie interrupted.

Toots, who Percy later found out was a few years older than Queenie, looked at her husband. 'No one's too old for that sort of thing. Age has never got in her way. But you would've thought she'd have learnt how to behave by now. She's a public nuisance. She should be put away.'

John Conway, dark red in the face, was tottering around the bar, reaching out for support now and then, hanging onto the backs of chairs and bar stools. Hanging onto Percy's jacket. Percy had come to the Links Hotel hoping to find John, hoping to find John with Toots and Charlie Wharton. He had wanted to be introduced to the Whartons, he had wanted to find out more about Toots Wharton's sister with orange hair. And it had worked, on the fourth night. He now knew her name, Queenie.

Percy knew John, like many widowers, spent most evenings in the Links Hotel, which had long ago ceased to function as a hotel. Unlike St Edmunds the Links Hotel shunned outward extravagance. There were no black beams, no fancy lights, no hopeless face-lifts. It was a plain brick, flat-roofed building, with rusting metal windows and creaking regulars who enjoyed the bar food reductions for pensioners.

Over the last few evenings Percy had watched John tell

the aging barmaids jokes. They seemed never to understand but they would laugh politely. And he watched John relay the same muddled catch-lines to strangers quietly sipping their drinks in the darker corners. Percy was becoming quite familiar with John's intonations, his gesticulations, his attempts to communicate, when the Whartons walked in at last. After some confusion Percy was introduced to Toots and Charlie. He was sure Toots recognised him from his Cliff Lane excursion. It was the way she looked at him. He soon realised she was the sort of person who remembered everything. He also realised she was the sort of person who liked to be remembered, who like to be recognised.

'Are you sure I don't look familiar?' she asked Percy. Her cheeks were flush with powder. Her eyelids a light metallic blue. Her hair quite purple, quite splendid. Unforgettable. She captivated the bar. John was no match.

Percy had made an effort to look smart all week. And he found it an effort without his wife's help, his wife's eye. She had always made him presentable, fussing over his appearance. He couldn't iron or sew or tell what went with what. He couldn't help the few stains and creases that had gathered over the last four days. What was important was the fact that he looked as smart as he could. He wanted to make an impression. He wanted Toots and Charlie to like him. He thought they might be helpful.

'Well just call me Toots anyway,' Toots said, after Percy refused to accept he found her familiar. 'Everybody does.'

Percy wanted to find out as much about Queenie as possible; he couldn't get her image out of his mind. But when he returned with a round of drinks Toots was talking about the Mercedes. 'Charlie's mistake,' she called it. 'A cousin of Charlie's said he could get one from Germany for half the price. So what happens? Charlie pays for the car up front and when it finally arrives at Yarmouth docks we find it's last year's model. And he still expects me to be driven around Gorleston in it, in last year's model. I tell you, Charlie's so stupid sometimes, he can't organise anything properly. Can you Charlie?' With that Toots poked Charlie in the stomach and cackled. Until then Charlie had stood there, almost motionless, looking at something somewhere at the far end of the bar, which was thick with smoke, or beyond.

'Toots, really,' he said. 'I thought you liked the car. You always said you liked the colour.' Charlie looked quite desperate. 'You don't know the trouble I went to.'

'Oh yes I do, Charlie, you're nothing but trouble.' Toots laughed again.

Country and Western music was playing, as it always did, and through the haze Percy could see Toots start to sway. *Deep within my heart lies a melody*. He had begun to appreciate the music, the desperateness of it. Country and Western fitted the Links Hotel, Gorleston even. *Where in dreams I live with a memory*. Still swaying, Toots told Percy she and Charlie used to own a farm in Cambridgeshire, a Fen farm which was rich and flat. 'I don't like real country,' she said, 'the Fens were just right. You always knew where you were. You could always see where you were going.' She threw her head back, the purple plume lilting, and lurched forward. Percy braced himself, but she pushed past him and made her way to the bar, where she joined a fancily dressed couple. He watched as she squeezed herself between them. 'Well I never,' he heard her say. And like some refrain he heard her say it again. 'Well I never.' *Beneath the stars all alone*.

Charlie shuffled closer to Percy. He too seemed to be swaying on his large feet, naturally, unconsciously. He kept looking at Percy, as if he wanted to say something, but didn't know what, or was too shy. But Percy wanted to talk to Charlie and he saw his chance. 'I don't have much of a family left.' He thought of his wife. Her face flashed before him. For so long she had been all the family he had known, but that had been enough. 'What about you Charlie? Tell me about your family.'

Charlie looked up at the ceiling, yellow with nicotine and damp, and then steadied himself. 'Family. There's only one family that counts around here,' he said, looking at Percy properly for the first time, his eyes as yellow as the ceiling. 'There's five of them, Doris, Poppy, Cassie, Toots and Queenie, five sisters. I married one of them but I might as well have married them all. It wasn't so bad when we lived in Cambridgeshire. But here, in Gorleston, it's another story.' He slurped his drink and beer started to dribble down his chin. 'We moved here because Toots said she needed to be with her family. I should have known better.' He swayed closer to Percy and lowered his voice so Percy could barely hear him above the sweet sadness of the Country and Western music. 'They quarrel.' He looked around and then continued. 'Sometimes disagreements go on for years. And sometimes they don't talk to each other for years. Toots hasn't spoken to Queenie for two years and Queenie hasn't spoken to Poppy for four. But that doesn't stop them from talking about each other all the time.' He sighed and looked around again, nervously. 'I try and keep out of it. Doris lives in Yarmouth so I don't see her very often, but if I see Queenie or Poppy or Cassie in their front gardens as I drive past I always wave. They don't always wave back. But you can't miss them. Certainly not Queenie.'

'Tell me about her,' Percy heard himself saying, shouting almost. 'Tell me all about her.'

'Queenie's the most colourful. She's the loudest. She lives just down the road from us, on Yallop Avenue, not that we visit her.'

John Conway appeared. 'Crazy,' he was singing, 'I'm crazy for feelin' so lonely, I'm crazy for feelin' so blue.' He smelt of whisky and pipe tobacco and staleness.

Percy wanted to tell him to shut up. But Charlie seemed relieved to see him, as though he had been rescued from saying something he shouldn't. Percy was annoyed. 'We were just talking about Toots's sister Queenie,' he told John.

'Queenie. Crazy,' John warbled. 'I'm crazy.'

'She drives too fast,' Charlie suddenly said. 'That's all I'm going to say. Along Marine Parade, sometimes up and down for hours on end. She's dangerous. I'm not going to continue but you never know where you are with her. Not that I've ever been interested, she's my sister-in-law. Whoo, whoo-ee I feel dizzy.' He coughed.

Percy thought Charlie looked pale. He thought he should perhaps sit down. But Toots came barging back, her hand brushing against Percy's bottom.

'Come on Charlie, it's time to go.' She started to tug at his arm. 'Everyone here is just so small minded. I'm not putting up with it for a minute longer.' She began bundling him out of the Links, winking at Percy just before she herself disappeared into the night.

The sky had cleared. The air smelt new. Percy could hear the lively tinkle of the sea. He could see the oil rigs, far out in the blackness, flickering. Words like stars filled his head. *I knew you'd love me as long as you'd wanted/and then some day you'd leave me for somebody new.*

2

The trees were not big but perfectly formed, the straight trunks branching out just above head height. They lined the edge of the pavement, evenly spaced, one outside every other bungalow. As Percy walked along Bately Avenue, his avenue, he could see the trees reflected in the windows of the bungalows' front rooms. A faint image. A shimmer really. All the bungalows were much the same along Bately Avenue, as they were along Youell Avenue and Buxton Avenue which both ran parallel. He liked the way the road had no markings, no white or yellow lines, and the way it was a light red colour. It looked as if it had been made with more sand than normal, as if it was part beach. The quartz glistened in the sun, which though low felt warm. He squinted in the heavy brightness.

Yesterday he had spent the morning in the carpark, looking out to sea. The tide had been out, leaving the top of the wreck visible. Seagulls perched on the twisted and blackened stump of metal that calmly rose out of the North Sea and that had once been a mast. They came and went amid much flurry. He had thought about Queenie and Toots and getting old. He felt time had quickened, yet he felt he wasn't getting older. And as he drove home he had realised he hadn't thought of his wife once, all morning. He had felt almost light-headed, a heaviness having lifted.

Usually Elizabeth was like a fog, everywhere, lurking even in the deepest recesses of his mind. But Percy knew the only way he could survive her death would be to try to not think of her. He would try to not think of the past. Of course this was impossible, and she appeared without his control. But he tried. He tried to numb himself by looking out to sea, at the seemingly perpetual dimness. The future.

Wading through the sun Percy turned into Yallop Avenue. It was a short walk. A walk he knew he could do if he suddenly went blind. A few cars and a bus passed. Yallop Avenue was busier, noisier, than Bately Avenue. Here he felt involved. The warmth of the sun on his cheeks. Movement. He saw the Mini Metro first, dark and gleaming, parked in the small driveway. Then the bungalow, Queenie's bungalow, which seemed alive in the sunlight. He couldn't see in. The frosted glass front door just quivered. He passed quickly, not knowing what to do for the rest of the day. Looking forward to tomorrow.

Gorleston Pier was covered in cracked and rippled concrete. A rough sea the night before had left large, oily puddles creeping inwards from the railed edges. Waves were still smashing against the sides sending up sea spray. Percy kept to the middle. It was a lonely pier, like a redundant runway, stretching far into the imagination. Grey clouds swept over the harbour-master's look-out. Seagulls waiting for trawlers wavered above the swirling waters of the harbour mouth where the River Yare met the North Sea. Across the harbour mouth workmen were repairing the North Pier which curved round the end of Great Yarmouth's South Beach before turning into Yarmouth docks. Looming in the distance was Great Yarmouth Power Station, its huge chimney splitting clouds.

Some children were cycling around and around the end of Gorleston Pier, laughing and yelling and splashing through the puddles. They ignored Percy sitting on a bench, the wind flapping the lapels of his coat and whistling through the metal ladder that ran up to the roof and on up the mast of the harbour-master's look-out behind him. He felt excited. He could see three oil rigs on the horizon. He tried to imagine what it would be like to be on one, out there. Surrounded by nothing but the wind and waves. He had nearly an hour to wait. He didn't mind waiting. He hoped a trawler or a ship would pass through the harbour mouth. He hoped he'd see the bright pilot boat. He hoped he'd see the seagulls' mad flurry for food. He hoped for all sorts of things. The children eventually cycled off, leaving him quite alone. He didn't think he could ever get used to being on his own. He got up and walked over to the railings. The sea eddying beneath. He turned inland and saw the rows of groynes running along Gorleston Beach. He thought they looked pathetic. Some protection, he said to himself. Gorleston's cliffs looked just so vulnerable. Gorleston looked so vulnerable. He knew enough about the erosion. He headed inland.

A few old men Percy didn't recognise were sitting in the damp concrete shelter at the beginning of the pier. One was reading a book. The others were smoking. Smoke billowed out and dissipated in the wet sea air. Percy passed them feeling self-conscious. A small row of amusements, Gorleston's only amusements, ran along the lower esplanade by the abandoned yacht pond. Most were boarded up for the winter. But Goldmine Bingo was lit up. Percy felt himself drawn to the bright lights. He walked up and, taking his glasses off, pressed his face to the steamed-up window of the small bingo hall. Through the condensation and smoke he could see the place was packed out. Old women sat behind consoles of flashing yellow and red buttons. Cigarettes burned in each of the ashtrays attached to the top of the consoles. At the back a man was picking up different coloured balls which were somehow being blown around a red wire-framed basket. Between the waves breaking Percy could hear screaming and shouting, laughter. The women were frantically pressing buttons and dragging on their cigarettes. Percy smiled. He had never played bingo. A woman with thick white hair turned and stared back at him. Her eyes were wide open, wild. He lifted his hand and waved gingerly before walking away, walking towards lunch. He knew he would be early. But then most people were early in Gorleston. And he was sure Toots and Charlie would be.

'Bingo,' said Toots, 'is just not the sort of thing Charlie and I would play.' She tossed her head back and smiled. 'We did go once, to the Granada Bingo Hall on the High Street. I can't think why. It was simply awful. All these people making such a dreadful sound, screaming and shouting. Charlie got a headache. Didn't you Charlie? He's so sensitive.' She pinched his cheek. 'Cassie plays. She loves it. But the poor dear can never find anyone to go with. I suspect she's bored everyone stupid.' She took another mouthful. And started to chew loudly.

Percy noticed a piece of meat hanging on her bottom lip. He began to wonder why he had asked Toots and Charlie to have lunch with him at the Pier Hotel. He began to wonder when the piece of meat would drop off. 'What about Queenie? Does Queenie play?' he asked. He felt strange saying her name aloud.

'Play what, dear?' Toots was still chewing.

'Bingo.'

'Queenie will play anything. Absolutely anything.' She wiped her mouth with her sleeve.

Percy had felt pleased that Toots and Charlie had accepted his invitation. He had telephoned them out of the blue and half thought they wouldn't remember who he was. He still wasn't sure they had remembered. Still, they had accepted readily enough and now they were here. He had worried that they might not have had anything to say. But he soon realised he shouldn't have worried. Toots didn't stop talking. Though she didn't always talk about what he wanted to hear. She seemed reluctant to talk about Queenie. He kept trying to bring Queenie back into the conversation.

The Pier Hotel was Percy's idea. He had thought it a rather novel idea. He had never eaten here before. He could see that not many people did. He also doubted whether many people stayed here. Just before the pier, the hotel followed the curve of Brush Quay. It was large and rambling and draughty, with weathered wood balconies and rusting fire escapes. Percy didn't doubt it had once been rather grand, in Edwardian times perhaps. It now appeared, like the rest of Gorleston, to be forgotten about. From the table he could see a side door and a sign stuck to the top of the door saying Ocean Room Dinner and Dance Hall This Way. A thick metal bar ran across the middle of the door, which was padlocked. A couple of sandbags sealed the bottom. The door looked as if it hadn't been opened for years, decades even.

'Tell me more,' Percy said. 'Tell me more about the games.'

Toots looked at Percy, as if he had said something he shouldn't have. Charlie looked animated though. 'There was a time when they turned the Ocean Room into the Polynesian Beach Club,' he said, not looking at Toots. 'There was a bar made from bamboo and dark ladies who danced. We came here once when we were staying with Queenie and her husband, Neville.'

'It was quite awful,' Toots said. 'The food was disgusting. They put pineapple and coconut on everything. That's what they thought tropical food was all about.'

'Yes,' said Charlie, 'but don't you remember Queenie?'

'I'd rather not.'

Charlie looked at Percy excitedly. 'She borrowed a grass skirt from one of the dancers and got on this small stage and did the limbo, or was it the hula hula?'

'Yes,' said Toots, 'I remember. I remember you couldn't keep your eyes off her.'

Charlie rolled his eyes at Percy. 'But you have to hand it to her,' he said, 'she entertained everyone for the whole evening.'

'I wouldn't hand her anything. She'd do anything to get attention.'

Percy started to feel a little uncomfortable.

'She said the next time she came back,' Charlie whispered to Percy, 'she'd black herself up. She said she'd get Neville's boot polish out and black herself up.'

'That's enough of that Charlie. You'll give our host the wrong idea. It's attention she's after, always has been. Nothing but attention.'

The old Gorleston lighthouse stood just behind the Pier Hotel carpark. Bricks were crumbling and the tower, capped by a red beacon, looked as if it would not stand for much longer. But Percy hoped it wouldn't be pulled down, not for a while anyway. He liked the way it stood there, watching over Lower Gorleston. A fragile piece of the past.

'Why don't you come over for Christmas lunch?' Toots said suddenly.

'Yes,' said Charlie unlocking his car, 'I could do with the support.'

'I'd hate the idea of you spending it all alone,' Toots added, before bending into the sky blue Mercedes Benz. 'Life's too short.'

Its name derives from the River Yare. The Celtic word 'gar' signifies rough or turbulent. Thus Gar-less-ton means the little town on the Gar or Yare.

The Romans built a fort here to repel the Saxons from the Elbe. They called it Garianonum. When they finally departed in 436 the east coast was left to the mercy of invaders from the Continent. First came Cerdieus, the Splashing Saxon. His descendants ruled until Lothbroe the Dane was driven here by a gale from Denmark. Lothbroe was murdered by King Edmund's henchmen, who were encamped in Reepham, further up the River Yare. Though the following year Lothbroe's countrymen revenged his death by returning with a mighty force and sacking Gorleston before establishing themselves in East Anglia, and then much of the country. The natives staged an uprising in 1002 and massacred the Danes. But the following year the Danish King Sweyn landed with a huge force and exacted revenge, sacking and burning Gorleston once again. From these very events arose the end of the Saxon dynasty in England.

And all the while the North Sea was attacking the chalky cliffs, slowly advancing on the settlement that was to become Gorleston, Gorleston-on-Sea. But no one saw the danger, for then Gorleston was many miles from the shore.

It was not cold enough to snow. And it was not warm enough to rain. Still Gorleston was glittering with fairy lights and Percy thought that made it special. Bately Avenue was particularly resplendent. He thought of oil rigs at night, fireworks, Oxford Street, children, as he looked out of his front window. He thought it was sad no children lived on Bately Avenue to appreciate the spectacle. The season. He thought of anything, trying not to think of his wife, or how it was only his second Christmas without her.

Toots answered the door and Percy thought for a moment she was going to lean forward and kiss him. Instead she squeezed his hand and pulled him inside. There was much noise and warmth. She hung his coat in the hall and then led him into the lounge. There were decorations everywhere, streamers and balloons, fairy lights and tinsel. Tinsel was draped over a picture that hung above the mantelpiece. It was a print of a horse and cart crossing a ford. The silver threads of the tinsel, like willow branches, floated down into the bright blue stream. A silver Christmas tree stood in one corner, waist high and sparkling. A group of people stood in another corner. Percy couldn't see Queenie. He didn't think it likely Queenie would be here, considering she and Toots didn't speak to each other, but he hoped, nevertheless. He really hoped she would be here.

'Everybody,' Toots shouted, 'everybody, this is Percy.' She pointed at Percy, who stood motionless in the centre of the hot room.

He was pleased Toots had remembered his name, he felt almost honoured, but he also felt embarrassed and shy. The group fell silent as they all turned to face him. He tried to raise his eyebrows in a friendly sort of way. A woman in a tight fitting purple dress, a shade or two darker than Toots' hair, walked over. She said her name was Linda. She said she was Toots and Charlie's youngest daughter. She said she used to live in Norwich but had returned to Gorleston when she married Burt. She had thick lips and a thick voice, almost a lisp. She pointed Burt out. Burt was huge. 'Burt, over here,' she beckoned.

Burt walked over and said 'hi'. He was an American. He put his arm around Linda as he stood there talking. He began to rub Linda's back. Percy watched as his hand moved further and further down Linda's back until he was caressing her bottom. The while he told Percy he was a valve specialist from Austin, Texas, and he worked on the rigs off Yarmouth. He said he worked two weeks on, two weeks off. In his other hand he held a sherry glass, making it look like a thimble. Toots was at the other end of the room, but Percy could see she kept looking over her shoulder at Burt. She couldn't keep her eyes off him. She then looked at Percy and winked. Percy turned away swiftly, embarrassed still.

Charlie appeared with a glass of sherry for Percy. He looked pleased to see Percy, but rather red in the face. 'Hello, old boy,' he said. 'Can't stop. I've been ordered to pour the sherry.' He pointed with his elbow to Toots. 'The boss keeps me busy alright.' He hurried off, Percy thought, looking rather frightened.

'What was your line of work?' Burt then asked. Percy was still thinking of Charlie, frightened and bullied by Toots. He watched him at the drinks cabinet, fiddling with the top of the cut glass sherry decanter. 'Your line of work?' Burt repeated.

'Yes,' said Toots behind him, 'what did you do for a living?'

Percy suddenly realised what he had been asked, by both Toots and Burt. He had come to hate that question. He had done little of interest. He hadn't worked on oil rigs. He hadn't seen any action in the war. And after the war he had moved to Walton-on-Thames and into packaging. He had taken the first job that he had been offered. He had been quite proud of it at the time, but his wife soon changed the way he thought about it. Elizabeth. He felt hot, his brow started to perspire, memories came flooding back. 'You're wasting your life,' she used to say. He could hear the sharpness in her voice now, the voice that could be so soft if she wished. 'You can do so much better.' Her father and her brother were lawyers, respected professionals. He was into cardboard. 'There's no history and there's no future in cardboard,' she once said. She had never made it clear what she thought he should do, but it was not what he was doing. Still, as the years passed it became harder and harder for him to leave. There was so much to worry about, his pension, their mortgage, their security. He just felt unable to change.

When he knew she was dying he started to look back on their life and he regretted not having made more of his career. He regretted the fact that he was not a professional or a professor even. That he had perhaps let her down. He wondered, as she lay struggling for breath, how different everything might have been if only he had been a little more adventurous. But how hard he had tried to hold it all together. Had she realised? He thought about lying to Burt and Toots. What did it matter? Nobody in Gorleston knew what he had done or not done, not now. Nobody anywhere did.

'I used to work for Birds Eye,' he replied. He couldn't lie. He never had been able to, well not often.

'Oh, go on,' Toots said, laughing. 'Captain Birds Eye.' She saluted Percy. 'I must tell Charlie. Charlie, Charlie, over here,' she shouted. 'Charlie, Percy used to work for Birds Eye.'

'I'm very keen on fish fingers,' Charlie said breathlessly, hopefully. 'Toots and I often have them for tea.'

Toots looked at Charlie scornfully. 'No we don't.'

'We do. What's wrong with fish fingers all of a sudden?'

She looked at Percy and Burt and then at her husband. 'You know I don't eat fish.'

'There's not much left of the fishing industry round here now,' Burt said.

'Shame,' said Toots before heading out of the room, her head held high. The purple plume swaying.

'Oil's the business to be in.'

'Actually I was on the packaging side,' Percy said at last. He didn't like fish much either, he didn't like the bones. Not like his wife. She had loved fish. He thought of oil, and the oil rigs that hung onto the horizon, but he couldn't help picturing Elizabeth waiting for the small fishing boats to dock down by Brush Quay. It was always early and cold, her breath thick in the fishy air. She would buy a herring or a plaice. Just one. 'This won't last much longer,' she'd say, 'lucky if these fishermen last as long as us.' And Percy then tried to remember when he had last seen fishing boats moored up by Brush Quay. He couldn't remember. And strangely, he thought, fishing boats hadn't docked there for years, decades perhaps. He wondered when he could have been there with Elizabeth. Momentarily he felt giddy.

Charlie seemed to relax when Toots was out of the room.

'Any of the sisters coming?' Percy asked looking around, casually. 'Queenie coming?'

'Ooh no,' said Charlie quietly. 'Lord no. Cassie's here though.' He pointed to a round woman with white fluffy hair eating crisps by the fireplace. She saw them looking and started to walk over. 'Doris is getting on and Poppy hasn't been out of her house for three years. She's got agoraphobia. It's incurable. She'll never come out.'

'I think you're right,' Cassie interrupted. Her face was covered with salt and crisp crumbs. 'Dear old Poppy, she's even retreated into her bedroom.' She looked at Percy sweetly and sighed. 'The only person she seems to trust is her doctor. She gives him a television for Christmas every year. She gets them cheap from her son Keith.'

Percy thought Cassie to be very open and friendly, and he thought it didn't matter in the least that she didn't care what she looked like, not like Toots. 'She'd be quite lost without him,' he heard her continue. Though his mind had started to drift again. He wondered what Poppy looked like, all pale and thin, bedridden and afraid of the outside. He wondered what Elizabeth would have made of him now. Enjoying himself with these people he hardly knew. He wouldn't have been here had she still been alive. They were not her sort of people. And towards the end, when he knew she was dying, he just wanted to be with her. He couldn't bear the thought of sharing her with anyone else, not after everything. She was his at last. They had grown closer and closer together, forced to in a way because they had no children. Because, Percy thought, they only had each other. He loved her more than he could ever tell her. He wasn't as good with words as she was, he was not as educated. So he would just sit with her, listen to her and stroke her wasted hands. She would tell him things about Gorleston and the sea and the cliffs and the erosion. He didn't understand everything, he didn't understand how she knew so much about the littoral drift, Joas Johnson, the shifting mouth of the River Yare. 'I know,' she would say, 'why the beach comes and goes. I know why everything changes so quickly here. Why nothing's as it seems.'

Percy didn't like change, never had. Yet he was beginning to feel things weren't as before. He was beginning to look at things differently. He thought of Queenie. She seemed such a mystery. Quite unlike anyone he had ever heard of. And for once he wanted to know more. He wanted to know everything. He wanted the mist to lift. He drank the rest of his sherry down in one.

'If there's one thing we are good at it's cheering people up,' Cassie was saying. She was still standing beside Percy looking warm and homely. 'Why don't you join me one evening? It's a hoot.'

Percy had no idea what she was talking about. He smiled at her, not wanting to appear rude.

'If you don't fancy the bingo at least pop round some time for a cup of tea. I live on Arnott Avenue.'

'Oh really,' said Percy, 'I live just around the corner.'

'Everyone, my dear, lives just around the corner here.'

After lunch Toots wanted to organise some games, but Linda said she and Burt ought to be getting home. She had told Percy over lunch that they lived on the new Mariner's Compass housing estate, and that the road they lived on was called The Boulters, which she thought was very fitting seeing as Burt was a valve specialist. 'He's only back for another two days,' she told her mother.

Percy noticed Linda's huge eyes for the first time. They were blue and expectant. He reckoned she was in her mid-forties. She was still attractive. And Burt still couldn't keep his hands off her.

'We see so little of each other.'

'I quite understand, darling,' Toots said, nodding her head, her plume. 'You just make sure you keep him happy.'

Percy had got lost in the Mariner's Compass housing estate a couple of times. He remembered he had seen children there. And pregnant women with push-chairs struggling along the tidy streets, bright with new tarmac and brick. He wondered whether Linda and Burt were trying to have children. He knew it wasn't all television and videos on the new estate. He knew where the oilmen and their wives, who would have liked to be younger, lived all right.

'It was terrible, terrible,' Toots said as she parted the pale green blinds and watched Linda and Burt get into their long American car. 'Just like that.' She turned round and pulled her right forefinger across her neck. 'Just like that.' She did it again. And then Charlie, who Percy thought was asleep in an armchair, perked up and did it too. Only his finger was shaking. 'Linda's last husband had his head knocked off,' Toots said, looking straight at Percy. 'He was a nice, simple chap. A bit thick up top. He stuck it out of a train window and it came clean off.'

'They didn't find the head until two days later,' Cassie added eagerly.

The room then fell quite quiet. Percy could hear the hiss

of the coal-effect gas fire, which looked like it was meant to flicker but just glowed a deep orange. And he thought he could hear the cliffs creaking and groaning, subsiding perhaps. Charlie and Cassie both soon fell asleep. Cassie started to snore.

'Come on Percy, I can't put up with this, let's sneak round to Poppy's,' Toots said. 'It's just around the corner.' She flapped her arms about excitedly.

Cliff Lane was enveloped in dusk. The sound of waves breaking died as they passed the bungalows and chalets, some displaying fairy lights, others glowing Father Christmases. No one else was about. They made an odd couple, Toots in her tight-fitting tweed jacket and skirt marching down the middle of the lane, Percy breathlessly struggling to keep up, slowed by his heavy overcoat, slowed by his age. He couldn't understand where she got her energy from. She's non-stop, he said to himself. They paused once they reached Yallop Avenue. Everything was still. Quiet. Percy felt he should say something. 'It's a lovely time of day.' It was his wife's favourite time of day. 'So peaceful. Don't you love the way the air smells so pure?' He mimicked her, almost automatically.

'Coo-ee. Coo-ee.'

Percy jumped. But Toots didn't even flinch. He looked around in the dusk. His heart beating. Across the road a small woman was standing outside a bungalow, yelling and waving at them.

'Coo-ee. Coo-ee.'

Even in the bad light Percy couldn't miss the orange hue of her hair. He knew who it was. She seemed tiny, much smaller than he had conceived. Her voice ricocheted off the surrounding bungalows, off the approaching night. She was like a beacon in the fading light. He had a sudden urge to cross the road and say something, anything. He wanted

Toots to introduce him. He wanted to meet her. He wanted to be invited in for tea. It was Christmas. But Toots started to march off. Percy stood where he was for a few seconds, looking at Queenie. He didn't know what to do. He watched as she turned and walked inside her bungalow, and closed the front door behind her. For a moment he saw her outline framed in the frosted glass.

'Gorleston's full of crazy people,' said Toots, once he had caught up with her halfway down Brett Avenue. 'Crazy, mad people. Still I suppose we should take pity on them at this time of year. Oh well.' She marched on.

Percy didn't know what to think. He was confused. But not too confused to feel sorry for Queenie. He couldn't stop thinking about her standing there, trying to attract their attention, trying to say hello, perhaps wanting to wish her sister a happy Christmas, wanting to make up for some silly argument that had raged silently for years. Thoughts raced around his mind. He hated himself for just walking away. He didn't want to think of what she would think of him now. Now he had walked away, walked away with Toots. He felt angry. Angry with Toots, angry with himself. Bugger it, he said to himself. Bugger it, rushing along beside Toots.

Percy was surprised by the exuberance of Poppy's bungalow. He thought someone so reclusive, so shy of the outside world, would want to live in anonymity. Poppy's bungalow stuck out a mile. It was the only one like it in the street. He had noticed it before. He couldn't have missed it. Like St Edmunds it had Tudor-style flourishes. Black beams were tacked onto the outside walls. The windows were a multitude of tiny panes. A street lamp now bathed the bungalow in yellow light.

The smell struck him first. He imagined it was like opening an oven that had for ever been keeping warm a roast dinner. A dinner that had long ago dried up. Toots walked straight in, and he had followed, the air thickening as they progressed. He was sure a window had never been opened. He followed Toots into Poppy's bedroom. And there she was, a shrivelled old woman propped up in bed watching television. It was incredibly loud. Toots waved at her.

'He makes me laugh. He's so funny, isn't he Toots, so funny. My doctor says it's good for me to watch television. He says it keeps my mind active. He popped round this morning. Ever so nice of him, what on Christmas Day and everything. He's got his own family you know. I gave him a television. It's the least I can do. I don't know what I would do without him. He's my saviour. Who's this then?' She lifted her withered hand and pointed at Percy with a thin, crooked finger.

'Oh, he's a new friend,' Toots shouted. 'Lives around the corner.' Toots turned round. 'She's a bit deaf,' she said loudly, pointing at her own ears. 'She's getting on.'

'Queenie came this Christmas.' Poppy was struggling to sit further up in the bed. 'Or was it last year. My mind is going.'

'You can say that again,' Toots said.

'I do like to see her. She always cheers me up. She's always so gay. We've made up. We're the best of friends now, or are we?'

'Well we're not.' Toots sat down on a small chair by the bed, while Percy hovered awkwardly by the door.

'I often remember those parties. It seems like yesterday. Perhaps it was.' Poppy sighed. 'And that glorious house they once had in Yarmouth. Nothing seemed to matter then. One could behave as one wished. So gay.'

Percy struggled to listen above the television as Poppy's voice trailed off into lightness.

'We know who behaved as they wished.' Toots tossed her head back. 'And don't forget about Neville, her poor husband.'

Poppy suddenly looked alert. 'You would say that. I know.' She looked about. 'If a man can't look after himself, that's his problem. He was soft.' She lifted her withered hand again and pointed to her head. 'He was soft up here.'

After a while Toots went to make tea. Percy tried to initiate a conversation with Poppy but they both soon found it was easier to watch the television. Percy, however, had difficulty concentrating. The heat was wearing him down. The air was so thick. He felt drowsier and drowsier. He sat back in an armchair. Sometime later he realised he was holding a plate with a piece of cake on it. The cake was dry and tasted of plastic. He had great difficulty swallowing. Toots handed him a cup of tea. Small balls of milk floated on the oily top. The television started to hum. The room got hotter and hotter. He loosened his tie. He couldn't hear the sisters talk any more.

Queenie drifted into his view. But it wasn't Queenie. She was older and smaller and she had lank white hair. He was watching the sea and she suddenly appeared. She brushed past him and hurried down the cliff. She reached the beach huts, a blur of colours, pinks, blues, greens. Then he lost sight of her. Though it wasn't her.

'She's always had everything she's ever wanted. And she's got away with murder.' Percy recognised Toots's voice.

3

Percy had dreamt something that made him feel uncomfortable, excited. It wasn't the first time he had felt this way recently. But he couldn't remember what exactly he had dreamt. Images of his wife, her brown eyes, Queenie, a strange woman with long white hair, eddied about his mind. But he was thick with sleep and nothing made sense.

As he walked to the corner shop he thought for the first time about the shop's name, Happy Shopper. When he got closer he looked up and could see the O of Shopper was fashioned out of a smiling girl's face, with a flop of hair blown across her brow. The face and the lettering were bright orange. Was he a happy shopper? He was not unhappy, he thought, far from it. He felt something deep inside him, loneliness perhaps, lifting. It was early and crisp. The air was light. Percy was just waking up.

It was New Year. Percy never made resolutions. He had never had to. He wasn't going to make any resolutions now but he had a feeling things would change. He had a feeling life wouldn't be like before. From the corner shop, from the Happy Shopper doorway, he could see clearly down Bridge Road to the sea. The sea was calm and cold, shimmering under the winter sun. He thought it quite beautiful. A Coca-Cola can lay half crushed on the pavement. For a moment he thought about kicking it.

'Of course it's not the sort of place we would normally come to,' Toots whispered loudly. 'Everyone's so old. They're all so everyday, aren't they Charlie?'

Percy could see the woman on the next door table look at Toots and then nudge her companion, an old man who was having trouble with his soup. Percy had felt rather proud of himself walking into St Edmunds with Toots and Charlie. He had wanted to see the old faces look up at him. He had wanted to be seen having lunch with Toots and Charlie, who weren't just anybody around here. John Conway didn't think so anyway, and he had looked surprised when he saw Percy walk in with them, Toots resplendent as ever. But Percy began to wonder whether it was such a good idea as Toots carried on in her peculiarly loud way. So what, he said to himself. He hadn't cared what anybody here thought about him before, why should he start to care now?

'Toots, they'll hear you. Quieten down. You get it from Queenie. You know how much she likes to be heard,' Charlie said rolling his eyes at Percy. He kept doing this. But it made Percy feel slightly uneasy, as if he were taking sides. And he didn't want to get on the wrong side of Toots.

'Do you think he needs a straw?' Toots questioned, not even bothering to whisper. The woman looked up and nudged the old man again. But the man remained bent over his soup. 'I say, does he need a straw?' The woman looked away and busied herself with her plate of food. 'Honestly, do they have to stare?'

Charlie was blushing. 'Toots, that was not kind.'

'They can't hear. They're all quite deaf.'

Charlie rolled his eyes again, resignedly. It was as if he knew he was never going to quieten down his wife, that whatever he said wouldn't make the slightest bit of difference. Percy watched Charlie look around the Mascot Suite dining room. He seemed to be looking for some sort of help, or hope. His eyes began to follow Rachel the waitress. Indeed, many eyes were following Rachel, as she rushed around, serving up the usuals. Percy didn't know why the place bothered with menus. Everything always tasted and looked the same, whether it was chicken or beef or pork. Rachel lent over Charlie as she put his plate of light brown food in front of him. From across the table Percy noticed a couple of brown stains on her white shirt. He noticed her black bra straps as her shirt fell forward. He looked up and caught Toots's eye. He was sure she had seen him looking at the young waitress and he felt himself go red with embarrassment. He always went red just like that. That was why he could never lie.

After a while he looked at Toots again. She was concentrating on her food now, chewing quickly. Close up, her nose was too big for her face which was too long. Her cheeks were smothered in rouge and powder, both applied in uneven quantities in quite a random way. The powder cracked and remoulded as she chewed. Her eyes were encased in bright blue eye shadow. He realised he had been staring at Toots for some time. Toots suddenly looked up and winked at him. She was still chewing. And as he stuck his fork into a wafer thin meat slice he felt his own cheeks flare up, again. This time though he sensed Charlie was looking at him. He wondered whether Charlie might think something was going on between himself and Toots. Though he thought Charlie was probably used to it. To Percy Toots seemed to be the sort of person who had spent her whole life looking elsewhere. And Charlie, Percy thought at the end of the day, was probably thankful.

Commotion in St Edmunds was a rare thing. And when Percy returned from the toilet the Mascot Suite dining room was in turmoil, as far as the Mascot Room could ever be in turmoil. He immediately thought Toots must have said or done something. He just couldn't imagine what. He saw Charlie sitting alone at the table eating banana custard. Then he saw Toots, at the window, surrounded by men, all clasping onto each other for support.

'It's nothing to be proud of boys,' he heard Toots shout. 'You've all seen her do it before. It's not very clever is it? Come on, back from the window now.' He could see Toots trying to push a couple of the frail men away. 'Though I suppose if you wait here long enough you'll see a bus come round that corner and crash right into her. Flatten her. Ha, it would serve her right.' Percy walked over to see what was going on. He had an idea.

Toots carried on lecturing and jostling the men, who refused to be pushed out of the way and continued to stare out at Marine Parade. They continued to stare at Queenie's Mini Metro swerving in and out of the white lines in the centre of the road. Backwards and forwards it went. Every now and then a gravelly cheer went up. Percy watched, mesmerised. His heart beating. The third time the car passed he noticed Queenie had a cigarette hanging from the corner of her mouth. Her orange hair swept back. He felt Toots tug indiscriminately at his arm. He turned to face her. Her make-up, thick as it was, could not hide her anger. Her face was turning purple. She was looking at him again, though she could have been looking right through him. Her eyes were black.

The car hadn't returned for some minutes and everybody slowly went back to their tables. Some men still chuckling. Others wiping tears of excitement from their tired eyes.

'I don't know what all the fuss is about,' said Charlie. The corners of his mouth yellow with custard. 'It's not as if she hasn't done it before. And every time you work yourself up Toots. What do you think everybody thinks of you?' He rolled his eyes at Percy. 'I should think they think you're as mad as she is.'

'Don't be so ridiculous Charlie. I was merely seeing what all the fuss was about. If she wants to kill herself, fine. It's the old men I worry about. Egging her on like that, I am surprised some of them don't just drop dead.'

Rachel started to wipe the gravy and custard off the table. Charlie seemed too entranced to answer Toots back.

'Charlie. Charlie I think it's time for you to go home and have a rest. Percy and I are going for a walk. Percy will drop me home later, won't you Percy?'

Percy couldn't say no. Toots was patting his knee.

'I've never let arthritis prevent me from going for a walk. I'm as strong as I've ever been. I'm a strong woman, Percy. As you can see I've looked after myself. Charlie moans if he walks to the end of the garden. Ha ha, not much chance of him walking too far.' Toots hurried along the upper esplanade in the cold stillness. 'I can't bear moaners.'

The sea was glassy. Small waves broke quietly along the shore. Percy saw some people milling around the shelter by the pier. The sun, wavering behind thin, wispy clouds, was turning the sky a soft red. Yarmouth Power Station ahead, its towering chimney, was turning a soft red too. He loved it when the sky started to burn slowly. He wanted to be alone. At least, he didn't want to be with Toots. He couldn't think of anything to talk to Toots about. Though he knew that didn't matter, she'd do the talking. He shivered as he felt her arm slip through his.

'The trouble with Charlie, Percy, is that he's got no sense of fun. He just can't stand up and enjoy himself. I like men with a sense of fun, with a sense of adventure. I like strong men.' She squeezed his arm with her arm. 'Tell me now, what do you think of me? Go on and don't be shy.'

Yarmouth Power Station seemed to turn a deeper red as Percy looked at it, as he desperately tried to think of something to say. A scarlet seagull swooped close by. Their shadows stretched long in front of them. Percy had a sudden urge to try to beat his shadow to the next lamp post. As he quickened his pace he felt Toots' arm tighten again. It was beginning to hurt him. 'Look, look. I think that's your sister down there,' he said, suddenly, excitedly, pointing towards the pier. 'There, just by the harbour-master's hut.' The little figure that he was becoming quite familiar with was walking beside a man, who was not much taller, near the end of the pier. Percy suddenly wished he was that man more than anything.

'Well I don't recognise the man,' Toots said, abstractedly. 'I can't for the life of me think who it could be.' She stood and stared for a while without saying anything else. Then she piped up. 'That woman is selfish. My God is she selfish. The trouble with her is that she's always been spoilt. She's always had her own way. And what's more she's a show-off. She won't change. Not now. Not that it bothers me of course. Oh no. I've never let it bother me. I get what I want as well, alright. Just you wait and see.' Toots smiled at Percy, the corners of her mouth almost curling into a snarl. 'But the reason I'm telling you all this, Percy, is that it's a warning. Don't be fooled. So many others have. What Queenie is is trouble. Big trouble. And don't you forget it, my man.'

What Percy couldn't forget was Toots's hand now clasping his arm. It might have been cold walking along the upper esplanade, between the thousands of retirement homes that all looked so alike that sometimes Percy felt he would never find his own, and the North Sea disappearing into the distance, but he didn't feel comforted by Toots' hand. He wasn't warmed by it at all. He wanted to thank Queenie for saving him from answering Toots's question about what he thought of her. He wanted to thank Queenie for lots of things. But he didn't want to offend Toots. What did she mean, what do you think of me? He muddled the question over. He had never really thought. He had never been asked such a thing in such a way. He couldn't answer questions like that.

He then started to worry about Toots's warning against Queenie. He didn't know what to make of it. In the darkening twilight he decided he wasn't going to make anything of it. Well, if anything, that Toots was jealous of Queenie and that was that. Though Toots, and Charlie, had been kind to him, he thought, and he wasn't suddenly going to forget about them. He wasn't like that.

They reached the end of the upper esplanade. Near by were a few bare flower beds. A dog, a small brown spaniel on the end of a long thin lead, was digging in the centre of one of them and an old woman was pulling at the lead with all her might. The dog just carried on digging, shooting lumps of earth onto the neat grass with its hind legs. 'Humphrey. Humphrey,' the old woman was calling from behind a head-scarf, 'if you don't stop it right now there'll be no supper for you.' Her voice was weak and seemed to drift hopelessly off in the wrong direction. 'Humphrey, Humphrey, come here this minute. Mummy's getting very angry.'

Percy drove Toots home. She said it was not the end of the world if she didn't find out who Queenie was with. She'd find out sooner or later. She always did, she told him. For a moment he thought she was going to ask him what he thought of her again, but she didn't. He dropped her at the beginning of her drive. He was eager to get away. He saw Charlie peering out of the lounge window, through the pale green blinds. He waved. He didn't want Charlie to think he was being rude by not going in. Charlie saluted back. As he turned his car round he felt sorry for Charlie. The sort of sorry he felt for people he thought were just hopeless. He had sometimes felt this way about himself.

* * *

The air was thick with salt and tar. Bately Avenue was empty. No one was about. No late night dog walkers. But inside the bungalows, one after another, by the warmth of gas fires and blazing radiators, people were watching television. Percy could see the blue-tinged flicker trickling round the edges of blinds and curtains. Brighter lights from the bungalows' porches and hallways, flooding through the frosted glass front doors, cast dim shadows on the dark road, shadows of trees and parked cars and Percy. He tried to imagine each lounge, each person glued to the television. Soon, he thought, they would be getting up from their favourite armchairs. Soon they would be putting on their kettles for tea and hot water bottles. Soon they would be getting ready for bed. Soon, for most of Gorleston, it would be tomorrow.

Percy didn't drink much. He had never been a great drinker. He had thought of himself as the sort of person who would never take risks, who would never get out of control. The sort of person with whom you knew where you were. But tonight he felt like getting out of his home. He felt like a drink. He couldn't explain it to himself and didn't try. The Links was not far. He was happy to walk, past Arnott Avenue and Buxton Avenue and out onto Bridge Road. He liked to walk in the peace of night. Small, frightened dogs barking in the darkness.

John Conway, as Percy had half expected, was standing at the bar looking like he had been there all day. Before Percy had even bought him a large whisky he started to ask questions about Toots. John wanted to know why he and Toots had gone for a walk without Charlie. He wanted to know if Toots had taken him as far as the model yacht pond. He wanted to know if Toots had made a pass at him, because she had once made a pass at himself. 'I bet she did,' he insisted, not slurring his words at all but enveloping Percy with a sodden whisky breath. 'Go on, you can tell me,' he nudged.

Percy told John to stop being so ridiculous. 'John, we're two old people who happened to take a walk after lunch along the Gorleston sea front. There's nothing unusual about that.'

'I don't know,' John said. 'Sounds pretty unusual to me.' He gulped his drink. 'Well then, what about Toots's sister, that Queenie woman?'

'What about her?'

'She's pretty unusual if you ask me. What does she think she's up to?'

'What do you mean, what does she think she's up to?'

'You know,' he said enthusiastically. 'All the antics. That business with the car.'

Percy said he had no idea, but that you had to hand it to her. 'Gorleston needs people like her,' he told John, feeling surprised with himself for saying it. Quite surprised.

By the end of the evening, with John's encouragement, Percy had drunk five brandies and soda. When he returned his home was still with cold. He was normally in bed by now, the heating having long expired. He lay down and listened to himself breathing in the quietness, in the darkness. He hoped that if he breathed quietly enough he would be able to hear the sea. It didn't work. Instead he thought of the day, quite a day. He thought of Queenie. Gorleston needs people like Queenie. The world needs people like Queenie. He started to laugh. Weaving in and out of the white lines. Honestly.

He hoped.

Why Gorleston was so fought over is quite a mystery. Many early invaders were attracted to Britain by the prospect of mines. But here the land was wet and chalky. The ancient forests had long been swallowed by the sea. The people were pagans. There were no such inducements.

The last megalithic stones were not removed until 1768, when they were dragged down and used to strengthen the harbour. They are believed to have been sited on land that became the Elmhurst Court Holiday Camp, and is now the Mariner's Compass housing estate. There was once a field here called Stone Close Field. In 1888 drawings of these megaliths were presented to the Norfolk and Norwich Archaeological Society by Fred Danby Palmer, whose son Andrew founded Palmer's, the department store in Great Yarmouth. The stones stood in a circular position and were some ten feet high.

Of course no one could explain how the stones got here, this being clay and chalk country.

It was the most miserable day, and Percy didn't feel like being miserable. Great drops of rain clung to his lounge window. He couldn't see far outside, just the thickness of the rain. But he knew there would be nobody out there. Nobody went out on days like this. It was the sort of day many people longed for. The sort of day Mrs Yarren, his neighbour, loved. She regularly told him so. She said on days like this she didn't feel guilty about not going outside. She said she was quite happy to sit inside by the gas fire and watch television all day. She even said Sandy, her Norfolk terrier, was quite happy not to go outside, though he got a little restless watching television all day. 'He needs dog company,' she would say, and wink. Indeed there was a time not so long ago when Percy was quite happy to sit inside by the television all day, whether the weather was bad or not. There was a time, Percy reflected, when he too felt like Mrs Yarren, or Poppy perhaps. But now everything was different. The weather was awful and he was still eager to get out. He was dying to get out.

The windscreen wipers were flapping at full speed. The car windows had steamed up. Percy found it difficult to see. He knew the sea was to his left, but it was lost in the rain and the cloud. As Percy struggled along the avenues and crescents he knew so well, it was as if the sky had fallen upon Gorleston. There were no mothers with push-chairs or large men with fierce dogs out walking on the oilmen's estate. Though now and then huge American cars would loom in front of him, tankering through the puddles.

Percy wondered why Linda and Burt had asked him over for Sunday morning drinks. He supposed Linda was asking Toots and Charlie and the others, and that a new face on the scene might liven things up. He supposed she was asking all the oldies over. Still, he didn't mind. He then considered the possibility of Queenie being there. He wiped the windscreen again, making a large Q with the back of his hand. He toyed with the idea of trying a little swerve. But he realised in the present conditions it would be extremely dangerous. He was a sure and steady driver but not an expert driver. He tightened his grip on the steering wheel and straightened his line. His mood sunk a little as it dawned on him that Queenie probably wouldn't be there. How could she be? He asked himself. She doesn't speak to Toots. And there was no way, he thought, no way that Toots would let her daughter invite Queenie. Then his mood sunk a little further as he began to feel uneasy about seeing Toots. He thought of their walk together. He didn't know what she might ask today. He didn't want to know.

The Mariner's Compass housing estate was a maze of small roads, some not yet finished, and crazy paving paths that led through communal gardens neatly dotted with shrubs and miniature lamp posts. It took Percy some time to find The Boulters in all the sameness, in the rain. He parked and walked down a winding path. Crazy slices of concrete sank unevenly into the earth. They squelched as he trod on them. By the time he got to Linda and Burt's house the bottoms of his trousers were speckled with muddy water. Their house was square, quite square, like all the houses nearby. Though he had noticed that the houses on the perimeter of the estate were grander, more elaborate, with architectural flourishes such as gables and vaulted roofs.

Linda and Burt's house was called Fair Rigger. The name was painted in pink on a highly varnished slice of log that hung dripping on the wet wall next to the front door. Percy thought the name was some sort of a joke. Then he wasn't so sure. He saw Linda coming to the door through the frosted glass. She was a bit taller than her mother and he realised she really had something of a figure. She made the most of it. She flung the door open. Her dress clung to her body. It was the same purple dress she had worn the first time he had met her, or at least the same shade of purple.

'Percy,' she said. It almost purred out. Perrrcy. 'Lovely to see you. So good of you to have ventured out in this weather. It looks just awful out there.' She stuck her hand outside, palm up. 'Errrgh. Daddy says he's never felt so damp. It's bad for his arthritis, and Mummy's in a flap because Daddy forgot to bring an umbrella. You'll have to cheer her up. Come in, come in, you'll catch your death of cold.'

Percy spent some time wiping his feet and acclimatising while Linda took his coat upstairs. He watched her waggle her way up the thin staircase. The warmth was tropical. He waited for her to return and then followed her into the lounge. Toots's hair had all but collapsed. Wet straggles stuck to the side of her face and he could see mauve trickles running down her cheeks. Every now and then she wiped her face with a paper napkin, which might once have been white, but was now quite purple.

'Percy, I must look a fright. Charlie forgot the umbrella. I said to him whatever you do don't forget the umbrella. And what does he do?' She wiped her face with the stained napkin, as if to emphasise how drenched she was. Though Toots was not as angry as he thought she could be. They chatted for a while longer and much to his relief she barely mentioned the walk the other day. She just said she had not found out who Queenie was with, how it could have been almost anybody, but that she would find out, eventually, she always did.

Percy soon found himself relaxing. Charlie, he noticed, however, was not his usual self. He was quieter than normal and slunk around the room. He looked like he was keeping out of Toots's way, which was not easy. The lounge was small. It was smaller than Percy's. The thick and creamy carpet seemed to swallow everyone up. So soft and comfortable was it in the humid heat that Percy wanted to lie down. One wall was taken up by a smoked glass bookcase which supported all manner of electrical goods, televisions, videos, hi-fi systems, and odd bits of china. There was even a china oil rig. The top shelf was taken up by videos in colourful cases. But he couldn't read the titles. He watched Burt. Burt looked very strange, so big and bluff, padding about the soft room. There was a dark brown velvety sofa pushed up against another wall. No one, except a few fluffy teddy bears and a rabbit, sat on it. Everyone, except Charlie, was crunched into the middle of the room. Crunched around Toots.

'I'm not in her good books,' Charlie told Percy to one side. 'I'm not looking forward to going home.'

'She doesn't seem to be too cross.'

'You're not me.'

'No, I suppose I'm not.' As Percy, too, padded around the room, he became aware he was leaving a faint trail. Mud was dripping off his trousers and matting the shaggy strands of the carpet. He picked a cheese straw from the tray on a side table and took a large step over to the sofa. A teddy bear landed on his lap as he sat down.

'Oh, I'm sorry,' Cassie said. She had sat down at the same time at the other end of the sofa and thrown a teddy bear out of her way. 'Oh, Percy, I say. I don't know why Linda's got all these things. It's not as if she's got any children, though I'm sure it's not for lack of trying. I can't think what Linda and Burt want with them. Though I suppose some people never grow up.'

Percy thought Cassie looked as fluffy as the carpet, the part he hadn't walked over anyway. She must have had an umbrella. Her white hair was dry and downy.

'A visit would have been nice,' she said.

Percy was momentarily distracted by Burt, who was running his hand over Linda's bottom. 'A visit. Oh, yes. Of course you live just around the corner. No, I haven't forgotten. I just seem to have been rather busy.' He sat back in the sofa. He felt something lumpy, but soft, press into his back. 'It's funny really. Until recently I never thought you could ever be that busy in Gorleston. I'd always thought of it as a sort of huge rest home. I don't mean to be rude, but the sort of place you come to when you want to just get on with the rest of your life, quietly. But when you get to know it a bit better, when you get to know everybody a bit better, things certainly seem to liven up. It's a strange place.' He looked at her, the whiteness of her face, her hair. She was looking at him intently. 'In an odd sort of a way it makes you feel younger. It makes me feel younger anyway.'

'The thing about Gorleston, Percy, is that it's by the sea. The sea's the key to it. It keeps you fresh. It rejuvenates you, if you let it. You have to get out and breathe it. Walk by it if you can. I've lived here nearly all my life. But I don't get out enough now. My legs aren't what they used to be.' She looked down at them, bulging out from the bottom of her dress, bulging in thick beige stockings. 'And look at Poppy. She doesn't get out at all. Look what's happened to her. All frail and thin.'

Linda came over and squeezed in between them. Her

dress rode high up her left thigh. 'Oops,' she said. Her stockings were the same colour as the carpet, but shiny and without the muddy tracks. She didn't make much effort to push her dress down. It just stayed were it was, revealing a lovely leg. 'What have you two been talking about? Tell Linda everything.'

'Percy was telling me he thought Gorleston was making him feel younger.'

'I can't say it's ever made me feel younger.'

'You look lovely, dear. And besides you've got Burt to look after you,' Cassie said.

Percy could see Burt was talking to Toots, or rather Toots was talking to Burt. Burt turned to Linda with a helpless expression on his face. Toots seemed to have pushed him right up against the side table with the tray of cheese straws on it. The backs of his legs were nudging it. He wondered what Burt, being an American, made of Toots. He wondered if Burt's mother, if she was still alive, was at all like Toots. He tried to imagine an American version of Toots. He couldn't. The tray of cheese straws looked as if it might fall off the table at any moment.

'Mummy tells me auntie Queenie's been misbehaving again,' Linda suddenly said. 'She amazes me. How old must she be now?' Linda looked at Cassie.

'I don't think age gets in her way.'

'No, I suppose it doesn't. I hope I'm like that when I'm her age, though.'

'I doubt you will be dear. It's got nothing to do with age. Queenie's always been like it. She was born like it. Mother used to say she was high spirited. I'd say she's certainly that. Your mother's high spirited but she could never keep up with Queenie, however hard she tried. I've never met anyone who could.'

They chatted for a while longer about Queenie and high spirits. And then Cassie said, talking about high spirits,

Linda and Burt's house was built on the site of the old Elmhurst Court Holiday Camp. She said she could clearly remember the blue and white chalets. She said they used to stretch from Links Road to where the Great Yarmouth and Lowestoft District Hospital now was. And in the centre, she said, about where they now were, was a huge pavilion. On Friday and Saturday nights, she said, bands from Great Yarmouth came over. The big bands that played on Britannia Pier. 'It was not what you would call classy, but it was just after the war and we had a ball. Oh yes.' Her white face turned quite red with excitement. 'Queenie always caused a stir. She loved to dance, with everyone. They couldn't keep their eyes off her. I could tell you some stories about Queenie and Gorleston holiday camp. I could tell you some stories about Queenie. But it's not for me to go digging up the past. What's happened happened.'

The top of the next morning's tide reached quite lazily the base of the lower esplanade, where it teased the cracked concrete for over an hour. Later in the day, when the tide had ebbed, officials came to look at the beach. Beds of flints and stones pocked with stumps of long-buried beach works scarred the wet sands. They moved on to lower Gorleston, walking with care, a huddled mass in the heavy rain. Puddles of sea and rain water, stained with oil and oddly beautiful, sat on Pier Walk and Brush Quay. Parts of Riverside Road remained underwater all day. The officials agreed that tomorrow lower Gorleston might be under five feet of water.

The army was called in. Along the coast, from Winterton through to Hemsby, Newport, Scratby, Caister, Yarmouth, and finally Gorleston, they began sandbagging. Barricading the lowlands of Norfolk.

For that night it was a full moon. The first spring tide of a full moon. The rain continued all day and as darkness fell the wind from the east freshened. Then as the sea began to edge up the beaches and over the quays, the sirens started.

Percy woke with a fright.

4

'Coo-ee, coo-ee.'

Percy didn't have to turn round to know who it was. But he couldn't help it. He swung himself round on the sawdust, just like that, before his heart had a chance to catch up with him. He wasn't old. Not now. Then, oomph, his heart began to bounce in his concave chest. There she was, standing in the doorway of the butcher's. Holmes, The Family Butcher, Bells Road, Gorleston-on-Sea. The sudden centre of Percy's universe.

'Cooo-eee,' she went again, taking more time over it, making it sound almost like a question.

The sun shone through her hair. Framed in the doorway she looked like she had an orange halo. She was smiling, a broad, happy smile. Smiling at Percy. Blood rushed to his head. Why had he not realised? She was calling him. She wanted his attention. She was wearing a lime green coat and her small cream-coloured clip handbag matched her cream shoes. He noticed some sawdust from the floor had already got on them. Her tiny feet were encased in creamy flakes. But he found he was struck by fear. She wanted something from him. She wanted him, and he had no idea what to do. He felt incredibly hot. It was like Linda's house in the butcher's shop, or Toots and Charlie's house, or for that matter any house he had ever been in in Gorleston.

Hot and humid. Much of Gorleston was indeed tropical, he often thought. Impervious to the cold winds that blew in off the North Sea. He felt his brow moisten. He wanted to wipe it. He didn't want Queenie to see him standing there, staring, sweaty and red faced. Much longer and he thought the sweat would start to drip off and clog the sawdust, or he'd faint. He could not move. In this intolerable heat he had frozen solid. He was stuck to the sawdust and he couldn't even open his mouth. His mouth felt dry, dry as a desert. Then she walked further into the shop. Queenie, a small flash of orange, lime green and cream, stopped just short of Percy. She was so near, he knew if he stretched out his arm he would be able to touch her, stroke her lime green sleeve. He could clearly hear her breathe. Raspy and uneven, a smoker's breath. He could even feel it, cutting through the tropics, disturbing the humidity.

'Good afternoon Queenie,' Mr Holmes said.

Percy sighed audibly. The oppressive atmosphere lifted. He felt he could move again. Wiping his brow on the sleeve of his coat, he turned back to the counter, this time trying not to looked startled, trying to look natural, calm. The butcher was still facing the white-tiled wall, working the slicer. He had not changed his position, he had not needed to see who or what was making the coo-ee noise. He knew exactly who it was, Percy thought. Everyone in Gorleston must have heard it, must know the source. It must be as familiar as Gorleston's fog horn, booming on misty nights. The slicer purred as it spun into Percy's bacon.

As Queenie stood there, looking around the small shop, up at the electric blue hue of the fly killer, the ordered counter of cuts of meat, the floor patched with sawdust, Percy felt relieved. He felt relieved that she was not going to come up to him after all, and say something he would have been unable to answer. She was there for the same reason as himself, he realised, to buy some meat. He was glad he was not going to make more of a fool of himself than he had already. He had never felt so relieved. He wiped his brow again, this time with a handkerchief, a dark red one his wife had given to him in a Christmas stocking years ago. He was cooling down. But he also felt sad, let down and a little bit lost. He wanted to stamp his feet. He might not have wanted to meet her out of the blue, in the butcher's shop, just like that. He was shy, inexperienced even. But he wanted to meet her. Best, he wanted Queenie to meet him. He knew he was being ridiculous. How could she want to meet him? She didn't know who he was.

The butcher turned round with Percy's bacon. He was a small, bespectacled man with a huge stomach. A bloodied apron stretched across it as it rested on the counter. He wrapped the bacon in grease-proof paper. Percy picked the package up, it felt cold and soft, looked at it for some time, turned it over in his hands, and then put it back on the counter.

'Is anything the matter, sir?' Holmes asked.

'Errgh, no, no.' Percy didn't want to go. He wanted to stay in the butcher's, with Queenie. He could have stayed here forever. He stood thinking of something else he could buy, anything. His mind was not working smoothly. It was like Queenie's breath, erratic. He could sense she was moving around behind him, becoming impatient. He fumbled an order for two lamb chops.

'Two?' Holmes questioned, so used to single orders.

Holmes was already walking towards the door at the back of the counter before Percy muttered a faint yes. As the butcher disappeared through the door to where Percy presumed the carcasses hung, cold and stiff, in neat rows, he turned to look at Queenie. She smiled. This time he knew she was smiling at him. She bore little resemblance to Toots. Where Toots's features, her nose, her mouth, her forehead, were too pronounced, Queenie's were well balanced with her small frame, her fine bone structure. Though she had perhaps spent too much time in the sun, Percy reflected. Her face was awash with wrinkles, rippling out from her petite nose. Her skin, a yellow brown, was speckled with freckles, some in large clusters. But he didn't mind. In fact she looked all the more exotic for it. He was sure her eyes were sea green. But he had never been very good at discerning the colour of people's eyes. He hoped they were, though. He liked the idea of Queenie having sea green eyes. Living by the sea. It didn't matter that the North Sea was never sea green, just grey.

Quite suddenly he realised he was doing something he thought he would never do again. He was looking into a woman's eyes, for something more than companionship, for love. He shrugged his shoulders. OK, he said to himself, I'm an old man, I can dream. And it was then he realised he was alone with Queenie in the same room. They were alone together for the first time in the butcher's on Bells Road. In the midst of the white tiles and marble, brightened by the fluorescent fly killer and strong strip lights, Queenie was resplendent. He could feel his face warming. He knew he had to say something. He knew this was his chance. He caught Queenie's eye again. She smiled, he smiled.

'He takes his time,' she said. 'What on earth can he be doing in there?'

'I think we've met before,' Percy croaked. He tried to clear his throat.

'What on earth can he be doing in there?' She repeated.

'He's getting my lamb chops. I think we may have met before,' he tried a little louder, feeling hotter, feeling his face redden. He looked up at the fluorescent fly killer, as if this were what was making his face glow. He then fiddled with the buttons on his coat, trying not to look at her. She opened her bag and took out a packet of Consulate. As she lit up and exhaled a fat plume in the vague direction of the fly killer that Percy had been studying, Holmes appeared back behind the counter, offering apologies for taking so long, but saying there had been a run on lamb chops that morning and he had had to prepare Percy's specially.

'No grandchildren today?' Holmes said, looking at Queenie. Queenie shot another plume at the blue hue and tipped some ash onto the sawdust.

'No, I'm pleased to say, and no dogs either,' she said.

'Well, you know I've always got the odd thing or two for children or dogs.' The butcher smiled.

Percy noticed a large No Smoking sign on the wall and presumed the butcher just made allowances for Queenie, her spent smoke now drifting over the counter, over the cuts of meat. He presumed everyone just made allowances for Queenie. He paid for the grease-proof paper packages and put them in a crumpled plastic bag he pulled out from a coat pocket. He thanked the butcher and turned to Queenie. 'We have met before,' he said, surprised that his throat had cleared, surprised with his own clarity. 'Well not exactly met, but I saw you on Christmas day, outside your house. I was with your sister, Toots.' He then knew he shouldn't have mentioned Toots. 'I've seen you elsewhere, around Gorleston, too.'

'Toots,' Queenie said, 'I haven't spoken to her for years.'

'Well I hope I'll see you again,' Percy said hurriedly. 'My name's Percy.'

Holmes started to rearrange the cuts of meat, packing the bits of poultry tighter into one corner, squashing the drum sticks and chicken wings together.

'Well,' said Queenie, exhaling, 'Gorleston's a small place. You seem to know where I live.'

Percy sat in his car without turning the ignition. He sat in the mustard coloured Vauxhall Cavalier across the street, across Bells Road from Holmes, The Family Butcher, thinking. He noticed a few yards ahead on his side of the street was another Happy Shopper. He had not noticed this one before and he smiled at the thought of a chain of Happy Shoppers throughout Gorleston, throughout the country. The bright orange lettering, the smiling girl's face with a flop of hair blown across her brow, smiling down on shoppers, on pensioners. Then Queenie sped past in her Mini Metro, up Bells Road. And on along Marine Parade. Percy thought in his stationary vehicle, sea green eyes by the grey North Sea. He made up his mind. If he didn't bump into her within the next week he would go and see her. He would call round to her bungalow, with its crazy chimney and chain fence, frosted glass front door and tidy front lawn. He knew he would do it. He knew he would have the courage. He realised something in the butcher's. He felt something he thought he would never feel again, a rush of anticipation. It is not all over yet, he said to himself in the rearview mirror and smiled. Not by a long way. He blew his nose on his handkerchief. Elizabeth would understand. She would. She would. She left me here. He felt his eyes water. Though he didn't know whether it was through sadness or excitement. Or just from blowing a sore nose.

'We have been shopping for today, we'll do tomorrow's tomorrow,' Percy heard an aged woman tell another aged woman in a corner of The Feathers. Their husbands, or friends, were by the fruit machine, smoking and frantically pushing buttons. The machine flashed now and then and played an electronic tune as coins clattered out. The men left the coins in the chrome tray and the even older looking man kept fishing out other coins from the side pocket of his fawn cardigan and pushing them into the machine. It was beginning to annoy Percy. He had never been able to work fruit machines. He never knew what to do when the nudge and hold lights flashed up, when the cash or chance light came on.

Percy usually called in at The Feathers when he needed to go to the toilet, while shopping. Though The Feathers was next to the public toilets at the beginning of the High Street, he preferred going in the pub. He liked to have a coffee, and occasionally a brandy as well. Today he had seated himself by the window. He had a splendid view of the toilets, the cross junction with England's Lane, Boots, and the public library, the busiest area of Gorleston. He had finished his first brandy and was halfway through his second when he thought he saw Queenie's Mini Metro pull out of England's Lane and into the High Street. But the car was going too slowly. It crawled round the corner and into the High Street, stopping by Boots to let a parked car pull out. The woman inside the Metro had fluffy white hair, not dissimilar from Cassie's, and thick black-framed spectacles. As the car moved up the High Street he could see a LIFE sticker on the rear windscreen.

Percy was now into the third day of his stake-out, as he liked to think of it. The third day of looking for Queenie, the third day of hoping to bump into the woman who now preoccupied his conscious thoughts. He had been all over Gorleston, to the butcher's every day, and twice yesterday, to the pier, the Pier Hotel, the Links, St Edmunds. He even drove up to the golf club for a sighting, for an encounter. Coins carried on clattering out of the fruit machine irregularly as he pondered the geography of Gorleston, the establishments Queenie might frequent. His travels invariably took him forwards and backwards, past Queenie's bungalow on Yallop Avenue. Sometimes the Metro was sitting there in the miniature driveway. Sometimes it wasn't. Then he would feel twinges of jealously. That morning, at seven-thirty, the car had not been there. He had driven to the thin carpark, his carpark, edging

Gorleston cliff top. The carpark that had once felt so secure, so final. He had got out and scanned the length of the lower esplanade, each deserted beach hut, and the pier, for a flash of orange. But everything was calm and grey in the chill early morning air. The Vauxhall, perched on the edge of Gorleston, was little comfort. He revved the engine in frustration and let the wheels spin in the sandy gravel as he whipped the car round and back onto Marine Parade.

Two young lads came into the lounge. They slouched by the bar waiting for their lager. The smaller one, the sleeve of his tasselled leather jacket dripping into an ashtray, surveyed the room. 'This place is full of old gits. Stupid sods.' Their lager came and they slurped it for a while before the taller one turned to his friend. 'I'd hate to be fucking old. Fuck all to do.'

Percy flinched in his window seat. Not so long ago he would have perhaps agreed with them. Not now, however. They don't know what it is about at all, he said to himself. They couldn't be more wrong. He put his coat on and walked out of The Feathers and into a crowd that had gathered by the corner of England's Lane and the High Street. People stood staring at something in the middle of the road. They put their shopping down on the pavement and stood and whispered to one another. He couldn't see what they were looking at or make out what they were talking about. He became entangled in the crowd as it grew. He had difficulty keeping his balance amongst the shopping bags and small dogs smothered in tartan blankets. A Jack Russell started to pee on a Superdrug carrier bag, though nobody did anything about it. Everybody was too busy looking into the middle of England's Lane. A siren sounded in the distance. The crowd began to shuffle back as it got louder, and Percy found himself near the kerb looking down on an old woman seated in the road. Her shopping was scattered over the asphalt, tins of dog food, fruit salad, tuna fish. A younger woman squatted beside her, holding her hand. Someone had placed a blanket over the older woman's shoulders. A car had been left in the middle of the road just short of her, with its doors wide open. He presumed it must have hit her. The old woman didn't look like she had been hurt badly, but she just sat in the road, pale and vacant. He could see that one of her legs, with a thick white support stocking on the ankle, was shaking.

'It was a near miss. It was near miss,' he heard someone say nearby again and again. The ambulance men placed another blanket over her shoulders and scooped her up into their new white and green wagon. The younger woman got in too and the ambulance headed off, back up the High Street. Its siren emitting the odd yelp. A noise quite like The Feathers' fruit machine made just before it ejected the jackpot, Percy found himself thinking.

The swamp to the north of Gorleston gradually assumed solidity, pushing the mouth of the River Yare further and further south. On this sandbank, bounded by the North Sea on the east, by the Yare on the west and by a small outlet known as Grubbe's Haven to the north, was built Yarmouth.

Grubbe's Haven silted up some time after the Norman Conquest and access to the natural harbour of the Yare estuary some way to the south was bitterly contested between Gorleston, which at this time had no seaboard, and Yarmouth.

Administered by an official of the Crown, Yarmouth obtained a charter which decreed that all merchandise be unloaded on its side of the Yare, for which it would pay the king a rent. The Earl of Richmond, the Lord of the Manor of Gorleston, petitioned the King, Edward I, claiming that Gorleston had anciently held the right for the reception of ships, together with all fairs, markets and franchises. The case was eventually referred to the Lord Chancellor, who in 1332 after a visit here himself, made the decision under Great Seal in favour of

Yarmouth. The King's rights to customs were to be preserved in Yarmouth.

Over the centuries the dispute would manifest itself in many ways, whether over ferry dues across the river or fishing rights, but Gorleston's hopes of ever becoming an independent port were wrecked in 1332. From that date many have said the town declined in consequence.

With two days to go Percy was becoming increasingly anxious. Rather than exhaust him, his continual searching and hoping only increased his energy and heightened his sense of anticipation. He would perhaps stop for tea or a bite to eat, but he never let his guard down, he was always alert, always looking. He would sip his tea too quickly and burn his tongue, get terrible indigestion from half-eaten cheese and pickle or ham and mustard sandwiches. He now went shopping two or three times a day, making excuses to himself for reasons to go into town, buying far too many packets of biscuits, tea bags, cartons of milk, rashers of bacon. His kitchen cupboards began to fill up with things he knew he would never have time to use. And in this heightened state he began to notice things, appreciate and re-evaluate things, parts of Gorleston he had always taken for granted, parts of Gorleston he had not known existed.

He realised how much he liked Bells Road and its small and friendly shops. There was Kenley's Footwear and Kersey's Electrical Goods. He had bought a new kettle from Kersey's shortly after his wife had died and he had been so disorientated he had been unable to put the plug on. Not that he was ever any good with electrical problems, that was Elizabeth's forte. She was practical. Until now Percy had forgotten how polite the man was when he had returned it for assistance. He had felt foolish and inept and the man, who wore brown overalls with pens in the chest pocket, had acted as if it were the most normal occurrence. 'You'd be surprised with the number of people who can't put plugs on,' he had said. 'Nothing wrong with that.'

Then there was the greengrocer, unable to contain the wealth of his goods on his trestle tables and boxed shelves that looked as if they were built from driftwood. Vegetables spilled onto the pavement. Percy had heard people complaining about this in St Edmunds. Complaining that they had nearly slipped or tripped and that one day someone would be killed. But he enjoyed the colour, the vegetation. He would never complain. And he enjoyed the toy shop next door, its window of Meccano cranes and Hornby trains, model World War II aeroplanes and Fifties sports cars. The promise of timeless entertainment. He had never seen children enter, only men mostly his age. And he had seen only men emerge clutching great packages, wrapped in brown paper. Smiling.

He wandered the High Street with new eyes. Changed the prescription of his glasses. He'd start at the busy beginning, the congested corner of England's Lane and the High Street, the corner where the pavement had been extended to accommodate the crowds and the toilet. Then he would move swiftly up the slight hill, past first Boots, then Superdrug, Addison's The Chemist, and two other chemists he could never remember the names of. Now his wife was no longer alive, now he no longer had to stem her pain with a cocktail of prescriptions, his visits to these chemists were irregular and infrequent. He noticed the resigned look of the shoppers entering Boots trailing their shopping baskets on wobbly wheels, a look pale with fatigue. The dull, smudged rouge, hiding little and telling of the great effort of getting up and going shopping. Of getting up and making the life-sustaining visit to the chemist.

But he also noticed the same faces emerge enlightened from the High Street's two travel agents. The travel agents' windows were plastered with last-minute offers for holidays of a lifetime; holidays to end a lifetime, Percy thought. Extended winter-warmer breaks for weeks, sometimes months, in resorts that enjoyed daytime temperatures that rose to 70 degrees and English food and beer at half the price. Tenerife, Madeira, Gibraltar, Malta, Cyprus. The world of winter warmth seemed vast to Percy, and far, far away. He had been to Spain and once to Malta, though for summer holidays, when he and his wife would sit on small beaches in the soaring heat. He always found the heat uncomfortable and hated getting sand in the picnic. Elizabeth would gaze at the Mediterranean Sea and daydream. He never knew what she was thinking, wishing, and he would not disturb her. He found she could look so delightful, so charming when she was like this, he preferred to just watch her. As they grew older they stopped going abroad, and went no further than the North Sea for holidays. 'I found the Mediterranean so predictable,' Elizabeth used to say, 'here at least you're never sure of the weather, or what to expect.' Percy found that by the North Sea, with the unpredictable weather and unstable beaches, their own sense of security was reaffirmed. Though he was never sure whether Elizabeth felt the same way. Or whether she just preferred the unforeseeable.

Percy had let his mind wander. He concentrated on the corner of the larger travel agent's window. He perused the exotic and tropical locations, the year-round hot spots, from Florida to Bangkok and countless islands with names like Polynesian dances in between. Nothing excited him. He had no wish to go on holiday, no desire to visit a tropical island. He wanted to stay here, in the damp cold, in Gorleston, by the North Sea. Everything that mattered was here.

Further up the High Street, further towards Great Yarmouth, past the banks and building societies, past the post office which always had a queue outside and Radio

Rentals, which had a queue outside also, the High Street narrowed. The pavements shrunk and the shop fronts became dotted amid small terraces of houses, the odd detached house and bigger buildings, some with Rotary Club, or Gorleston Conservative Club, or Women's Institute, inscribed above the front door or on fading plaques attached to the façade. Percy had seldom come this far up the High Street before. Now he found it fascinating. Just near a shop selling artists' materials, easels and brushes, rows of paint tubes, was Joe's Tattoo Studio. The tattooist's front window was swamped by a giant painting of a naked woman with purple hair and a green snake entwined around her body. A note in the bottom of the window listed Fine Line, Custom, Japanese and Traditional Designs. Privacy Guaranteed, it stated in equally large letters. Percy imagined Burt and other riggers coming here, the far end of Gorleston High Street, to be forever marked with images of naked women, the names of lovers past and present. Slightly further up and across the street was Sally Smith's lingerie shop. He marvelled at the size of the slight pink knickers, the lace camisoles, the short nighties. He thought of Linda, then he thought of Queenie.

That evening, as he slowly lowered himself into his bath, he looked at his thin right forearm and visualised a tattoo of Queenie, unfurling from his elbow. He visualised Queenie naked and curvaceous, her hair, more blonde than orange, falling over her breasts.

On the last day, the last day of hoping for a chance encounter, Percy found himself in Lower Gorleston. He had parked his car in the Pier Hotel carpark, scanned Gorleston Pier, and the North Pier opposite, just in case, and briskly set off along Brush Quay. There were no fishing boats in sight, but seagulls followed gaily and noisily overhead. The River Yare calmly reflected the hazy blue sky and Yarmouth Power

Station's chimney. The image of a bright yellow salvage vessel, moored to Yarmouth's East Quay, also rippled across the river, its funnel merging with the chimney as Percy reached Gorleston's lifeboat station. He felt warm as he walked, now along Riverside Road. It felt like spring. He wished he hadn't worn his thick overcoat. Workmen with a digger were moving earth and mud, building up the quay between two wooden jetties. He stopped briefly and chatted to one of the workmen who was leaning against the digger smoking a cigarette. Percy remarked on the fine weather and asked him what they were doing.

'Big tides are coming,' the workman said, breathing smoke out of his nose. 'We're plugging the gaps. Last autumn this road was a foot under water.'

Percy knew Lower Gorleston was prone to flooding. As he continued along the uneven and pot-holed road with the flurry of gulls he tried to imagine the River Yare swollen, Gorleston under siege from the sea. He knew no one who lived on this side of town. He had no idea who lived in the ramshackle homes that stretched along Riverside Road just a few feet away from the water. But he found them appealing. He appreciated the danger, the precariousness of their situation. Yes, he said to himself, the unforeseeable, how appealing.

Queenie's Mini Metro was parked on the dirt track leading to the harbour pilots' headquarters. The building, a modern two-storey block, sat incongruously on the weatherbeaten waterfront. Moored up were three pilot boats waiting to guide the large ships in and out of the harbour. He stood in the road, looked at the car, then the pilots' building, then out across the River Yare towards the busy docks of Great Yarmouth and the towering power station. He looked out and across to a different town. He could feel his heart beating. He stood on Riverside Road and felt himself almost vibrate with the hum of the digger and his heart. His energy suddenly seemed to dissipate and he felt slightly faint. He walked slowly over to the car to check he hadn't made a mistake, even though he knew he hadn't. An opened packet of Consulate lay on the front passenger seat and a lilac silk head-scarf was draped across the back seat which was covered in black dog-hairs. The car was quite filthy inside and out. He noticed a number of dents on the wings. There were more dents on the front and rear bumpers. Rust sprouting here and there. One of the headlights was cracked. He then walked over to the building. He just wanted to see if he could see anything. See what the pilots did while waiting for the short trips out of the harbour mouth, out into the North Sea. He didn't feel he was snooping. He didn't want to spy on anyone, certainly not Queenie. He just wanted to see what was going on. Heavens, he said to himself, Gorleston was full enough of Peeping Toms, all at it full-time. As he walked along Bately Avenue, Buxton Avenue or Youell Avenue, even Yallop Avenue, he would catch sight of shrivelled faces peeping out from behind curtains and blinds, peering at him and the street, peering into a world they were no longer part of. If they saw him staring back they would suddenly disappear, shut their curtains or close their blinds, shrink back into the artificial light and warmth and security of their homes.

A bell started to ring just as Percy reached the nearest ground-floor window. Because of the glare he couldn't see in. He immediately turned around. He no longer felt faint but slightly sick, the bell still ringing, louder and louder in his head. A wave of panic washed through his body. He stumbled to the quay where the pilot boats were moored. He didn't know what was going to happen, why the bell was ringing, how he could explain his presence. He stared at a pilot boat trying to think logically, calmly. Close up it was big and bright, bright orange. A cabin led off from the wheel-house. He crouched down on the cold concrete quay by a bronze capstan and tried to look in one of the small dark portholes. He saw nothing at first then something moved. He could make out a figure, perhaps two or three. As he stood up, the hatch by the wheel-house opened and a man hurried out. He was wearing what Percy thought must be a captain's uniform, a navy jacket with gold stripes on the sleeves and epaulets. The captain was carrying his cap. Queenie then emerged out of the hatch behind him. She lifted up her dress to step over the gunwale and onto dry land, a few feet from Percy. 'So long,' she shouted after the captain, who reached the door of the pilots' building just as two similarly dressed men came out.

'It's quite something,' she said looking at Percy and straightening her dress on the dock side. 'They're very complicated, much more so than they used to be. There's an extraordinary amount of navigation equipment, monitors, depth sounders, radars. It's all in there.' She moved closer to Percy.

'Look interested,' he thought he heard her whisper. Though he wasn't sure. He was aware of the digger, still chugging and humming in the distance. And he was aware of the shortness of his breath. The two other captains boarded the same boat. They nodded at Queenie and then at Percy.

Queenie turned to Percy. 'I'm sure I recognise you.' The boat's engine choked into life, drowning out the digger. They stepped back. 'Yes, you do look familiar, but I'm sorry dear, I can't remember your name.'

'It's, it's Percy.'

'Have we ever met?'

Percy wiped his brow. 'Urrgh, yes, twice, sort of,' he replied staring at the ground. 'Most recently a week ago, in the butcher's, Holmes' on Bells Road.' He moved up to the capstan. He felt more sure of himself than he had thought he would. After all the anticipation, the week of watching and waiting, Queenie's sudden appearance was even more surprising than he could have imagined. Oddly it calmed him.

'Oh, yes,' she said. Though Percy was not convinced she remembered. 'Queenie,' she said, holding out her tiny, wrinkled hand. The pilot boat pulled off. 'Coo-ee,' she shouted to the captain piloting the orange vessel. 'Coo-ee,' she went again, waving. 'I've known a lot of pilots,' she said turning once again to Percy.

Percy tried to remember the conversation that followed, everything Queenie and he had said, word by word, as he walked back along Riverside Road. As he walked back to his car alone. She told him she had always been fascinated by the pilot boats and had watched them for most of her life, meeting ships, guiding them home. She had smoked three Consulate cigarettes consecutively. She said she occasionally visited the pilots, though nowadays they were always so busy. But when they had time they still loved to show her around, show her the latest pieces of equipment. And take her out to meet the ships sometimes. But she said it used to be more fun, when they were all a little younger. 'They are now much more careful,' she had said, he remembered. She kept brushing her orange hair away from her eyes. A sea breeze must have got up. She asked Percy to drop by for an early evening drink and perhaps a game of cards next week. Then she left in a cloud of smoke and dust, roaring down Riverside Road. But he couldn't be sure of anything, his mind was unclear, thick with flotsam. The pilot boat was speeding back into the harbour as Percy climbed into his car. He thought he would just sit here a while, and watch it safely home.

5

Percy woke earlier than normal. He had indigestion. He felt anxious. He lay in his bed in the thinning darkness, worrying. He believed he felt guilty. He realised that over the last few days he had thought of little else but Queenie. What a difference from just a few weeks ago, he thought, smiling. Then a wave of pain swept up from his stomach and into his chest. He thought of the other people still alive he had neglected recently. Linda and Burt, who he hadn't thanked properly for their party. Toots and Charlie, his new friends. They were friends, he insisted to himself. He even started to feel guilty about not visiting Cassie for tea and not dropping by the Links for a drink with John Conway. He didn't want to appear rude or exclusive, Gorleston was too small for that. Gorleston was suddenly full of friends. And now that he had made contact with Queenie, now that that was sorted out, he wanted to be a part of Gorleston, to be a part of the life here. For the first time.

His mind moved ahead quickly. Queenie's image floated in front of him, quite life-like. He began to think about the rest of his life. How it would all fit together. He wanted it to all fit together. He was used to order. He understood it. He caressed the neat triangles of the quilt, ran his fingers along the stitching. He was worried about Queenie and Toots, though. The fact that they didn't get on. Here, he thought, there might be a problem. Still, in his warm bed, surrounded by the dampness, he could imagine them all going out as a foursome, Toots and Charlie, Queenie and himself, strolling into the Links. Perhaps they would go to Great Yarmouth. The Star Hotel for tea.

It was six-thirty in the morning and he could hear Mrs Yarren moving around her bungalow next door. Gorleston was full of early risers. He heard her walk from one end of the bungalow to the other. And back again. He imagined Sandy, padding loyally behind. And further away, further down Bately Avenue, he thought he could hear the hum of someone hoovering. He lay on his back listening. Savouring the sounds of the new day. Of life. He breathed as quietly as he could, trying not to miss anything. He shut his eyes and the room rocked gently, as though he were at sea. He couldn't quite believe what was happening around him. That all this was real. That Queenie was real. He couldn't help but be swept along. He felt like a thousand particles of sand suspended in the littoral drift that scoured the Gorleston sea-shore.

He had a sudden urge to ring everyone up. He wanted to hear the voices of his friends. He wanted to make sure it was all real. But he knew he should wait an hour or two. And he knew he should stop thinking about Queenie all the time or he wouldn't get anything done. He decided not to think about her until eight-thirty, which would give him something to look forward to. He thought he might do some housework. When his wife was alive they used to have a cleaner who came on Tuesdays and Thursdays. Elizabeth enjoyed chatting with her. But since Elizabeth died he preferred to do the cleaning himself. Apart from the fact that he was better at it and younger than the cleaner, there was only himself and he didn't make much of a mess. He never entertained. As he started to dust Elizabeth's dressing table in his frayed blue pyjamas he thought not of her, but that perhaps it was time he held a small party, a drinks party. He drew up a mental list of the people he would invite, if he were to have one. The list ground to a halt at eight including himself. It seemed to be all couples. He wondered mischievously about pairing Cassie off with John Conway. You never know, he chuckled to himself. Strange things do happen. Strange things certainly happen here. He tried to yelp like The Feathers' fruit machine when it was paying out the jackpot.

The rumble of Mrs Yarren's washing machine started to permeate the wet early morning air. Someone somewhere else had turned on a transistor. He then heard Mrs Yarren open her back door. He heard Sandy rummage around the small frosty garden, separated from his by a wooden fence. A few seconds later he heard Mrs Yarren calling. 'Sandy, Sandy.' He thought of the dog, alone at last in the dark garden. A few more seconds lapsed before he heard her calling again. This time she sounded quite frantic. A torch beam traced across the top of his window and he heard Mrs Yarren join the rummaging in the garden. 'Sandy, where are you, treasure? You know Mummy loves you. Where are you, treasure? Arrgh, there you are, darling. Do come inside now. You'll catch your death of cold. Be a good boy.' Percy was thankful his other neighbours didn't have a dog. They had a cat which they didn't let out of their bungalow for fear it would run off.

He let up the kitchen blind with a bang, he never could control it, and saw light emerging from the eastern sky. He went over the kitchen floor with a dust pan and brush, his back not aching as much as usual, and moved onto the hall with the Hoover. He banged into the hall table and knocked the handset off the telephone. He replaced it and went to look at the kitchen clock. He had just over half an hour to wait before he could politely make his first telephone call and over an hour before he could think of Queenie.

But he couldn't help wondering what she might be doing right now. If she would be looking at the brightening sky. It was going to be a clear day. He tried to wipe the thought of Queenie from his mind. He thought of blue sky, repeating blue sky, blue sky, in his head. He followed the Hoover into the sitting room.

He was trying to push the Hoover away into the hall cupboard when the telephone rang. He jumped.

'Toots here,' she shouted. 'Where have you been hiding?'

Her voice rung in his head. 'Actually I've been running around all over town. I'm surprised we haven't bumped into each other,' he said hastily, feeling rather clever with himself.

'Are you telling the truth?' she said, sounding like a concerned parent. 'Are you sure you're telling the truth?' she repeated.

'Of course.' He was thrown off course. 'I never lie, Toots. You can count on me. I'm as reliable as the tide.'

'Well, I hope you have not been hiding from me. There is no escaping,' she said threateningly. 'No escaping, you know.'

He felt concerned and sat down on the small stool by the hall table. He couldn't imagine what she meant. He couldn't imagine what was in store.

'It's turning into a lovely morning, I thought I might pop round for an early morning coffee.'

'I'm still in my pyjamas. And besides, the house is in a terrible mess. You couldn't possibly come round now. Not possibly.'

'Have you got someone there?'

Percy laughed, nervously. 'Don't be ridiculous.' He laughed again. 'I'm far too old for that sort of thing.' He looked at his bent body, the thin white ankles protruding from his pyjamas. His moulting Marks & Spencer slippers. He knew he should tidy himself up. Buy some new slippers, pyjamas, a silk bathrobe, perhaps. Instead of a dressing gown he had taken to wearing an old camel-hair coat around the house when the heating wasn't working properly.

'Well then, you had better come round on Thursday evening.'

'I can't, I'm busy.'

'Busy. Nobody is ever busy in Gorleston. Are you sure you are not just avoiding me?'

'Of course not, I really am busy.'

'I believe I'm becoming rather jealous. What are you up to? Where are you going? Who have you been seeing?'

'Oh, it's just that a distant relative is taking me out for supper.' He tried to sound as casual as possible, knowing he would not have been able to lie had he not been on the phone.

'You told me you didn't have any relatives.'

'Oh, well a few, distant ones. Very distant.'

In the end Percy invited Toots and Charlie round for a drink a week later, a week after his date with Queenie. 'Do bring Charlie,' he insisted, and wondered whether to invite everyone else.

He put the phone down and wondered why he had felt guilty at all earlier that morning, why he had even contemplated ringing Toots. Was she really a friend? What was she really after? And he began to wonder if Toots knew something about Queenie and himself. If she knew he was going round to Queenie's on Thursday evening for a drink and perhaps a game of cards. Why had she asked him round on Thursday? Why Thursday of all days. No one is ever busy in Gorleston. Toots said so.

He telephoned Linda. She took a while to answer and sounded very out of breath when she did. 'I hope I haven't disturbed you,' he said. She said she was saying goodbye to Burt, who was due back on the rig. She said he was late but that she couldn't bear to see him go, even though he was only going for a week this time. Percy said he just wanted to thank her properly for the party, sorry it had taken him so long, and that he was having a small drinks party on Thursday week. He felt oddly embarrassed for mentioning it and put the phone down quickly. He dressed and made himself a cup of instant coffee. He counted eight jars of Nescafé in the cupboard, and ten jars of Marvel. He couldn't believe he would ever be able to use it all. He opened the back door and stepped into the garden with a mug of coffee. The grass glistened with frost in the early morning sun. Steam rose from the mug. He lifted his face to the summery rays and thought of Queenie. It was eight-twenty-three, but he always kept his watch a few minutes fast.

For more than 200 years attempts were made to stabilise the mouth of the River Yare. Then in the reign of Elizabeth I an ingenious Dutchman, Joas Johnson, built a wooden pier that stretched far out into the North Sea from the south bank of the Yare. The vast structure not only fortified the harbour against the sea, and secured the Yare's exit, but over the centuries it became a beloved feature of Gorleston.

Curving out into the water the old wooden pier caught the sun throughout the day. Crowds of anglers, families and courting couples would clamber over the weathered planks and pilings, and rest in the cosies between the great timber knees, which also provided shelter against the cold northerly winds. The pier was lined with capstans, for so long used to warp schooners into harbour.

For 400 years the pier survived. Each gap opened by the pounding waves lovingly patched. Finally the North Sea and a particularly nagging worm, Teredo Navalis, got the better of it. The rotten, worm-riddled timbers were replaced in 1964 by a solid concrete pier.

Many hydrological experts blame the new pier for the dramatic disappearance of much of Gorleston beach. They claim the new pier directs the littoral drift out to sea, sweeping the sand with it.

Clothes shopping was new to Percy. He had never had to think about it. Elizabeth had just done it for him. She knew what went with what. She was quietly stylish, elegant. And she did her best with Percy, but Percy occasionally wondered whether she was trying too hard. Of course he always wore what she purchased for him, he was always grateful for the time and trouble she went to, though sometimes he didn't quite feel like himself in his new clothes. 'It's what's inside that's important,' he'd joke with her. 'Yes, of course, dear, but we could all do with a new coat of paint from time to time,' she'd reply.

Percy entered Marks & Spencer as if for the first time. The shop was bright and warm and packed. He was immediately relieved to notice that there were quite a few men present. He didn't feel too out of place. Nevertheless he felt conspicuous, wandering the aisles and the racks, wandering over the carpet squares, on his own. Most men seemed to have female companions to guide them. He felt he could do with some guidance too. He had an idea what he wanted. What he wanted to look like. Indeed, what impression he wanted to make. But he had no idea where to start. After some time lost in the haze of green and cream he came upon shelves and shelves of pyjamas, in every imaginable colour and style, neatly wrapped in plastic. For some reason Elizabeth had always bought him blue pyjamas. He picked a green and white striped pair, presumed he was a medium, and put the packet in a basket. He moved onto the racks of dressing gowns. Here he thought he would go for a silk one, perhaps in burgundy. He had long imagined such a thing. He wanted to feel and look rather decadent. Standing by the rack he took his jacket off and put on a silk burgundy dressing gown over his pullover. But he found it was not at all what he expected. The material felt sticky, almost salty. He looked at himself in the tall, smudged mirror. The dressing gown draped lifelessly over his thin shoulders, clinging to his pullover. It stopped well short of his knees. He imagined walking through his home, out into the garden on a summer's morning, with his thin legs looking whiter than ever against the dark red hue. He hung the dressing gown back on the rack. He found a fawn towelling one that he much preferred. The colour and the thickness of the material were more comforting. It was also a good deal longer, reaching nearly to his ankles. He turned round, trying to see what it would look like from the back.

'That's the right choice.'

He knew the voice instantly.

'Looks great. Who's the lucky lady?'

Blushing, Percy turned to face Linda. His red face and neck coordinating nicely with the fawn towelling. She smiled broadly. He wasn't sure where to look so he looked down at her shopping basket, overflowing with black and white lacy frills.

'Mmmmm.' Her eyes sparkled under the bright lights.

'Hello, hello,' he said, feeling the heat on his face. 'Just doing some shopping. Awfully crowded and hot in here. I thought it was about time I bought a decent dressing gown. My neighbours can see everything. You know how nosy people are around here.' He cleared his throat.

Linda agreed. 'I'm spied on all the time.'

Percy could imagine. Though he thought she was not perhaps the most discreet person he had ever met. He looked again at her basket and imagined her parading around her hot house, even hotter than Marks & Spencer, dressed in skimpy pieces of black lace, lingering as she passed the windows.

'Let's pay up and grab a coffee.' Linda tugged at his

arm, still encased in fawn towelling. 'I love my elevenses.'

He said he would love to do that, but that he had intended to buy a pair of slippers and a jacket as well. He told her he couldn't remember the last time he had had a new jacket. He could, but he didn't want to think about it.

'Well, if you're quick,' she laughed. She led him to the suits and jackets area, crowded with men stiffly trying jackets on, all being advised by their wives, or female companions. He looked at the men struggling with their jackets and the women picking other jackets off the racks. He thought he recognised a few from St Edmunds or perhaps the Links. He could see them looking at Linda and himself. He knew they would be wondering whether Linda was his daughter. He knew they would be looking at this younger woman with her basket of frilly underwear and wondering what she was doing with him, a much older man, quite red in the face. And oddly he found himself liking the idea of being thought about in such scandalous terms. A few people were now whispering to each other. It made him feel important, something he was not used to. Aware of the looks they were getting, Linda whispered in his ear, 'I wonder if they think I am your daughter or mistress.'

'Oh, mistress, I hope.'

In full view of everybody Linda theatrically chose Percy a navy blue double-breasted blazer with real brass buttons. 'It makes you look very handsome,' she said loudly.

Percy looked in the mirror and agreed. It did suit him and it reminded him of the harbour pilots' uniform. It was exactly what he wanted. He worried about what he could wear the jacket with though, what shirt and tie, what trousers. And he anticipated a few more visits to Marks & Spencer.

As they waited to pay a couple walked past and both

nodded at Percy before looking quizzically at Linda who was unloading her basket onto the counter. Percy had once had lunch with them at St Edmunds, a long time ago. He remembered the woman was rather pleasant but her husband a bully, never letting his wife finish a sentence. He couldn't remember their names. He nodded pleasantly and vowed never to go back to St Edmunds if he could help it. He shuddered at the thought of the Mascot Suite dining room, the hopelessness of it. He could even smell the room, the sweet smell of pee. He shuddered again.

'Burt's very fussy,' Linda said, as if explaining why she was taking so long at the till. 'He goes through phases, one minute it's black, then white, then black again. Still, I like to please him. I like to make an effort. My mother always told me to make an effort with my underwear. She used to say it keeps men keen.'

Percy was becoming used to Linda's frankness but he was surprised to see that her total, flashed on a green extension to the till, came to twice as much as his. 'It's not cheap,' he said, then wondered if he had said quite the right thing.

Yardley's Cafe, on the corner of the High Street and Baker Street, was where everyone went for elevenses. At this time of day the front window was thick with condensation, so much so that the interior was lost to passers-by. Inside, the large room was warm and damp and smoky. They had some difficulty threading their way to a small table at the back, minding shopping bags and small dogs, umbrellas, walking sticks, and two Zimmer frames.

'Gracious,' Linda exclaimed. 'Rush hour.' She ordered a milky coffee and a chocolate eclair. Percy settled for just a coffee. He didn't have a sweet tooth. 'So Percy, you never answered my question. Why all the new clothes, is it the party, or are you trying to impress someone?'

He was reticent. He looked around the room casually. 'Oh, the party,' he said loudly.

But Linda was quite persistent. 'You can't fool me,' she said, fingering her chocolate eclair. 'I saw the way you looked in the mirror when you were trying on that blazer.'

He took a sip of his coffee and burnt his tongue on the pale watery liquid. 'Well, you know, it's the time of the year. Good for a change. The party's a good excuse.'

'Yes?' She wiped some cream from the corner of her mouth with a paper napkin. Her big blue eyes staring at him.

'I've never held a party. Not on my own. I thought it was time I repaid everyone who has been so kind to me, you and Burt included of course. You have all meant so much to me. More than you could imagine.' He sipped his coffee, still piping hot. 'My life has quite changed,' he said, thinking of Queenie. And he began to imagine the party of his life, his coffee table full of crisps and nuts, even cheese straws. He liked those. The room crowded, chatter and laughing, noise.

Linda offered to help Percy with the food and drink, or in any way she could. 'Who else is coming? Will it be big?'

'Well, not that big. But I'm asking all the people who matter.'

Linda was looking about, as if for the waitress. 'Can I get you anything?' He thought she might want another coffee or chocolate eclair. She ate the first one so quickly.

'Oh no, no thank you.' She rubbed her stomach. 'I thought I saw Auntie Queenie.'

Percy leapt up then sat down again. A wave of panic rushed through him. He scanned the smoky room frantically. He wasn't sure what to do. He wasn't sure what Linda thought of Queenie or what Queenie thought of Linda. He knew he wouldn't be able to just sit here if Linda ignored her, like Toots had. He would say something. He would have to say something.

'But it wasn't her. I don't think I've ever seen her in here. It's not her sort of place. She can be very choosy.'

Relaxing, Percy sat for a while trying to breathe calmly. 'Isn't it hot and stuffy?' Linda agreed and asked if he wanted to leave. He said there was no need to leave immediately. His legs were shaking. He knew he wouldn't be able to walk just yet. 'I thought I would ask both Cassie and Queenie to the party.'

'I didn't know you knew Queenie.' Linda's eyes seemed huge. She was wearing blue eye shadow, not a dissimilar shade to the one her mother favoured. 'Well, I suppose everyone knows Queenie. Do you know her well?' She raised her eyebrows.

'Oh, not that well. I've met her a few times. But we get on terribly well.' Percy knew they would get on terribly well even if they didn't yet. 'She's a remarkable lady.'

'She is, certainly. But I am not sure whether it is such a good idea asking both Queenie and my mother. You must know they don't see eye to eye. They don't even talk to each other at the moment. I'm quite sure they wouldn't go to the same party if they knew each other was going to be there.'

'Well, yes, I did know there were some differences. Perhaps there's a way around it.'

'I don't think so. Heavens, over the years I've tried countless times to solve their squabbles. The trouble is they go on for so long they both forget what they're squabbling about. Who knows why they're not speaking to each other at the moment. Nobody can remember. I try not to get involved any more.'

'What if neither of them knew the other was coming?'

'Oh, they'll know. They might not speak to each other but they have a pretty good idea what is going on, what the other is up to. They find out. They have their spies, quite literally. Just look down Yallop Avenue, you've seen the old faces peering out from behind those net curtains.'

'Yes,' said Percy sadly.

'Of course.' Linda looked animated. 'They're both very jealous of each other. Neither would want to be left out. I'm sure neither would want to let you go.' She winked at him. 'But then do you really want to invite them both? Do you really know what you're letting yourself in for?'

Percy wasn't quite sure. But he told Linda he was and said the more the merrier. And in many ways he did think it would all work out. 'Besides,' he told her. 'I haven't asked Queenie yet. She might not be able to come.' He hoped she would, though. He had almost taken it for granted that she would. The party wouldn't be a party without her. It wouldn't feel complete. She must come, he said to himself. She must.

As Linda waggled down the High Street, a stuffed green Marks & Spencer plastic bag swinging from each arm, she turned and shouted to Percy, 'I just hope you know what you're doing.'

'Just make sure your father comes,' he shouted back.

Percy wanted to drive faster. A car and a bus in front were holding him up. He was excited. He couldn't help but rush. He had so much to look forward to. His evening with Queenie, his party, the spring. Along Marine Parade he looked out over a flat sea, speckled with shade from the cumulus floating overhead. A ship was inching its way to port. It looked so majestic. At that moment Percy would have given anything to have been the captain of the ship. The stories he could tell. The respect. He moved his eyes back to the road. He imagined standing on the bridge. 'Maybe', he said aloud, the Vauxhall Cavalier trilling in the background, 'maybe I could come out of retirement'.

6

Dawn came noticeably earlier, in the rush for summer. Soon the hour would move forward. Each morning the insomniacs, and there were many insomniacs in Gorleston, would sit by their open windows and look up at the dark sky waiting for the first whisper of light. Their wait, however, would never get shorter as they took up their vigil earlier and earlier each day. They knew exactly when to expect the light. Why then wait? Gorleston was all about waiting. Everyone waited for something. Even Queenie, though she was never sure what she was waiting for. She was never satisfied with the present. She was always wanting to get on with the next thing, not that she knew what the next thing was. Though someone always turned up. Always.

When Percy was younger, much younger, Saturday night was the night everybody went out, to a film or a dance, a club for a drink. He would meet friends or occasionally take girls out on dates. He was very shy and awkward and it was never a great success. Until he met Elizabeth. She was strong and decisive, she new exactly what she wanted. She would arrange things for them to do, places to meet. She was cultured and entertaining. Once they were married they continued to go out often, to dinner with local friends, sometimes colleagues from Percy's work. They were popular. Elizabeth was popular. And as they started to grow older together, as they couldn't have children, they carried on going out to dinner, the pictures, the golf club. Wednesday night, Friday night, Saturday night. Elizabeth was keenest to get out of the house. And Percy understood, realising how she missed not having children. How she needed distraction. He, of course, followed her, wherever she wanted to go. He would do anything for her, to help her with her loss, their loss. But sometimes he felt it was not much consolation.

Now, so much later in Gorleston, there was no favoured evening to go out. There was no Saturday night or Friday night or Wednesday night. Every night was the same. Every night people went out, if they could, if they were mobile, to console themselves for some loss or other. There was nothing special about a particular night and indeed nothing to miss if you didn't, or couldn't go out. Unless, of course, you were meeting Queenie. In his timeless retirement Percy found that many things quickly assumed extraordinary dimensions and proportions, with scant regard for the past. He had little control. For in Gorleston people lived for the moment. The past was hazy. There was not much future.

Percy knew it was going to be a long day. A long, frantic day. He had woken up in his new green and white striped pyjamas long before he heard Sandy rustle in the next door garden. Long before he heard Mrs Yarren's desperate calls. Yet he got straight out of bed. For he knew it would have been useless to try and go back to sleep. He decided to have his tea and digestive in the kitchen. Sitting there, in his new fawn towelling dressing gown, in the near silence except for the tick of the clock and the intermittent hum of the fridge, he wished he had something proper to do. A proper job. Somewhere to go in the mornings. He turned on his transistor just in time to catch the end of the early morning shipping report. He loved the shipping report, news of the sea. Though as the night turned to day he knew it would not be easy to be the captain of a ship. He imagined himself on deck in oilskins as waves crashed over the bow. Shouting orders through thunder and driving rain, lashed to the wheel. Of course, he knew he would never really be the captain of a ship, or for that matter come out of retirement. Whoever came out of retirement here? He laughed at his own wishful thinking, his stupidity, his childishness, as he dunked a second digestive into his tea. But he was not without hope, not without ambition. For though he had spent much of his life readjusting his dreams, or Elizabeth's dreams, coming to terms with thwarted ambitions and disappointments, there were still things to do. Things he had to do for himself. Now more than ever. In fact the future was brighter than he could ever remember. He loved to have things to look forward to, now he had so much. Everything. Nothing was going to get in his way. Nothing was going to stop him now.

Sandy announced his presence in the garden with a little high-pitched woof. And then Mrs Yarren followed, frantic as ever, frantic as Percy. This calmed Percy, however, and he made and set breakfast methodically, even placing his napkin in its silver ring by the place mat on the small formica-topped kitchen table, his table now. By the time he finished breakfast the day was luminous. Not that it could have been anything else.

Stretching from Church Road to the High Street by Priory Lane and School Lane there once stood an Augustinian Priory. It is believed to have been built on the site of a Roman temple, on the rising ground of the estuary shore, by William Woodreve and his wife Margaret in the reign of Edward I. The Priory was one hundred feet long and twenty-four feet wide with a square embattled tower one hundred feet high that served as a good sea mark.

After the Dissolution much of the ruined Priory was used to strengthen the harbour. The tower survived, however, until 1813 when it was blown down one night during a fierce gale.

The only known surviving relic of the Augustinian Priory is the Gorleston Psalter, engrossed and illuminated in the priory around the year of 1306. It contains the Sarum Calendar and noted is the Feast of the Dedication of Gorleston Church, March 8th.

This copy, decorated with the coat of arms of Gorleston, a shield overlaid with a cross set between four leopards' heads, found its way to Norwich Cathedral, eventually becoming the property of the distinguished East Anglian Sir Thomas Cornwallis. The Cornwallis family presented it to Lord Baybrooke of Audley End in 1823. In 1904 it was acquired by Charles Dyson Perrin of the sauce family, who left it to the British Museum in 1958.

Percy looked at himself in the bathroom mirror. He had to bend his body this way and that and at one point stand on a stool to get some idea of the overall effect. He had been back to Marks & Spencer that morning. He had rushed around looking for a new shirt and a pair of trousers, moving from rack to rack, pulling off things here and there. He was told off for taking seven items of clothing into the changing room at once. But he came away without buying anything. He walked out of Marks & Spencer without a tell-tale green plastic bag. He was not able to concentrate on clothes, his mind was elsewhere. And as he surveyed his attire in the small mirror he was pleased he hadn't wasted his money on the orange trousers or the dark blue shirt. His new blazer would do, anything else new and he would have felt uncomfortable. His grey flannel trousers were fine, as was his old blue shirt. He felt enough of a new man as it was. At three-thirty in the afternoon he tried a little skip on the bathroom stool.

He had wondered for days what time early evening actually was and variously settled for five-thirty, six, six-thirty, seven and seven-thirty. As evening neared he became increasingly nervous. He had a glass of sherry at five as the sun was setting in a beautiful bronze band behind Mrs Yarren's bungalow. He watched the light slowly fade from the kitchen window. His stomach began to feel tight and he thought he might be getting indigestion. He took some tablets and had another sherry at six. But he downed the second almost in one and, feeling rather flushed, left home shortly after.

The air was cool and salty and calmed his cheeks. Bately Avenue was a patchwork of shadows cast by the bungalows, aglow with exterior and interior lights. Almost everyone, it seemed, was at home. A few bungalows remained in the dark, however, awaiting new old occupants. Awaiting replacements. Some people had closed their curtains and some had yet to do so. He could see people walking from room to room, sitting watching the television, or just watching the gas fire. And some, he knew, would be watching nothing at all, just staring blankly at the walls or carpet, biding time before bed time. He strolled briskly down Bately Avenue, a bunch of flowers under his left arm, feeling alive and important and pleased to be outside. He had waited long enough. The waiting was over.

Queenie's bungalow was ablaze with light. So much so it seemed to radiate amongst the other dwellings of Yallop Avenue. Even her car headlights were bright and shining, Percy noticed. His pace quickened and he was drawn in and up the crazy path, like a moth to a naked light bulb. He didn't have time to feel nervous or feel the waves of panic that had swept through him throughout the day. Before he had realised what he was doing he had his finger on the bell. It made a two-tone ding-dong sound. He stood there for some time, perfectly still. He thought if he moved before she came to the door it would all be a dream, and he would wake somewhere else, perhaps back in the carpark on the cliff top. He tried to breathe quietly, evenly. She didn't come to the door and eventually he pressed the bell again. Ding-dong. 'Coo-ee,' he heard emanating from somewhere inside the bungalow. 'Coo-ee.' It came again, louder this time, from the shallows of the lighthouse. And then he saw her, through the frosted glass. She looked like she was straightening her skirt, smoothing down the crumples, front and behind. He didn't dare move, not until she opened the door. And then he found he couldn't.

'Why, hello,' she said. 'Percy, isn't it?'

'Yes, yes, Percy . . . This is the right evening?'

'Oh, yes.' She blocked his path into the hall. 'Why not?' She giggled. He handed her the flowers. 'Daffodils. Why not?' She laughed again. 'Well, you better come in. No point standing there all night. No point at all.'

Percy followed her deeper into the hall. There was a slight sweetness in the tobacco scented air, but he couldn't place it. It was also rather chilly. He had assumed, as it was so bright, it would be warm. They passed the kitchen, which led off to the left, and a large hall lamp. It was an extraordinary lamp consisting of a naked women holding a large globe. It looked like it was made out of marble, though he couldn't be sure, and the globe, containing the bulb, was flushed a speckled ochre. A gilt-framed mirror hung at the end of the hall. She led him into the lounge, then she disappeared back down the radiant hall with his coat. He stood in the middle of the large room. A dark brown sofa lined half of one wall and two matching armchairs sat in the chimney recesses. The fireplace had a marble mantelpiece, the same hue as the hall lamp. An elaborate gas fire, with an iron and brass grate and imitation logs, stood idle. He noticed there were no pictures on the cream walls and the curtains were still open, revealing a half open double window and the next door bungalow, battened down for the night. An antique-looking bureau in dark wood stood on the fine royal blue carpet against the far wall. A small brass chandelier hung from the ceiling. It was complemented by four brass wall lights in similar curvaceous style, all sparkling with life. It was a room quite unlike any he had seen in Gorleston. Quite unlike any he had seen anywhere. He was completely entranced. He walked over to the mantelpiece which had a number of china and other objects scattered along it. He carefully picked up a small china figure of a woman carrying a basket of grapes. The back of her pleated dress had a small hinge and flap. He inserted a nail and lifted up a section of the dress. Underneath was the woman's bare bottom, a fly perched on her left buttock.

'Charming, isn't it?' Queenie was just a few inches behind him. He felt her breath on his neck.

He nearly dropped the figurine. 'Yes . . . quite extraordinary.'

'She's part of a couple. Look, that's her partner.' She pointed to the small figure of a man. He was propping himself against his basket of grapes. A crook in the other arm. 'There are no flies on him. No tricks at all. Most disappointing.'

She had placed a tray with some glasses, a decanter and a couple of bottles on the long, thin coffee table. Percy hovered by the mantelpiece, thinking of the china couple. The man relaxing after a hard day's work, and his companion, a smile, or was it a smirk, on her glazed face and a fly on her bottom. He wondered what she was thinking.

'Sit, sit.' She sat on the edge of the sofa, which all but swallowed her small frame. 'Help yourself to a drink. There's sherry in the decanter. Pour me some, will you?'

Percy poured Queenie and himself a sherry. The other two bottles both contained whisky, the same brand. He thought a whisky would be too strong. He had already had a couple of sherries. He sat in one of the armchairs, so he almost faced her. She was wearing a tight light-green skirt and matching jacket. She was wearing brown stockings and dark shoes. Numerous rings sparkled on her tiny fingers. A heavy gold bracelet hung on her left wrist. Another drooped around her neck, complementing the quiet orange of her hair. He noticed that her hair was not as bright as he had remembered, and it also seemed more controlled, groomed into light curls.

'Well, isn't this nice,' she smiled, her face wrinkling right up, just as he had seen it do a number of times before. He found it more appealing than ever. She lit a cigarette and puffed smoke into the middle of the room, where it quickly dispersed in the breezy cold. 'I hate crisps, so I didn't bother to get any. I hope you don't mind. I don't like nuts either. Proper canapés, yes, but who can you find to make those nowadays?' She blew another huge plume into the centre of the room. 'We used to have staff.' She smiled at him, her face wrinkling up again. 'So here we are then.'

'Err . . . yes.' At last, he hoped he heard her sigh in response. But it could have just been the wind. He was glad it was chilly. Even at this temperature he could feel he was perspiring under his new blazer, the brass buttons shining madly. The palms of his hands were sticky. He found he had almost finished his sherry. 'This room, what a lovely room. You have the most unusual things.' He still felt quite overwhelmed.

'Well we used to live on Marine Parade, number fifty-four, and before that in Great Yarmouth. In what's now the Carlton Park Hotel, actually. They were much bigger houses, of course. Oh, over the years I suppose you could say I've accumulated a few precious things. I've chucked many away, but I like to keep the odd thing. It's moving I suppose.' She lit another cigarette. 'This little bungalow is quite a change. I don't think I'll ever get used to it. But it's much easier to manage you know, without staff.' A plume, almost of dismay, funnelled out of her mouth.

Percy told her his bungalow was much smaller than hers, then he regretted telling her that. It didn't sound impressive and he wanted to sound impressive. 'But I don't notice the space,' he added, 'that's not what's important. What's important is to be on your own, to be yourself.' He felt himself becoming muddled. He couldn't think clearly, looking at Queenie, so attractive in her tight light green suit. He finished his sherry. 'The wife's gone. It can get quite lonely. I'm not one for homes, though. Oh no.' He tried to laugh. Queenie smoked on, a huge tube of ash drooped from the end of her cigarette. He admired the way the ash clung there.

'Oh, I can't imagine a young man like you getting lonely. Nobody should be lonely here. Why do you think they build places like Gorleston? My father was a builder and he told me why, to keep people on top of each other.' She looked at him and raised her eyebrows, which were mere whispers. 'And happily out of the way.'

Percy had not thought about this before, why places like Gorleston were built. To keep people on top of each other. Happily out of the way. He thought of his road, Bately Avenue, and then Buxton and Youell Avenues. He thought of the rows upon rows of bungalows, all with windows affording views of the avenues and next-door bungalows. He thought of the small gardens, just big enough for a flower bed or plastic rockery, and the low garden walls, low enough so you could chat to your neighbours while planting or weeding. And then he thought of the stories his wife used to tell him about the history of Gorleston, how it was once a Roman settlement, the marauding Saxons, the Augustinian Priory and the old wooden pier built by a Dutchman. How Gorleston was once many miles from the sea. And how the sea now threatened the town. 'But parts of Gorleston are very old,' he said. 'And parts are falling into the sea.'

'Yes. And thank God. I've never much cared for the place.

It's too fussy. It's too small.' She took a last healthy drag, 'still I've never let that get to me,' and stubbed her cigarette out, somehow managing to reach the ashtray with nearly a full cigarette length of ash attached to the butt, which was ringed with red lipstick. 'I've always done as I've pleased. Nothing's ever stopped me. Then I suppose I've got health on my side. I don't feel any older than when I was, oh, in my twenties. I certainly don't behave any differently. Why should you behave as if you're old if you don't feel it? Everyone here behaves as if they're about to die. Just look at them. You'll never catch me having lunch in St Edmunds. Never. I'd rather be dead. Though I suppose that's the same thing.' She shifted around on the sofa, brushing ash off her lap, and lit another cigarette.

To Percy she looked so alive, so full of life. And at that moment he too felt younger and more alive then he could ever remember. He knew exactly what she was saying, he understood everything, except he didn't feel like behaving how he did when he was younger, when he was in his twenties. He felt completely different. He wanted to do what he pleased. He wanted nothing to stop him. He wanted to be like Queenie. He wanted to be with Queenie. He worshipped her. 'Do you mind if I have a cigarette?' he asked, pouring Queenie and himself another glass of sherry. He hadn't smoked for years, decades. He lit a Consulate. The menthol soothed the impact. He didn't inhale the first few puffs, but tried to look as if he did. He couldn't get the smoke to come out in plumes like Queenie. He exhaled puffy clouds that hovered around his head. 'I must confess I have been to St Edmunds.'

'Oh.'

'Well just a few times. More by accident. But only since my wife died.' He could not remember whether he had told her his wife had died. He wanted to be sure she knew he was single. He felt a twinge of disloyalty to Elizabeth, but not much, he was far too excited, far too alive. 'It was never my sort of place. Quite disgusting food.'

'Been here long?' She sat back in the sofa.

Percy looked at his watch.

'In Gorleston?'

'Oh, oh, no. Just a few years. We moved here from Surrey. It was my wife's idea. She knew the place. She first came here just after the war. She had friends here and she loved this part of the coast. I expect it's changed quite a bit since then.'

'Not really. Just more Americans. They're so uncouth.'

Percy liked them. He liked Burt. But he was not going to say so now. 'Yes, aren't they. And so big.'

They then talked about the beach, how it had a habit of disappearing then building up again, and how no one knew why. The desperate attempts of the local council to control the erosion and how Cliff Lane was already falling into the North Sea. 'My sister Toots will be next,' Queenie shrieked with laughter.

And as the bungalow lights burned they talked on and on and finished the decanter of sherry and filled up the ashtray with Consulate cigarette butts and long stems of ash which Percy thought looked like fossils. He didn't find out very much about Queenie's past. Not the immediate past that he wanted to know about, anyway. He learnt, however, that her husband died some years ago, but that it had been expected for a long time. And he learnt that she had a daughter and two grandchildren who lived in Wales. She didn't see them very often and she didn't mind. 'Gorleston's not the place for young children,' she said. He worked out that her grandchildren must have now been in their twenties or even thirties, but he didn't say anything. And then she talked briefly about her sisters, Cassie, Poppy and Doris. 'They live roundabouts,' she said simply. 'Sometimes I see them. Sometimes I don't. Poppy never goes out of her house at all. She's afraid of the outside.' She didn't mention Toots again, leaving her about to fall down the cliff. 'I have a few friends,' she said at one point, obliquely. 'I like company.' She didn't ask Percy much. But he managed to slip into the conversation that he used to work for a major corporation, as a manager. He didn't mention frozen fish, it didn't seem relevant. The playing cards were never brought out, much to Percy's relief. He hated cards and was a useless player. She shifted around on the huge sofa, her feet barely touching the carpet, looking sweet and he thought a little vulnerable. He wanted to go over and sit next to her, put his arm around her. They made a promise to go to Great Yarmouth. 'We must go to the pleasure beach,' she said. 'We simply must go. It has the greatest big dipper.'

At nine-thirty Percy said he really must be going. He didn't want to go, but thought he had better out of politeness. He was there just for an early evening drink after all. They could spend longer evenings together later. As he stood up he felt his head spinning. She showed him to the front door. On the doorstep the cooler air cleared his head a little. The spinning slowed. 'I am having a drinks party, next Thursday,' he said hurriedly. 'It would be lovely if you could come.' He knew he should say something about Toots and Charlie coming. But he couldn't, he didn't want to ruin everything. It had all gone so well. He knew she would find out before, anyway.

'Yes, I know. I was wondering when you were going to ask me.'

'Oh, of course I was.' He was shocked the news had spread so fast. 'You'll be the most important guest. You will come, won't you?'

'I'll see,' she said, Percy thought rather coldly. 'I might be busy.'

'You have to come.' He tried not to sound desperate. 'Perhaps I can see you before then anyway?'

'Perhaps,' she replied. 'Gorleston two five two four.'

'What?'

'Gorleston two five two four, my telephone number.'

'Oh yes, of course.' He repeated the number in his head, his spirits lifting, soaring. 'It was a lovely evening,' he said, still thinking of the number. He stooped to kiss her on the cheek. He was not sure what happened next, whether she was turning to go back inside, or what, but his lips touched hers. They felt soft and slightly moist. He quickly straightened himself and backed down the crazy path, the smell of her sweet perfume coming with him. By the gate he waved to the small figure closing the frosted glass door. The shadow disappearing down the hallway. He thought he heard a muffled coo-ee as he headed along Yallop Avenue, leaving the lighthouse behind. The Metro's headlights still happily shining into the night, guiding him.

His legs felt tired and his throat felt fuzzy and dry, but he knew he wouldn't be able to sleep. He decided to walk the long way home, to the end of Yallop Avenue and along Marine Parade as far as the Links. It was a beautiful clear, crisp night. The sky was full of stars and as he was looking up Toots drove past in the Mercedes. She hooted, but by the time Percy turned and looked she had cruised round the corner. The road was then quite empty. From Marine Parade he could make out three oil rigs, their lights matching the stars for brilliance. He stopped at number fifty-four. He had noticed the house before. It was a big house and paint was peeling off the gate posts. A balcony jutted out over the garage. The house was in darkness. There were no cars in the driveway. It look deserted, forgotten. It was from another time.

He was home by ten. As he was taking his coat off, the telephone rang. He let it ring while he jotted Queenie's number on a pad before picking it up.

'Out late,' Toots boomed.

'Oh, hello. What do you mean?'

'I saw you walking down Yallop Avenue.'

'Did you. I didn't see you. What were you doing?' He felt angry. He felt she was spying on him. He felt he couldn't do anything he wanted to. He felt small and frightened.

'I was driving home after my whist evening and I saw you out walking along Yallop Avenue. I hooted but you were looking at something in the sky. You should watch yourself. You'll fall over and break your neck.'

'I suppose I was on my way home from the golf club. I had supper with, errgh, Peter, a relative, remember. We had a very pleasant evening, very pleasant indeed.' He knew it was only half a lie. He had had a very pleasant evening. A wonderful evening, and Toots was not going to spoil it now.

'Well anyway,' Toots said. 'I just thought I'd tell you that unfortunately Charlie will be coming next Thursday. I hope you can cope. I'm not sure I'll be able to.'

'Good. Actually a few other people are coming as well. It's turning into quite a party.'

'Great,' she said sarcastically. 'We can always sneak out and leave them to it.'

'No we can't. Good night.' He put the receiver down and thought about ringing Queenie, just to thank her for a wonderful evening. But he decided it was rather late and he understood that he shouldn't appear too keen. He would ring her in the morning.

Sandy was having his late-night rummage when Percy climbed into bed. He heard the little dog scratching at the wooden fence, as if it were trying to escape. And he heard Mrs Yarren's frantic calls. He thought of Queenie, how she had looked so vulnerable on the big brown sofa. How he had wanted to put his arm around her. How he wanted to protect her. From Gorleston, from Toots. He knew one day he would get closer to her. He knew. He wanted it to be tomorrow. He had so much to look forward to. First he would call Queenie. He would suggest a walk at the weekend, a stroll along the cliff top. He felt there was so much left. Life was wonderful. Quite wonderful. He turned his bedside lamp off, for once without looking at the photograph of his wife on the dresser, and rolled over in his new pyjamas.

Most of Gorleston was already deep in troubled sleep. Bately Avenue, Buxton and Brett, thick with coughing and spluttering and struggling for breath. The Mariner's Compass housing estate was still ablaze though. The Americans and their youngish wives thrashing about.

And Queenie's bungalow could still be seen by sailors. A lighthouse warning them not to come too close, warning them of danger. Inside Queenie was watching snooker on the television, which was kept inside the fake antique bureau. She loved to watch snooker. And after the snooker she would watch American football, nothing else was on. Then, she thought, she might dye her hair, do some ironing, smoke more cigarettes, think about her boyfriends. She loved having boyfriends.

7

It has been said that Oliver Cromwell resided here before becoming the Lord Protector. Many would have it that the White Horse Inn was the place. Though others have said in a merchant house long since demolished on Riverside Road. It is true, however, that Bridget Bendish, a granddaughter of Oliver Cromwell, lived in Gorleston and was a well known member of the community.

In 1782 a fort was erected on Gorleston Cliffs for the defence of the harbour during the Napoleonic wars. It was armed with a number of 24-pounders and a battery of nine 18-pounders, but a shot was never fired in anger.

At the foot of the White Lion steps is a well, sunk for Admiral Duncan in 1797, for watering naval vessels.

In 1812 the population of Gorleston was 1,714. In the same year the meadowlands of the village were enclosed by an Act, under which any waste land rising from the river between Breydon Water and the Feathers Inn was to be cultivated as gardens. These were the first allotments in Gorleston.

On October 24, 1884, William Moore severed his wife's head from her body with a carving knife. She had a habit of going out at night with other men and on the fateful evening she teased her husband about her affair with neighbour Tom Casey.

In 1890 Marine Parade was known as Belle Vue Road.

Heavy rain held off. The morning's fine drizzle gave up

leaving just a stony greyness. It was one of those Gorleston days when the sea and the sky merged in stillness. It was not so cold but the dampness permeated everything. The day could have belonged to any season. It was a typical day.

Percy looked down onto the beach, the tops of the groynes piercing the flat, grey sea in neat rows. The top of the tangled wreck further out. He looked at Queenie walking beside him, her hair restored to its full orange glory, and smiled. They walked along the upper esplanade past the full carpark. Faces gazed out of the cars, straight through Percy and Queenie and out to the merging of the sea and the sky.

'I've never understood why people do that,' Queenie said as they ambled on towards the pier. 'What are they looking at? It's hardly the greatest view in the world.' She turned her head and frowned at the cars. 'Hopeless. They're just hopeless.'

'I suppose it gives them something to do,' Percy said. 'It's better than sitting at home all day.' He remembered the hours, the days he had spent in his car, looking out to sea. Feeling lonely. Feeling sorry for the people in the other cars. Feeling sorry for himself. Numbing himself in the greyness. Thinking life was over. And he remembered, not that he could ever forget, the day he first saw Queenie from the carpark. Her orange hair. Skipping along the lower esplanade, in and out of the beach huts. He had thought she was a young girl, playing with her father. That was the day everything changed. The day he found a new meaning. Everything was quite different now. It was as if he had stepped into a new life. He couldn't imagine ever returning to the old times, to how it was. He couldn't imagine ever returning to the cliff top to stare out to sea.

'I don't know. I would rather they stayed at home. At least then we wouldn't have to be reminded of their existence.'

Her sea green eyes sparkled. She never wore glasses, she had told Percy. She had never needed to. 'I'm as fit as a fiddle,' she'd say.

Beyond the carpark, the upper esplanade trailed along the edge of a strip of grass, tough, thick grass, hardened by frosty winters and damp salty summers. Odd mounds stuck up here and there. Relics, Queenie told Percy, from when this land was a crazy-golf course. He knew the real golf course occupied the cliff top further south.

'I don't know why they had to grass it over,' she said.

'Seems a terrible shame,' he replied.

'Life's full of people who want to stop you enjoying yourself. Just full of them.'

'Yes, I suppose it is.' Percy thought about this as he watched dogs run this way and that. But some dogs just trailed along slowly beside their muffled owners.

Queenie suggested they go down to the lower esplanade. The promenade, she called it. They descended one of the paths that ran down diagonally, so as to lessen the gradient. It was still steep and Percy had some trouble traversing. The path was damp and slippery. Queenie skipped ahead. 'Come on, Percy,' she shouted. 'Come along, you old man.'

He was quite out of breath by the time he got to bottom. Queenie was sitting on a bench and trying to look as if she had been there for ages. 'Where have you been? I've been here for ages. I was beginning to think you might not be coming.' They both laughed.

Sand had blown or been washed onto the lower esplanade and had heaped up under the bench. Percy noticed Queenie's shoes were speckled with it. They were the same shoes she wore the day he bumped into her in the butcher's. Then they had been speckled with sawdust. A railing ran along the edge of the lower esplanade. The drop to the beach was in places quite considerable, many feet. Percy remembered seeing children last summer jump off here onto the sand. Or was it a summer many years ago? Queenie walked over to the railing and lit a cigarette. She leaned against the railing and smoked. Percy had bought his own packet of Consulates and lit one too, before walking over to the railing and joining her on the edge of Gorleston's small sea defences. He could see that south towards Hopton and Lowestoft, where the cliffs were crumbling most, large rocks had been piled up at the bottom in a haphazard attempt to stem the erosion. They both watched a middle-aged couple walk along the beach holding hands. It was an unusual sight. A dog carrying some driftwood sloped behind. The sea lapped the shore pathetically. Queenie flicked her cigarette butt onto the beach and Percy did likewise. They then set off along the lower esplanade, in places streaked with sand, towards the pier. The chimney of Great Yarmouth Power Station loomed in the grey distance.

'Catch me if you can,' Queenie suddenly shouted. They had reached the first beach huts. She then skipped behind a hut. Appearing some moments later from behind another hut further down the row. Large rusted padlocks, and in places metal bars, were attached to the huts' front doors and shuttered windows. The huts were faded, their pastel colours bleached by the sun and the salt. They had the same seaside names as the houses along Marine Parade, Clear View, Sea View, Bay View. One, however, had simply Pilots painted on the front door in orange. It was a dark blue hut. Weathered but still solid, still dark. Percy looked at it for some time and walked down the narrow gap between it and the next door hut. 'Coo-ee.' Queenie's head popped round the far corner. Her head disappeared, then reappeared. 'Coo-ee.'

Percy said 'coo-ee' back. It sounded strange. 'Coo-ee,' he said again, getting used to it.

'I think I'm stuck,' she said.

He squeezed to the end and looked around the corner.

She seemed to be wedged between the end of the hut and a grass bank.

'I think you'll have to go around the other side and pull me out.' She was not at all distressed.

He walked sideways back down the side of the hut and onto the lower esplanade. The couple with the dog were seated on a nearby bench looking at him. He smiled, then crab-walked down the other side, between the Pilots hut and a tatty pink one. Its double-doors had been kicked down and planks of wood were nailed to the frame in a half-hearted attempt to stop further intruders. The passage-way smelt of urine. He reached Queenie, who seemed to have resigned herself to her predicament and had lit a cigarette. The air was quite still behind the hut and smoke hung there, overcoming the smell of urine. 'Oh, I say,' she said, smoke pouring out of her nostrils, 'what are we going to do?'

'Here, let me take your arm.' Percy tenderly took hold of her arm and started to pull her. Her bottom seemed to be stuck though.

'I think you're going to have to pull a bit harder, young man.' She stubbed her cigarette into the grass bank. He increased the pressure. She shifted a bit, but he thought he might be hurting her arm. 'Pull from here,' she said. He put his arms around her waist and tugged her. She came loose and fell against his chest. Time slowed and Percy thought they remained like that for ages. Queenie in his arms. It was in fact only momentary. They disengaged and squeezed back out into the open. The back of Queenie's coat was covered in mud and grass. She started to rub it, but then asked Percy to. He gently brushed the loose stuff off, still catching his breath. 'Lower down,' she said. 'Lower down. I can still see some dirt.' His hand curved down her back and over her bottom. She felt so small and slight. He looked around, oddly feeling he was doing something he shouldn't. He had no idea why. The couple on the bench were looking at them and Percy smiled again. The dog was chewing the driftwood, growling with joy.

'Do you often play this game?' Percy asked. He wondered how many other times she had been stuck behind the beach huts. He wondered how many other men had pulled her out and stroked the dirt off her back, her bottom.

'Only when I feel like it. It's fun isn't it?'

'Yes.' He thought of only holding Queenie in his arms. Not the other men who might have held her in their arms. He loved the game.

The chimney did not appear to be getting any closer as they walked on, towards the pier and the model yacht pond, towards Great Yarmouth. They came across more strollers the nearer to the pier they got, wrapped up with scarves and head-scarves, hanging onto each other. Percy wanted to link arms with Queenie but was afraid to make the first move. He tried to walk as close to her as possible. Occasionally brushing her shoulder. His gloved hand brushing hers. 'Nothing like sea air,' he said. His throat felt awful and the air smelt of tar. Further on much more sand had been washed onto the lower esplanade, washed off the beach. People shuffled through it, as if negotiating a snow drift. 'There was no sand on here last year,' he said. 'I am sure of it. It must have come this winter.' They passed a large shelter, built into the low cliff. A number of old couples and some frail, single women were seated inside, staring out to sea. He could hear faint muttering.

Percy was pleased to find he was not as unfit as he had imagined. Queenie was still bounding along happily, and he was managing to keep up. He kept looking around, looking at her, taking everything in, soaking it all up. It was the best walk of his life. He filled his lungs with air and coughed. He was not going to start worrying about smoking, not at his age. Besides, he couldn't imagine Queenie worrying about smoking. He couldn't imagine Queenie worrying about anything.

A man and a young boy were crouched by the model yacht pond, which arched out from the lower esplanade and over the beach. Percy was sure the last time he had noticed the pond had been empty. Dry and forgotten. It was now half full. He wondered whether a high tide or the council had filled the pond up prematurely for the summer season. The man was fiddling with a boat, the boy looking on. 'Hurry up, Dad. I want a go,' the boy screamed.

Queenie and Percy sat down on a bench overlooking the pond. 'What fun,' she said.

At last the engine ticked over and buzzed into life. The boy, who looked about eight, jumped up and smiled. 'Let me have a go, let me have a go.' The man put the boat into the water and it shot off, bouncing wildly on the small ripples. He handed his son the remote control unit and the boy sent the boat into a dizzying series of circles. The buzz of the engine filled the still afternoon.

'Did you have a happy childhood?' Percy asked.

'Oh, yes. I've always been happy.'

'Mine was very quiet. I was an only child. Though I feel I'm making up for it now.' He smiled at her.

The buzz suddenly stopped. Percy looked up and saw the boat bobbing in the middle of the pond. 'Go and get it, Dad, go and get it,' the child screamed. The father didn't look happy. 'OK, son, OK,' he said. He was an American. He took off his shoes and socks and rolled his trousers up. 'For chrissakes,' he said, stepping into the grey pond. The child started to laugh. 'Ow. There's something sharp in here. For chrissakes.' The man began hopping about. He reached the boat, grabbed it, and hopped back quickly. He put the boat down, picked up his shoes and socks and came over to Percy and Queenie's bench and sat down.

'Nice day,' he said. 'This is the last time I take the kid boating.'

'It looked so much fun,' Queenie said. 'I was going to ask you if I could have a go.'

'If I get it fixed, sure you can.' He tried to dry his feet on his trousers. They had gone white and were turning blue.

Percy presumed he was an oilman. He had to be. He was surprised Queenie was being so polite to him though, after what she had said earlier about Americans. In a way he was disappointed, because he liked Queenie's intolerance. He found it appealing. He thought people their age were allowed to be intolerant, not that he ever was.

Queenie looked at Percy, the American's feet, then back at Percy. She squeezed her nose with her fingers and nudged Percy with her elbow. Percy then offered her a cigarette and they both smoked and watched the man get up and start fiddling with the toy boat again. His son becoming increasingly impatient. 'This is boring, Dad. Can we go?' The man looked cross. 'I've nearly got the thing fixed. No we can't.' The child had sat down on a bench on the other side of the pond when the boat buzzed back into life, he didn't even look up. His father sent the boat across the pond and back and turned and smiled at Queenie.

'Come and watch,' she said to Percy. She sprung up and raced over to the man. Percy followed, feeling rather nervous. He knew he wouldn't be able to control the thing and hoped he wouldn't be offered the chance. He had no idea whether Queenie would be able to control it. It looked like an expensive toy. The man explained the controls to Queenie. She nodded and said, 'Oh, yes, yes, very simple.' She kept reaching out, trying to grab the controls from the man.

'Here you go then,' he said at last.

The boat shot off and swept round the perimeter of the pond. It was expertly done. Queenie then sent the boat into a series of figure of eights. 'Light me a cig,' she said to Percy.

'Unbelievable,' the American said.

With a cigarette in the corner of her mouth Queenie put the boat through a number of increasingly complicated patterns. The boy had now come over to where they were standing. 'It's my turn,' he said. 'That's easy.' He tried not to sound impressed. Queenie looked at the young boy, ash drooping from her cigarette hanging in the corner of her mouth. There was then a squeal and a thud as the boat crashed into the wall across the pond. Bits of plastic floated out into the pond, bobbing on the ripples, and Percy could see the hull was starting to sink. The boy burst into tears and the man ran round to retrieve the remains. He carried it back, stroking the plastic hull.

'I say, I'm terribly sorry,' Queenie said stubbing out her cigarette. 'It suddenly didn't seem to respond.'

'I'm sure we can mend it,' the man said. 'It could have happened to anybody.'

The boy was crying, 'She's broken my boat, she's broken my boat.' He started to sob uncontrollably.

'How unfortunate,' Percy said as they walked off, and he started to wonder whether Queenie had done it on purpose. But he couldn't believe she would do such a thing. No, he said to himself as they strolled on. He saw the middle-aged couple and their dog get into a car parked by the small strip of amusements at the end of the lower esplanade. They looked happy and content and he wondered whether he and Queenie would get a dog one day, a black Labrador that would carry driftwood along the beach and growl with pleasure as he chewed it. Percy was beginning to think of the long term. He knew he hardly knew Queenie, but it seemed so right. He thought it must just have been meant to happen. That they had found their true match at last. Yet somewhere, deep down, he couldn't help feeling that he had known her before. He couldn't explain it. He thought it was perhaps the sudden familiarity. Maybe it was just that he had seen her darting around Gorleston a long time ago.

They had a cup of tea in the Seaside Cafe, which was wedged between Marine Bingo and Goldmine Bingo on Gorleston's sad amusement strip. The air was smoky and two children were playing on a video machine. There was no sign of whose children they were. The tea was too hot to drink at first. 'You wait until you see Yarmouth,' Queenie said, making her contribution to the smoky atmosphere. Percy helping as well. 'They have proper amusements there. Not just kid's stuff.'

He looked at her, her left hand resting on the sticky formica table speckled with tiny, glinting sugar granules. She was wearing a large ruby on her wedding finger, but no wedding ring. Percy's marriage had lasted thirty-eight years. He had never had an affair. 'I'm so glad I ended up here. Gorleston grows on you more and more.'

The video game was emitting shrill electronic tunes and Queenie winked at Percy. 'This place is full of surprises,' she whispered.

They walked past the Ocean Rooms Dinner and Dance Hall and onto the damp pier. 'Look,' said Queenie, 'a ship's coming in.' She trotted to the end, past puddles and capstans and the harbour-master's look-out. A ship sat on the grey sea in the grey distance, its blue funnel exhaling plumes of black smoke. 'I wonder where it's from,' she said, when Percy had caught up with her. 'Let's guess.' They stood there, on the end of the pier, reciting all the ports they could think of. Percy came up with Rotterdam, Gdansk, because he had seen a ship from there before, Le Havre, Copenhagen. Queenie thought of Cape Town, Rio de Janeiro, Havana. A pilot boat sped out of the harbour mouth. Percy watched its wake rippling back down the

River Yare and into the concrete of Gorleston Pier and the wooden stakes and steel girders that made up the end of Yarmouth's North Pier. Queenie started waving, but the boat was soon far out to sea.

She went over to a couple of fishermen who had propped their rods up against the pier rail. They were wearing green anoraks with the hoods up. They both stood beside large buckets of worms, smoking. Smoke oozed from their hoods They seemed to know Queenie. They looked up and smiled as she approached. 'All right lads?' she asked. They nodded. 'Any luck?'

They both said no, shaking their heads.

'Few tiddlers,' one of the men then said, lifting his head. 'Nothing worth taking home, though.'

'No fish out there today,' the other man said dejectedly.

'Big ship coming in, though,' Queenie laughed. She walked back to Percy, who was staring out to sea. 'They're here almost every day. They never catch anything.' She then went over to the harbour-master's look-out. There was a small ladder running up one side. For a moment Percy thought she was going to climb it. 'Why don't you climb up, and see what you can see?' she said, gesturing. 'There's a great view.'

Percy said he had a great view from where he was. He was a little afraid. It was a long way up.

'Well, I'm going up.' She clambered up the metal ladder which started to clang and shake. Up she went above the hut and on up the ladder which became attached to the hut's mast. Halyards rattled in the wind and with the disturbance. There was a small platform near the top. Here Queenie stopped. Percy and the fishermen watched from below as she scanned the horizon. She then started to wave madly, both arms and hands flapping above her head. 'Coo-ee,' she started to shout. 'Coo-ee.' The pilot boat was speeding back to port, well ahead of the ship. As the small orange boat came closer Percy could see the man at the wheel wave back. 'I'm not sure who that was,' Queenie said once she'd climbed down. 'I can't seem to keep up with all the new pilots.'

Eventually the ship reached the harbour mouth and glided into port at a walking pace. Black smoke still puffing out of the chimney. It was huge and tatty and rusty. It carried containers, and deck-hands were running about the deck between the containers, so close Percy felt he could say hello to them. 'Coo-ee,' he shouted to three lads in oily overalls. They looked at him but they didn't wave. As the ship rounded the slow corner by Brush Quay the stern came into view. Gdansk was painted on the stern in huge blue letters in English and below in smaller letters in Cyrillic script.

'You're right,' Queenie said. 'You're right. Well I never.' She stood on tip-toes and kissed him on the cheek. He felt very proud. He felt himself start to flush. 'Where's Gdansk?' she said. 'I've never heard of it before.'

'Poland,' he told her.

She still looked a little unsure. But she put her arm through his, as if to be sure of something, as they set off back along the lower esplanade, back home. Percy was sure they had become lovers. He was sure of it.

Percy didn't feel like spending an evening at home on his own. Not after Queenie had kissed him for the second time in a day, when they had said goodbye in the carpark. He felt far too restless. He was looking forward far too much to the next time he would see her. He smoked a cigarette in the kitchen, on his own, trying to blow smoke plumes. He wasn't very good at it, but he felt strangely naughty. He thought some alcohol might settle him, perhaps help him sleep. He had become increasingly restless at night, waking up earlier and earlier. He set off for the Links in the evening quietness, in the damp stillness.

The pub was flush with warmth. John Conway, as Percy had expected, was standing at the bar. Percy felt he had the upper hand with John now, now that he knew Toots and Charlie and Linda and Burt and Cassie, and Queenie of course. He asked John to the drinks party and told him that he was sure it would be an interesting evening. He then told John about Queenie, Toots's younger sister, and how she had climbed the mast at the end of the pier. He told John it was quite unbelievable. That she scampered up it as if she were a young girl. 'She's not a bit like Toots. She's quite something.'

'Yes,' John said. 'I can believe that.'

Percy felt very proud for the second time that day. He lit a cigarette. 'She's just great.'

'I've heard the odd thing or two about her.'

'What do you mean?' Percy said defensively. 'What do you mean?' Country and Western music was playing in the background as usual.

'Someone once told me she used to strip on Britannia Pier, for the troops in the war.' He looked at Percy as if to say sorry. 'But people say some strange things around here. You know how they like to talk.'

'That's ridiculous.' Though the more Percy thought about it, the more he found it believable.

'Do you know,' said John, 'I think it was Toots who told me. She would know.'

Percy decided that even if it was true it didn't matter. It was a long time ago and besides, what he loved about Queenie was the fact that she was so different. That she did what she wanted. That she knew how to live her life.

The rain, which had held off all day, started and Percy heard its gentle patter on the window panes in between the mournful Country and Western tunes. He walked home in the wet, still cheerful. He tried to imagine Queenie taking her clothes off, Queenie stripping. But he couldn't without feeling jealous and it reminded him of a time when he had felt jealous before, a long time ago. He couldn't remember the year, but could still remember the feeling, almost desperation. It was summer, and Elizabeth had visited Gorleston without him. She still hadn't taken him to Gorleston at that point. It was then a place that belonged to his wife's former life. Somewhere she talked about in the past tense. It could have been any seaside town remembered from childhood. He recollected saying goodbye to her at the station, not sure why she had decided to go. She had recently miscarried for the second time and he thought he would be of more comfort than friends, a distant cousin. But he let her do anything she wished, he always did. He convinced himself the sea air would be good for her, the rest. They had been in a rush to catch the train. But he recalled lingering on the platform after the train had pulled out, feeling helpless and that something vast was missing. The image of her, her pale cheeks, her deep, almost piercing brown eyes, her dark hair falling out of a rather old-fashioned hat, stayed with him clearly all week. Until now he supposed. He had mentioned nothing to her about feeling jealous when she returned, he didn't like discussing such difficult things, and put it down to the fact that it was the first time they had been apart since they were married. She meant everything to him then. He cleared his mind, not wishing to dwell on Elizabeth, or Queenie stripping.

By coincidence Queenie was stripping at that very moment. Pulling off her cardigan, her blouse, her brassiere. Unzipping and sliding off her skirt. Her stockings had gone baggy at the knees. She admired herself in the bedroom mirror. She never cared to close her curtains and occasionally her neighbours would admire her as well. She was used to people admiring her body. She still had quite a figure. A little small nowadays, but trim she thought. She wanted to slip into something more comfortable. The night was young. There was not much on television, it being a Sunday. She hated being on her own. She hated entertaining herself. But she would find something to do. She always did.

8

Time was going quickly now, so quickly that Percy found there was never enough time to do everything. Never enough time to think of everything. Linda rang wanting to know if he needed any help. He did, and he wasn't going to ask Queenie. He couldn't imagine Queenie being any help at all. It just wasn't her sort of thing. Besides, he wanted to impress her, to surprise her. He told Linda that he didn't want to be any trouble, but actually he didn't know where to begin. Except that he wanted canapés.

'Well what sort of canapés?' she asked.

'Oh, I don't know, the normal sort. Nice ones.' He was not entirely sure he knew what canapés were.

'Are you sure you want to go to all that bother?'

'Oh yes. I'm sure it won't be that much bother,' he said, worried. 'We'll make the simple ones. I am quite used to the kitchen now. I know my way around. It'll be fun.'

'Very well then.' She said she would bring some cookery books over.

Percy thought he would love to have a daughter like Linda now. He missed not having children more and more. He wondered what Queenie's daughter was like. He doubted she was very much like Linda. He doubted whether she was as helpful. Though he knew she would have other qualities. That she would be special. She had to be. He thought of her upbringing. But he had difficulty imagining Queenie as a mother. She just didn't seem the type.

He washed and shaved and dressed and laid his best clothes out on his bed to change into later. He looked at his bedroom with the two single beds, his and his wife's, separated by a small, knee-high cupboard, covered in dust like fine sand. Elizabeth had used this cupboard. It was her cupboard. He never touched it now.

He looked at the black and white photograph of her on the dresser. It had been taken some twenty years ago. He liked the picture. It was part of the room. She looked at him, her eyes dark and sharp, but somehow distant. He often wondered what she had been thinking when the picture was taken. He angled it away so she no longer looked over the room, so her face could not be spotted by someone entering. He hung his new dressing gown on the back of the door, and folded up his pyjamas and put them away. The room smelt stale. He wished he had some flowers or a pot of those scented dried flowers that everyone seemed to have nowadays. He opened the window. It creaked and he found the edges were encrusted with salt.

He went through the bulging kitchen cupboards, seeing what he had and what he didn't have. He opened the kitchen window as well to get the air circulating. And then he walked round and round the rest of his bungalow, moving pieces of furniture, removing then replacing photographs. He repositioned the lamps and the cushions, pushed the television into the corner. He kept rearranging the ornaments on the mantelpiece, a small wooden shelf above the gas fire. But whatever he did he couldn't get the bungalow to look exactly how he wanted it to look. It never would. He sat down and had a cup of coffee and a cigarette. He was sweaty and out of breath and resigned.

Linda arrived laden with cookery books and cooking implements, bowls and trays. 'I thought some of these might come in handy,' she said, swinging a tray. 'You've got to put the food on something.' Percy hadn't even thought about it. 'What a dear little bungalow.' She sat down eventually, having first wandered around Percy's home, picking up various objects, looking at photographs. She had even gone into his bedroom and found the picture of his wife. 'So this was your wife. What an attractive woman. I imagine she was quite formidable. You must miss her.'

Percy didn't answer. He rushed into the kitchen and pretended to look for something in a cupboard. He didn't know what to say. Linda followed, lighting a cigarette. She said they should decide what to make before they went shopping. Percy picked up one of the cookery books. He didn't know what to look for. He too lit up, rather self-consciously. He was shaking slightly.

'I didn't know you smoked.'

'Oh, I smoke now and then, when I'm a little nervous or excited or just busy.'

'You seem a bit on edge. Is something the matter?'

'No,' he replied as calmly as possible. 'I've just been very busy. In fact I'm extremely happy.' He was, truly. And he wanted to tell someone why. Indeed, he wanted to tell Linda all about his love affair. As if it would somehow make it more real. So he told Linda he had seen her aunt Queenie a couple of times over the last week. But he played it down. He knew that that was what Queenie would expect him to do. And he wasn't going to let her down.

'So how is she?'

'In fine form. Funny, healthy. Smoking like a chimney.'

'Yes, it's never done her any harm.' Linda, however, told Percy to expect a scene tonight if Queenie and her mother were both coming. 'There'll be a scene all right.'

Percy was not so sure. Queenie had reassured him that

she would try her best to come, and that she was looking forward to seeing her sisters. 'We've got a lot of catching up to do,' she had said. He didn't think she would cause any trouble. He knew she was not like that. He knew it would all work out.

It was not until they got to the High Street that Linda started to talk about Queenie and Queenie's men-friends. 'She's like a siren,' she said as they entered Spar. Percy found a trolley. 'She's always had men running after her, even now,' she said by the cheeses. 'I do wish sometimes that my mother would have more luck though. OK, I know she's had a few affairs. I can't imagine who hasn't at her age.' Percy looked away. 'But compared to what one hears about Auntie Queenie.' She picked up half a Brie and poked it furiously to see how ripe it was. 'Oh, I shouldn't go on.' She looked at him sweetly. 'It's not fair.' She put the Brie back on the cold shelf and dropped an Edam into the trolley. They moved on up the aisle to the pâtés. 'You never knew her husband, of course. I felt sorry for him. He must have had a lot to put up with.' She picked up a tube of liver sausage and started to squeeze it. 'He lost a fortune, you know. I must say I occasionally wonder how responsible she was. She loved to go on holidays, especially cruises. Cruises were her thing. And she never went with him.' The liver sausage was put back on the shelf. 'I never knew why they stuck together. Habit I suppose. A different generation.'

Percy wondered about Linda's past. She rarely spoke about it, but he knew that she had been married three times and that it was her second husband who had been killed.

'How's this?' she beamed, showing him a slab of fine Brussels pâté.

He was beginning to think there must be more to canapés than cheese and pâté. They reached the dips. A big sign helpfully said so. There were rows of cream cheese dips, with all sorts of additives, blue cheese, chives, prawns, garlic. This was all quite new to Percy. He had never been so far down this aisle before. 'Do we really want dips?' he said, thinking of Queenie.

'It's easy.' She was already dropping tubs on top of the Edam and the Brussels pâté.

They moved on to the bread section. 'If Queenie wants to live like that then it's up to her,' Percy said. And he meant it. The more he thought about it the more he realised just how judgmental everyone was about Queenie. He knew Toots was jealous of her and he was beginning to think Linda might be too. Maybe Linda longed to have love affairs. Maybe Burt was not enough.

'I just think you should know,' she told him. She sounded hurt. 'It's all very well Queenie carrying on, doing as she pleases, but there are always other people involved. There are always other people who get hurt.' They moved to another aisle. 'How about some jelly?' She looked at him. Her wide eyes pained. 'Mother loves it.'

'What about the cookery books?' Percy protested. 'What about the devils on horseback?'

Linda took charge of the trolley and continued to haul items off the shelves, napkins, cocktail sticks, crisps. She was swinging down the crowded aisles, dodging the other shoppers, many of whom were having great difficulty with their trolleys and shopping baskets. Percy rushed behind her and the trolley. He knew what he had with Queenie was special. That it was different. She had almost told him so. 'I don't meet many people like you, Percy,' she had said.

'Things can change,' he told Linda at the check-out desk. 'People can change.'

'I suppose you're going to tell me she used to be a stripper next,' Percy said in the car on the way home, laughing.

They were stuck in a traffic jam on Bells Road, just by the butcher's. He looked in just in case. The shop was empty, except for Holmes, who was standing quite still behind the counter.

'It's funny you should say that,' Linda replied. 'Mind if I smoke?'

Someone was having difficulty trying to park. The man in the car ahead got out and started directing, occasionally slapping the roof of the car in difficulty. All seemed to be going well until the car suddenly lunged forward and into a parked car in front of it. There was a sound of breaking glass and the man directing put his hands on his head. An old man got out of the car. He was shaking.

'Damn, I forgot the cream,' Linda said exhaling.

Linda was a whirlwind in the kitchen, finding everything from the cupboards without any guidance from Percy. 'You've got a lot of coffee, Percy, and Marvel, look at all that Marvel.' They cooked the sausages then because Linda said it would be easier to heat them up later. 'We'll just put them in the microwave.'

He helped spread pâté on oat fingers, which Linda topped off with olives. 'Are these really canapés?'

'Yes,' she insisted. 'They're just perfect.' She licked some paste off her fingers. 'Uhmm.' She covered the plates of food with cling-film and spread crisps and biscuits on trays around the tubs of dips. 'All we have to do is take the lids off.' They made cheese and pineapple cocktail sticks and then she was off, saying Burt was coming home early and she wanted to be there when he got in. They would both see him later.

Percy said he would be quite able to get the drinks ready on his own. But once he was on his own he started to worry about there not being much choice. What if someone wants a gin and tonic? What if someone wants red wine? he asked himself. He then worried about the canapés. They didn't look very impressive, the oat fingers were sweating under the cling-film. His stomach began to ache. He just hoped that everyone would drink enough. He took an indigestion pill and smoked a cigarette. What if Queenie doesn't come? What if something awful has happened to her? Questions, dreadful questions floated around his head. He wanted to ring her and check she was all right. Check she was coming. But he didn't. He knew he would sound too nervous, too concerned. He went to look at the new clothes he had laid out on his bed earlier that day. It was mid afternoon, but he put them on anyway. He went to sit in the lounge and wait with the second packet of Consulate he had ever bought.

The story of the Gorleston Kill Jews might never have been known were it not for a Spaniard who died a convict in New South Wales in 1826. Just before he died he confessed to the following and confirmed many a suspicion.

Having been shipwrecked off Gorleston the Spaniard stayed and joined a company of boatmen. One day, in answer to a signal from a vessel offshore, they set forth to land a passenger. The passenger was a Jew and he was in possession of a heavy chest, about which he was extremely anxious. The boatmen believed there might be valuable plunder in it, and when running their boat along the seaward side of Scroby Sand, they struck the passenger hard in the head with the tiller and rendered him unconscious. They then tossed him overboard and broke open the chest to find it contained gold and jewels and fine cloths.

They buried the chest in the sand south of the pier and divided the riches. They built themselves houses on Prospect Hill and the boatmen's wives were often seen wearing fine lace and jewels. Their sudden increase in wealth aroused the suspicions of their neighbours, who gossiped wildly about the source. But it was not until news of the Spaniard's confession reached Gorleston that their suspicions were confirmed. Those men still alive who helped thrust the tiller into the Jew's head were executed. Prospect Hill became known as Pilfer Hill and Gorleston obtained the name of Kill Jews.

Today Pilfer Hill is known as Cliff Hill.

A dollop of dip landed on Percy's left leg as he tried to remove the lid of a tub. His attempts to remove it from his grey flannel trousers were not successful. A damp creamy stain stretched almost the length of his thigh. He was changing his trousers when the doorbell rang. It rang again. He heard the flutter of the letter-box.

'Coo-ee.'

He struggled with the clean pair of trousers. He was not expecting Queenie to arrive first. 'Just coming,' he shouted. 'I'm on my way.' He was too overcome with panic to appreciate fully the fact that it was Queenie who had arrived. That Queenie had actually come. As he stood up he caught his reflection in the mirror on the dresser. His face was bright red. His thin hair was ruffled and had fallen forward. He smoothed his hair down. 'On my way,' he shouted again as he put his blazer back on. He noticed some dip had got onto his left sleeve. Well, it'll just have to stay there, he said to himself, and brushed his sleeve on the hall wall. His heart racing, he opened the front door as calmly as possible and found Linda and Burt standing there.

'Sorry we're so early. Did we catch you at an awkward moment?' Linda asked. 'Were you expecting someone else?'

'I didn't think it would be you.' He cleared his throat. 'Come in, come in.'

'Something I picked up from Auntie Queenie,' Linda was telling Burt as Percy took their coats. 'We thought we would come early just to make sure everything was all right,' she shouted after him.

In a way Percy was relieved it wasn't Queenie. He wasn't

ready for Queenie. He didn't know where to put the coats, so he dumped them on his wife's bed.

'Nice place,' Burt said. 'Real cosy.'

'Let me look at you, Percy,' Linda said, blocking him in the hall as he returned from his bedroom. 'You look very handsome. Great blazer.' She started to brush the sleeve that had picked up some dip. 'You've got something on your jacket.'

'Yes, yes,' he said. 'It doesn't matter. You'll never get it off.' But she kept on brushing his sleeve as if he were a small boy. He felt Burt watching behind him. And he started to feel embarrassed. 'Really, it's fine.' She eventually stopped. And he looked at her. She was wearing a purple dress with a slit up one side. He didn't want to stare, but as far as he could tell the slit went a long way up. She had tied her hair up and wore dark red lipstick. Her perfume lingered in the air as she swept from room to room checking everything was in order. Percy and Burt followed.

'There's no need to warm the sausages up until everyone is here,' she said. 'Oh good, you've remembered to take the cling-film off.'

Burt helped himself to a crisp and dunked it in a dip. He looked quite happy and casual as he smiled at Percy. Percy liked Burt and he hoped Linda was happy with him. And then he thought it couldn't be much fun for them going to parties like this. They should be with people their own age, he thought. They shouldn't be in Gorleston. He poured them drinks. Linda had a sherry and Burt had a whisky. Percy poured himself a whisky as well. He knew he would have to be careful. He was not very fond of whisky, but thought it was more manly than drinking sherry. Burt was drinking it after all. Linda and Percy then lit cigarettes. He began to relax a little. Though his stomach ached still. And shortly he found he was worrying about Queenie again.

Worrying whether she would come. And if she didn't come, why not?

John Conway was the next to arrive, at two minutes past six. Percy wasn't surprised. He introduced John and handed him a whisky that he asked for as soon as he took off his coat. Percy thought he smelt as if he had had a few already. John stood and talked to Burt, but Percy could see he kept looking over at Linda, who was sitting on the sofa, her shiny left leg protruding from the folds of her purple dress.

'Do you like the work?' John asked Burt. 'You must get very lonely, being away from home for so long. How do you cope?'

Burt said he had a very loving and understanding wife. Linda smiled from the sofa.

'I wouldn't leave her at home on her own for too long,' John said, laughing. Burt joined in, though Percy thought it sounded forced and was probably out of politeness.

Cassie arrived next, her hair luxuriantly white and fluffy. She looked larger, rounder, than Percy remembered. She seemed delighted, hugging Linda and Burt and smiling sweetly at John and Percy. 'How nice to be here,' she said. 'I haven't been out all week. And it's just around the corner. Literally just around the corner. I'm almost a neighbour.' She smelt of food, as if she had been cooking all day, and Percy noticed there was a large brown stain on her white shawl. Gravy, he thought. She asked for sherry. 'Just a small one. I don't trust myself when I've had a few.'

'Oh, Auntie,' Linda said.

John stared at Linda. The doorbell rang. It was quickly followed by a knock and then the flutter of the letter-box.

'Coo-ee, coo-ee.' Everyone looked towards the door. 'Coo-ee.'

As Percy walked out of the room, he turned and smiled back at his guests. He felt proud. He felt loved.

'What's going on in there,' said the voice through the letter-box. 'Let us in.' There was more rattling on the door.

He found Toots and Charlie jostling on the path. 'Calm down, Toots,' Charlie was saying. 'There's no need for all that. It's embarrassing.'

'Oh, don't worry,' said Percy, sadly. 'I'm used to it, come in.' He was becoming used to it. He hadn't realised it was a family trait. Coo-ee, he said to himself.

Charlie rolled his eyes at him as he walked in. 'Sorry we're late. She takes an age to get ready. An absolute age.'

Percy was glad to see Charlie. Very glad. And Toots looked extraordinary. He could see she might have spent an age getting ready. She was wearing a tight-fitting mauve suit with gold buttons, a pearl necklace, and a diamond-encrusted gold brooch pinned to her large breast. Her make-up was lush and florid. Her hair had been teased into a magnificent bouffant and shone purple in his bright hall. She smelt of violets. A field of damp violets. She kissed him, leaving a cracked impression of her lips on his cheek. He felt the lipstick on his cheek and tried to wipe it off with his sleeve as he followed her and Charlie into the lounge. It was six-thirty.

'What a charming little home,' Toots said. Percy handed her a sherry and she strutted around the lounge, studying everyone, the mantelpiece ornaments and the canapés on the coffee table. 'Are we all here then?'

Percy lit a cigarette. 'Not quite.' Smoke filtered out of his mouth. 'No. There might be a surprise yet.'

'Really.'

He knew she knew who else might be coming. But he didn't feel like telling her.

As if reading his thoughts, though, Toots continued, 'I'm not very keen on surprises. They're never very pleasant. Not round these parts anyway.' People stopped talking and turned towards Toots, as if they knew who she was referring to. 'Still, the surprise I'm thinking of never turns up.' The others started to pick at the canapés nervously. 'She's the most unreliable person I've ever had the misfortune of coming across. She loves to keep people waiting. She'll never come.' She put an oat finger smothered with pâté and topped with an olive into her mouth. A few oat flakes stuck to her bottom, lipstick-smothered lip. She licked her lips. 'She just doesn't know how to behave.'

Percy looked around the room. Everyone looked away, perhaps out of kindness. Toots sidled up to him and started to whisper in his ear. 'Queenie's not the only woman in Gorleston, you know.' She pinched his arm. He was sure the whole room smelt of damp violets. 'Don't you forget.'

'I think I'll warm up the sausages,' Linda then said loudly. Percy said he would help. He needed to get out of the room. In the kitchen Linda told him it was a lovely party. She said she had been talking to John and Cassie. She said they seemed to be getting on very well. She then said she was sorry Queenie hadn't arrived, but that at least there wouldn't be any trouble.

'It's still early, she'll come,' he protested, though he was losing heart. And he was drinking too fast. 'She'll come.' He watched the sausages in the microwave, hissing and spitting.

'Well never mind if she doesn't. Mother's very pleased to see you.'

He knew that, but Toots frightened him. She was so different to Queenie. Queenie he could trust. Toots was devious, so much more calculating. He wondered whether Linda would end up like her mother.

Percy fetched more bottles of sherry and Scotch from the kitchen. Burt was entertaining Toots. And John was entertaining Cassie and Linda, telling his awful jokes.

Charlie was sitting in an armchair struggling to keep his eyes open. Percy watched them as they closed for longer and longer stretches of time. Then Charlie's head would loll forward and he would wake with a jerk, his eyes suddenly opening. Watching this made Percy feel dizzy. He was now quite drunk. And quite sad. But he was pleased that most of the food had gone. There were only a few oat fingers left, the pâté now a charcoal grey. He moved over to where John and Cassie and Linda were sitting. Cassie's cheeks were bright red. They nearly matched John's. She was drinking whisky. As was Linda.

'Where did you find him?' Cassie asked Percy. 'He's hysterical.' John smiled. Cassie had him pressed against the arm of the sofa.

Percy remembered what she had said when she first arrived. I don't trust myself when I've had a few. Linda, he thought, however, looked a little bored. She was lounging in the armchair, her left leg protruding into the room, the white top of her stocking clearly showing. He pushed aside empty plates and sat on the coffee table, trying not to look at her leg.

'Hi,' she said. 'I think my mother has a crush on Burt. It's quite common, you know, for older women to have younger lovers around here. Queenie does, plenty.' She sighed. 'I like older men, though. But maybe I'll change when I'm older and start liking younger men.' She looked at Percy and smiled. 'Oh, I think I've had too much to drink. You'll have to excuse anything I say. I won't be held responsible for anything I say or do.' She swooned and slunk further into the armchair, revealing her bare thigh, above her stocking. 'Light me a cig,' she said softly.

Just like someone else, Percy thought. He saw that Toots had nudged Burt into the mantelpiece. She was whispering into his ear. John started to read Cassie's palm. Cassie giggled. Percy helped himself to another whisky, spilling some on his stained trousers and the coffee table. Someone had stubbed a cigarette out on the plate containing the last few charcoal-grey oat fingers. He lit another Consulate and blew a thick plume into the centre of the room. 'Did you see that, did you see that,' he shouted.

'See what, did I see what?' Linda lifted her large eye lashes, heavy with mascara. 'I can't see anything.'

Percy blew another perfect plume. 'Look, there.' He pointed vaguely to the ceiling, the smoke slowly dispersing. There was a tapping at the window. Linda looked confused and lazily blew three perfect smoke rings. She sent a fourth through the third. 'Oh please teach me how to do that,' he begged. 'I'd love to be able to do that.' The tapping grew louder, more frantic.

'Someone's at the window,' Burt shouted. Percy and Linda looked at him. Burt walked over to the window and drew back the curtains. 'My God,' he said, leaping back. Charlie stirred. They all rushed forward. Queenie was staring in, smiling. Percy saw her mouth coo-ee. Her eyes were wide open, her forehead wrinkled and pressed against the window, her hair standing up.

'She's here,' Percy said, and leapt out of the room, knocking the plate of oat fingers and cigarette ends to the floor. Two oat fingers landed face down on the carpet. But he didn't notice in the rush to the door. Just wait there, he said to himself. I'm coming. He threw the door open. 'You're here,' he said to the darkness. 'You're here.' He tried to focus. The night air engulfed him. It was cold and refreshing. 'Queenie, Queenie?' It was dark and silent and eerie. Then he thought he had lost her. He thought she had disappeared back into the night. Gone forever.

'Coo-ee.' She sprung out of the darkness, right into him. He felt the lightness of her small body. 'I thought I'd surprise you all,' she said, laughing. And stood on tip-toes to kiss him. He bent down and breathed in her sweet perfume, her smell. She was wearing a fur coat and carrying a small brown leather handbag. He followed her into his home. 'I'm sorry I'm so late. I'm normally very punctual. But I couldn't start the car. The battery must have gone flat or something.'

He took the coat and carefully laid it out on his bed, not Elizabeth's. He had no idea what fur it was but it was the most luxurious thing he had ever handled, so lush and dark, so soft. She was still standing in the hall when he returned from the bedroom. She was wearing a light pink suit. So much more subtle, more elegant than Toots's suit, he thought.

'So this is where you live. How very practical.'

'I'm afraid we've all had rather a lot to drink, and most of the food has gone.' But in a way he was pleased the food had gone. He knew it was not quite right. He was pleased he had had so much to drink too. He felt confident, gregarious even. He led her unsteadily into the lounge. 'Everyone,' he shouted as if he was about to launch into a speech. 'Queenie has arrived.' He had a broad smile across his blotchy face.

Everyone turned and John half stood, still holding Cassie's hand. 'I'm John,' he said, holding out his other hand. Queenie, however, just smiled at him and then Linda. Percy didn't think she even noticed Charlie slumbering in the armchair. She headed straight for Toots and Burt.

'Burt, aren't you going to kiss a young lady hello?' He lent down and kissed her on the cheek. Toots looked on, imperviously. 'Hello Ruby,' Queenie then said, looking at Toots.

'Hello Elizabeth. How unfortunate. We're just about to leave.'

'What do you mean? The party's just beginning.' She asked Percy for a Scotch. He walked towards the kitchen. 'Coo-ee,' she called after him, 'on the rocks.'

'How stupid. I didn't realise you were called Elizabeth,' he said breathlessly, handing her the drink.

'I'm not often any more. Though Ruby calls me that sometimes. But then she's just awkward. I'm Queenie really. Of course I'm Queenie.'

He knew he would always think of her as Queenie. He couldn't think of her as Elizabeth. Elizabeth just wasn't right. Though he thought Ruby quite suited Toots. The two sisters started to talk to each other, not unpleasantly Percy thought. Toots or Ruby started to complain about Charlie and Queenie complained about Gorleston. How there was never enough to do, or the right person to do it with. They stood by the mantelpiece. Queenie was shorter than Toots. But she seemed to Percy so poised, so stylish, standing there smoking a cigarette. He thought she looked sophisticated. He was delighted they seemed to be getting on, after the frosty start. He watched Queenie and he watched her finish her Scotch in one. He found himself quite unable to take his eyes off her. He thought her glorious. He hovered nearby, staring.

'Are you going to refill my glass or carry on standing there looking like a fool?' she asked in the sweetest way.

'Of course,' he said, fumbling for her empty glass, 'of course.'

Over the next hour Percy somehow managed to keep Queenie's glass full and only stand on one oat finger.

'Why don't we play a game?' Queenie said loudly, looking round. The room was in some disarray. Nobody having yet left. She walked over to Charlie who hadn't moved for a long time. 'How about a game?' she shouted in his ear. Toots laughed. Charlie opened his eyes, then quickly shut them, without moving his head.

Cassie sat up though. 'I'd love to play a game,' she said. 'I'd love to play.' John didn't look up to it. He seemed mesmerised by Cassie's puffy hands.

'I only know one game,' Linda said, yawning, 'sardines.'

'What about strip poker?' Burt said, looking at his wife.

'That doesn't count.' She blushed.

'Why not?'

'Well we can't play that here.'

Percy looked at Queenie. She was smiling. He remembered what Linda and John had said about her being a stripper on Britannia Pier. She looked back at him and winked. He wondered whether she knew he knew. He had never played strip poker. He didn't want to take his clothes off here, now, even if Queenie was going to. He never even used to undress in front of his wife.

'I don't see why not,' Queenie said, still smiling. 'No one's got anything they're afraid of showing, have they?'

Percy thought Cassie looked rather disappointed. She was looking down at her hands which John was still fondling. Toots looked quite eager, though.

'Mind you,' said Queenie, 'I think sardines can be a lot of fun.'

'Yes, sardines,' said Cassie joyfully. 'Sardines.'

Percy said he was not sure that he knew the rules. Linda explained them to everyone. And said she would volunteer to be the first to go and hide. John tried to stand up.

'You always go and hide first,' Burt said.

'I'll go,' said Toots.

'No, I'll go,' said Queenie.

'What about me?' said Cassie, getting up. 'What about me?'

The four women started jostling by the door. Percy said perhaps his home wasn't really large enough. Toots said of course it was, trying to push Cassie out of her way. Cassie agreed and so did Linda, all pushing each other.

'Girls, girls,' Burt shouted. 'Girls.' He moved in to try and break them up.

'Uhmm,' Percy heard someone murmur. 'Uhmm, uhmm.'

'Well, we could always do some dancing?' Queenie

said, untangling herself from her sisters and niece and Burt.

Linda and Burt said they should really be going, straightening their clothes and hair.

Percy said he only had a transistor.

'Where, where?' Queenie demanded. She rushed to the kitchen and returned with the radio crackling loudly. 'I can never tune these things.'

John said he thought he should be going and Cassie said she ought to be going as well. But Queenie soon found a station. A ragtime jazz tune was playing. She pushed the coffee table away from the centre of the room and started to Charleston. Percy watched the locks of her orange hair fly up and down, in unison with her gold necklace. He thought she was brilliant. But it made him feel dizzy to watch her. He saw John and Burt were entranced. Cassie started to clap.

Charlie opened his eyes and slowly sat up in the chair. 'What's all the fuss? What's going on?' he said. 'Queenie up to her usual tricks? She can still dance then.'

Queenie waved to Percy. She was dancing furiously now, her arms outstretched, beckoning him. He didn't know what to do. He couldn't dance. He was hopeless. He then felt someone pushing him towards her. Queenie grabbed him and started to shake him into step. Behind he could hear Cassie clapping faster and faster. He started to sway and lift his feet to the music. 'Faster,' Queenie shouted, 'faster.' She tried to turn him around. This way and that. The song finally ended leaving him quite out of breath, panting. 'Wonderful.' She rubbed her hands. 'I'm just getting warmed up.'

'We're off,' Toots suddenly shouted. 'Come on Charlie, out of that chair. We can take you home Elizabeth, you'd better come with us.'

'But I don't want to go yet,' Queenie protested. She pulled a sad face, reminding Percy of a small girl.

'You're coming with us and that's that.'

Everyone suddenly demanded their coats. 'Come on Percy, we haven't got all night,' said John, 'and bring Cassie's with you while you're at it.'

He fetched the coats from his bedroom, leaving Queenie's until last. He was picking it up when he felt something touch his arm. He turned and there she was. Queenie, standing in his bedroom looking up at him in the faint light. He suddenly felt cold. Frozen. He couldn't speak or move. She looked at him, then reached up and pulled him down to her. She kissed him on the cheek, then gently on the lips. He was swamped by her sweet perfume. He tasted her lipstick and shut his eyes thinking he was somewhere else, not the bedroom he used to share with Elizabeth, his old Elizabeth.

'Elizabeth, Elizabeth.' Toots was shouting from the other end of the bungalow. 'Come along. We're waiting.'

Queenie pulled herself away. 'I'll see you soon,' she whispered.

'Elizabeth.'

Percy helped her with her coat and she walked out of his bedroom. He followed. His legs quite weak. The others were waiting by the front door. Cassie had put her arm through John's and Linda was leaning on Burt. Charlie was leaning against the front door and Toots was staring at them, her head in the bright hall glowing purple, glowing ruby.

'It was a lovely evening,' Cassie said, as the front door was opened.

'It's OK,' John said, 'I'll walk her home. I'm going her way.' They set off into the quietness of Bately Avenue.

Burt shook Percy's hand, a great strong handshake that left his hand ringing. Queenie was singing the ragtime tune, tapping her feet on the path. 'Ch, chew, ch, ch, ch, chew, chew.' Linda kissed Percy goodbye. A big wet kiss. And Burt led her away to their car, the American cruiser which was stretched between Percy's bungalow and Mrs Yarren's bungalow.

'Elizabeth, get in the car,' Toots demanded. Queenie danced over to the Mercedes, waving at Percy. Toots was standing by the front door and Charlie eased himself behind the steering wheel. Percy walked over. He wanted to kiss Queenie goodbye. But Toots grabbed him. 'Goodbye, dear.' She kissed him on the lips, and she held onto his shoulders so he couldn't escape for a number of seconds.

'Leave it out,' Percy heard Queenie whine. She was shuffling nearby. 'Leave it out.' He finally managed to pull himself away.

'We'll have a quieter evening some time soon,' Toots winked and then pushed Queenie onto the back seat, before Percy had managed to kiss her, and she got into the front, first hitching up her skirt.

Queenie did manage to turn and wave before the car veered into Brett Avenue.

'Will you please be quiet. Do you know what time it is?' Mrs Yarren was standing on her doorstep. 'You should know better. It's disgraceful.'

Percy could see Sandy cowering behind her. He ignored Mrs Yarren, feeling sorry for the dog.

The smell of cigarettes and whisky and violets and Queenie's sweet perfume, like some exotic sea mist, saturated the bungalow. He felt far too tired to clear up and struggled out of his clothes and into bed without bothering to put on his new pyjamas. He pulled the covers up, over his nose, pretending they were Queenie's fur coat. He smelt Queenie. She was everywhere. He kissed the air.

Toots made Charlie wait until Queenie had let herself into her bungalow. 'I don't trust her. I'm not having her running back to bother that poor old man,' she said. Charlie grunted.

*   *   *

Queenie lit a cigarette and flicked through the channels on the television. Nothing interested her and she soon switched the set off. She then sat in the silence of night-time Yallop Avenue, night-time Gorleston, the tune still in her head, puffing on a cigarette. How she loved to dance. She felt frustrated. And she made up her mind. Ruby was going to pay for it. Oh yes.

9

The clocks moved forward, which was a comfort to many, though it was still not very warm. It rarely was. The mornings were especially chilly, and misty. The damp Gorleston air rising off the North Sea in the twilight. The fog horn announced each new day, reverberating in the thick, heavy air. People would lose sight of their dogs, out walking along the cliff top.

Queenie waited for the fog horn while Percy woke with it. They saw each other often. Percy was convinced he was the only man she saw. She told him so. And of course he believed her. He felt more and more secure, more and more confident. Things were just gliding along. As he had hoped, as he had longed for all his life. They went for walks and they went shopping. He lit her cigarettes and she laughed and made him laugh. She would drive in and out of the white lines along Marine Parade while he held his head in his hands. 'Stop it, stop it,' he would protest.

She would place both her hands on the Mini Metro's windscreen and say, 'Look, no hands.'

'Stop it, stop it,' he would protest still louder. Though secretly he loved it.

He would always look in the sand-blown windows of St Edmunds as they sped past, often on the wrong side of the road. If he was looking for anything it was a reminder of how things might have been, of how grateful he was to Queenie. At these moments he would turn and look at her, perhaps touch her knee, just to make sure she was real. She was. She would slap his hand away and say, 'Oi, oi.'

The High Street was Queenie's heartland. Every shopkeeper knew her by name. Queenie. They loved to say it. Queenie. Again and again. They would remark on her good health, her good looks and fine clothes. And they would ask after her grandchildren, and some would ask after Ralph, her dog, not realising he was dead. Her curiosity and sense of fun continually amazed Percy. He would be pulled into the travel agencies and they would rifle through the brochures, Queenie demanding to know where he was going to take her. 'It has to be hot and it has to be a long way away,' she would stipulate. 'It has to be exotic and very, very expensive. I want to be spoilt rotten.' He would be shown glossy brochures and she would pick out the resorts. Some she said she knew well. And often she would ask the girl behind the computer terminal to see if a particular holiday or cruise was available for two. She would ask for the presidential suite or cabin. This always took some time and while they waited she would giggle and imitate the other customers queuing to book their summer package holidays. Yet they never booked a holiday, there was always something not quite right. And at the bottom of his heart Percy was glad. He would have been frightened to make any such trip, even if he could have afforded it. He liked it where he was. He liked Gorleston. He didn't want a change of scenery. He liked things how they now were. And occasionally he would tell Queenie so. 'Urrrgh,' she would go. 'It's horrible here.'

Queenie was even known in the small, specialist shops at the far end of the High Street. Joe's Tattoo Studio, Jenkins' Artists Materials, Sally Smith's. Joe the tattooist was fat and friendly and in his late fifties. It seemed to Percy that he had known Queenie for years. She never explained how she'd got to know him. He had a long moustache that curled up at the ends, which she would try to twist. 'Let me, go on,' she would demand. Joe would go through his designs again and again, telling them what were the most popular, and where people wanted them inscribed. His arms were thick with tattoos. The colours merging into a green grey, much like the North Sea on a good day, Percy thought.

'Which one do you think?' Queenie would ask. 'Which one would suit me best?' She wanted a tattoo on her shoulder or her thigh, her inner thigh.

Percy pretended he wanted one on his forearm and would pick out naked women with long fair hair, or swords with snakes curling round them. 'I might just have QUEENIE tattooed on my arm, below one of those hearts,' he teased.

'What will all your girlfriends say?' she'd tease back and wink.

She said she used to paint still lifes and seascapes, as she mused through Jenkins'. She would take the tops off the paint tubes and bottles of white spirit. 'Uhmm, smell that.' And as Percy bent down to smell the opened tube of paint she would squeeze a dollop onto his nose. It happened every time but he didn't mind. He thought one day he would buy her an easel and some paints. He would set it up on the beach or on the cliff top for her and watch her work. She was the most artistic person he had ever met.

And once they were at the far end of the High Street they would invariably pop into Sally Smith's lingerie shop. Sally Smith knew Queenie. She knew Queenie very well. Percy was far too embarrassed to go in at first, though Queenie eventually dragged him in and slowly he got used to it, he got used to the skimpy, lacy undergarments, the whites and pinks and blacks. 'My figure's not what it used to be,' Queenie would complain from behind the changing room curtain. 'It's just not what it used to be.' She rarely bought anything, and Percy presumed she just liked trying the things on.

Sally Smith never complained, she always seemed far too pleased to see Queenie. 'She's my best customer,' she would tell Percy. 'She's a trend-setter.'

And if they went anywhere near Bells Road, Queenie would insist they just nip into the toy shop. She was always thinking of her grandchildren, she told Percy, and there might just be something for them. And mostly she would buy something, joke toys mainly, gorilla masks, funny hats, plastic snakes, plastic dog turds, edible cigarettes. She had drawers of these jokes at home, Percy found out later. She never sent them on to her grandchildren.

Queenie didn't eat much and they would often keep going for the whole day on nothing more than a couple of cakes and cigarettes. Yet she never tired. Her energy staggered Percy. She was forever skipping and trotting. She told him she once had a donkey, called Peggy. She would imitate Peggy on pavements, trotting and bucking and ee-awing.

For a while Percy heard very little from Toots and Charlie. Not that he really minded. Queenie was all that he wanted. And she often said she would be quite happy if she never saw Toots again. Sometimes she called her Ruby and sometimes Toots. There seemed to be no difference in her attitude to her, her scorn for her, though Percy suspected she was fond of Toots really and he wondered whether she really meant what she said, that she would be quite happy if she never saw her sister again. When Percy thought of Toots, and Charlie, he often felt sorry for them. But he was not going to ruin his relationship with Queenie, not for anything, so he tried to keep out of Toots's way. He didn't want Queenie thinking he was disloyal. He avoided the places he thought she might be. He avoided the Links, despite invitations from John and Cassie, who it appeared now met there regularly. Even his friendship with Linda was strained, he felt. She seemed to have sided with her mother, who she said was quite lonely. 'She's much more lonely than you could imagine. Daddy's not the most stimulating of people. Why don't you take her out for lunch, tea even? She'd love that.'

On the evening of 18th February, 1807, the Snipe gunboat started to go to pieces within sight of the harbour mouth. Captain Manby, who had rushed on horseback to the pier, watched as body after body washed up along the shore. Two other ships close by went down that ferocious night and the next day 147 bodies were recovered within a 30-mile stretch of coast.

Captain Manby was so distressed by what he saw that he set about designing an apparatus to save lives imperilled by shipwrecks. A year later he had completed a prototype. When the brig Elizabeth of Plymouth started to founder in a violent storm some 150 yards from shore he brought his equipment to the pier and fired the first rocket attached to a line over the brig. The line was caught and a breeches buoy was attached, by way of which the crew of seven were all brought successfully to shore.

There is a plaque on the house he once lived in on the High Road that reads, 'In commemoration of the 12th February 1808 on which day, directly eastward of this site the first life was saved from shipwreck by means of a rope attached to a shot fired from a mortar over the stranded vessel.'

The Rocket Lifesaving Apparatus, however, never earned Captain Manby a knighthood or much money, which he bitterly complained about. He was constantly in debt and his wife fell in love with a Captain Pogson, who shot Manby in the head. Mrs Manby and Captain Pogson fled the country leaving Manby penniless and crippled.

* * *

Percy was waiting for the kettle to boil, staring into Mrs Yarren's kitchen, when he heard the door bell. He was not expecting anybody. He looked at the clock. It was eight-thirty in the evening.

'Percy, I knew you'd be in.' Toots was standing on the doorstep. 'I had to see you. I simply had to. Charlie thinks I'm at my whist drive.' She smelt as if she had been drinking. A bouquet of alcohol and violets filled the hall as she stepped inside. 'On your own?' she asked, sweeping into the lounge.

'I was just making a cup of tea, would you like one?'

'Not likely. How about a proper drink?'

'Sherry?'

Toots laughed. 'I said a proper drink.'

Percy went to the kitchen to hunt out the tumblers and whisky. The kettle had boiled and he looked longingly at the whisper of steam seeping out of the spout. Toots had taken off her coat to reveal a sleeveless blue cocktail dress. She was sitting back on the sofa. He poured her a drink and then sat down in the armchair, pulling up the coffee table, barricade-like, between them. He lit a cigarette and found his hand was shaking. All he could think of was Queenie turning up unexpectedly. She never had before, but he knew there could always be a first time. He knew he could rely on Queenie to do the unexpected.

'Oh, it's so nice and warm here,' Toots said, shifting around on the sofa, getting comfortable. She slipped a shoe off and tucked a foot under herself. Her mask of powder could not hide the fact that her face was flushed. Her hair was in disarray. Percy thought the purple bouffant had run out of puff. It fell to one side precariously. 'I haven't see you in ages, old boy. Tell me, what you have been up to. I've been concerned about you. Truly concerned.'

'I've been absolutely fine.' He felt increasingly annoyed,

realising that Toots's visit might not actually have been a matter of life or death. 'In fact I've been having a wonderful time. So what did you have to see me about so urgently?'

'Expecting someone?'

'No. It's just that I was hoping to have an early night.'

'So what did I have to see you about?' She started to run her fingers through her hair, as though she was trying to prop it up. 'Well,' she smiled at him, 'nothing in particular.' She slipped her other shoe off. 'I just wanted to see if you were well. You hear so many stories. Gorleston's such a small place.' She tucked her other foot beneath her.

Percy was quite surprised by her agility. 'What stories? What have you heard?' He knew there was concern in his voice.

'Just tittle-tattle. Nothing important.' She smiled again.

'Well why did you come round then?'

She sipped her whisky loudly. 'I don't want you to make a mistake. Come and sit next to me.' She patted the cushion next to her. 'Come and sit next to me.' She continued to pat the cushion.

'What mistake, what are you talking about?'

'You know perfectly well. I don't need to spell it out.'

'I've no idea what you're talking about. No idea at all.' He was determined not to go and sit next to her. Determined. He was not going to be ordered around. Not by her.

She suddenly looked very stern. 'You're making a big mistake. Elizabeth, or Queenie, or whatever you like to call her, is not to be trusted. Leave her alone, Percy. Forget about her. She's nothing but trouble.'

He felt like screaming, he was so angry. 'She's my business,' he shouted. He reached over and topped up his whisky, ignoring Toots's empty glass. 'Just leave me alone. She's mine, mine, mine. It doesn't make any difference what you say. She's mine. Leave us alone.'

'Oh darling, don't be like that,' Toots lisped gently. 'Don't be cross.' She unfurled an arm along the back of the sofa. 'Come and sit next to me. Let me calm you down. You need soothing.'

Percy felt horrified. He thought about running out of the room but realised he would have to pass close by her and she might grab him.

'I'm sure we could come to some arrangement.'

He didn't know what she meant and didn't want to know. 'I think you'd better go.' He wanted her out of his home, now. He was convinced she was drunk, very drunk, and he worried about what she might do next. He stood up.

'Oh, do come and sit down,' she gestured. 'Don't be such a bore.'

Percy didn't mind Toots calling him a bore. If Queenie had it would have been a different matter. 'Toots, I really think you should be going. You must go.' He was becoming increasingly anxious about Queenie turning up. 'You're putting me in a most difficult position. Now come on, get up, please, you're going.'

She looked at him and smiled sweetly. Then she yawned. 'Maybe I could stay? I'm feeling awfully tired. I'm never going to be able to walk home.'

'Yes you are,' he shouted. 'You have to go home, now. I'll drive you.' He got hold of an arm and tried to pull her up. She was heavy, but relaxed. She flopped forward. 'Please, Toots. It's not fair. You'll ruin everything.' He knew he sounded desperate. She untucked her feet.

'Where are my shoes then?' Percy found them and gave them to her. She put them on and stood up, unaided. Wobbling, she smoothed down her dress. 'Do you like my dress? I put it on specially for you.'

'Lovely,' he said, not even looking at her. He held out her coat. The coat smelt of violets and pipe tobacco. He couldn't remember whether Charlie smoked a pipe or not. He helped her put it on. She grasped his arm as they walked to the car. It was drizzling. The car took a while to start and the windows quickly steamed up.

'I only wanted to know if you were all right,' she said in the darkness. 'I only wanted to know if you were still alive.'

Percy looked at her, she looked away, and rubbed the door window with the sleeve of her coat. He suddenly felt sorry for her. She looked sad and vulnerable and helpless. In a way she reminded him of himself. He thought of Queenie. Queenie was never sad or vulnerable or helpless, even though sometimes she pretended to be. Perhaps, he thought, that was why he adored her so much. Such a strong woman. They moved off down Bately Avenue, the yellow street lamps refracting on the drizzle trickling down the windscreen. He leant forward to try to see more clearly. His mind was drifting in all directions.

Toots started to hum. 'Is it because she can dance?' He didn't answer and she didn't pursue the question and Gorleston being so small, they were at the end of Cliff Lane in no time. The Mercedes was in the drive and light poured out of the large bungalow. 'Charlie will be watching Sky,' she said, sounding more cheerful. 'Marvellous.' She clambered out of the car before Percy had time to go round and help.

'Look, Toots,' he said as she tottered down the driveway. He didn't know what to say. 'Let's have a drink another time?' He really hoped she would forget about the evening. He heard her laugh. He turned the car round quickly. Rain now was sweeping into the windscreen. He pulled into Yallop Avenue. He slowed as he passed Queenie's bungalow. It was quite dark. Not one light was on. He imagined her, tucked up in bed, fast asleep.

Queenie said she was tired. 'No, nothing's wrong. I just didn't sleep very well last night.' She said she would rather spend the day quietly at home. They had arranged to go shopping together. Percy was worried. Queenie had never told him she felt tired before, let alone expressed a wish to spend the day quietly at home. But she slowly put his mind at rest. 'Don't worry, dear. Really I'm fine. I'll be back to normal tomorrow.' She didn't tell him the Benson and Hedges World Snooker Championship was reaching a climax. Then she didn't tell him everything. She put the phone down before him, as she always did. He could never quite bring himself to put the phone down first.

Linda was surprised to hear from him. 'I thought you'd abandoned us,' she said on the telephone. Percy laughed, saying he'd just been busy. 'I've heard,' she said. He half-lied and said he was going to be in the area later that morning and wondered whether he could pop round for a coffee. 'A friend is coming over at lunchtime, so you better make it well before one,' she said. She didn't sound terribly pleased.

Still, he felt it was necessary to make the visit. He didn't want to abandon Linda and her family and he wanted to try and straighten things out with Toots as soon as possible. Before something really terrible happened. He didn't know what Toots might do next. She could do anything. And he thought the only person who might be able to help would be Linda. He knew Linda would understand. Besides, he needed her as friend.

He drove to the Mariner's Compass housing estate in a blaze of sunshine. The fog had lifted early, leaving the sea to reflect a clear blue sky. He knew the fine weather might not hold up all day, it rarely did, but it was a lovely morning. Sun poured into the car, warming him. He wound the window down. He could hear birds and children crying. There were a number of women in summer dresses pushing push-chairs along the wide pavements. Some had double push-chairs. He remembered the last time when he had been here it had been pouring with rain. He remembered everything had smelt new and wet. How he had found it all rather depressing. Now in the sunlight he found himself appreciating the estate, its newness. The thought that had gone into it. The way each house was slightly different, a red door here, a green one there. Some houses had porches and some didn't. He found it so much more uplifting than where he lived. And there were signs of life everywhere. Young life.

Linda answered the door in her dressing gown, a pink towelling dressing gown. 'You'll have to excuse me for a minute, I haven't quite finished my nails,' she said breathlessly. She was holding a nail polish brush in her right hand.

Percy noticed she had already made up her face. Her bright red lipstick clashed with the pink dressing gown. He thought she had perhaps applied a little too much make-up.

'Put the kettle on,' she said, rushing back upstairs, the dressing gown flapping round her long brown legs.

The kitchen was a mess, which surprised Percy. Coffee granules had melted on the white formica surface around the kettle and drifted into a large dark brown pool. There were bread crumbs everywhere and the microwave door was open, inside sat a plate of what looked like grey scrambled egg. He found two mugs in a cupboard, both were chipped and stained. He heard Linda walking around above him. A cork notice board above the fridge was covered in scraps of paper, video club newsletters and Chinese restaurant take-away menus. Shafts of sunlight poured through the kitchen window, highlighting stains on the linoleum floor.

After some time Linda appeared, wearing a pink summer dress, the same shade as her dressing gown. 'It's such a gorgeous day, isn't it? Phew.' She wiped her brow. They sat on stools by the breakfast bar. 'Sorry about the mess. I just can't seem to get on top of it.'

Percy was relieved to find her more cheerful and welcoming than when he had spoken to her earlier that morning. She smiled at him. She was not wearing any stockings and he couldn't help noticing that her legs were much browner than her arms.

'So how's life in the fast lane?' she said, before sipping her coffee loudly.

He laughed. 'Fast lane, here?' He didn't let her pursue the question and suggested they went for a brief walk in the sunshine, if she had time.

'Sure,' she said, 'but I have to be back by one. I can't be late.' She fetched a cardigan and they set off down the crazy paving path. The quartz glistening.

'Your mother dropped by last night. I'm not quite sure why she came round, or what she wanted. She was rather drunk. But I got her home eventually.'

'Oh dear.' Linda stopped walking. 'That bad?'

'Yes, it was rather awful. You see it could have been very embarrassing. I like your mother and Charlie, but people might talk. I don't know whether you could say anything to her. Of course she might not remember any of it. But I thought you might be able to help. I don't want to lose any friends. I don't want there to be a misunderstanding.' He looked at her. 'I don't really want her just turning up drunk.'

'The trouble is, Percy, I could say something, but I don't know whether it would do any good. She doesn't listen to me or anyone else for that matter. And what would I say?' She sounded rather angry. 'What on earth could I say?' They had to move onto the road to let two women with push-chairs and lots of children pass. Linda nodded at them. 'She's on her fourth,' she said loudly, pointing to one of the women. 'What would I say to her? Leave Percy alone, Mummy. She doesn't mean any harm. She's an old woman for chrissakes.'

Percy thought she said chrissakes in a very American way. He thought of Burt, on his rig, and he watched the women and children disappear round a corner.

'Really, Percy, I think you can stand up to her. Why don't you take her out for dinner and just let her know you want to be friends. And that's all. Explain yourself. Tell her you're taken. She doesn't give up easily.'

They reached the edge of the housing estate, where gardens backed onto the playing fields of the secondary school. Linda slipped through a gap in the fence and onto the edge of a games field. Percy followed. He could see some children far in the distance, near the school buildings.

'My father's never been very supportive. He's been useless really. And not altogether faithful. Poor mother. I think she's had a hard time of it. It's not been easy for her. Queenie's always been in the spotlight, you see.' She sat on the grass and stretched out her legs. 'And I suppose she thinks she knew you first and now Queenie has stolen you. It's not the first time something like this has happened.'

Percy said it was not like that at all. He didn't explain himself and he didn't tell Linda that it was he who had pursued Queenie. 'But there must be some way round it?'

'To be quite honest, Percy, you'd be better off not getting involved with either of them. Have you ever thought of moving to this part of town?'

He looked around at the unusual brilliance, the children, the seagulls. He looked at Linda, her brown skin against the pink dress. 'It's very nice here.'

'You'd never guess what goes on.'

'I think I'm too old for this part of town. I don't belong here.' He believed it too. He didn't belong here. He knew where he belonged. He belonged on Yallop Avenue.

Linda said goodbye at the top of the crazy paving path that led to her house and then she scampered off. Percy watched her go, a shimmer of pink and brown. He turned and bumped into a man walking down the path. Percy noticed he was about his age and he thought he recognised him. He thought he might have seen him in the Links or St Edmunds. The man said sorry and he thought no more of it.

Percy eventually made it out of the estate, having taken a couple of wrong turnings into neat cul-de-sacs. The sun was stronger now and he felt happy to be out of the estate. A yellow banana bus sped past. A huge plastic banana attached to its roof. He had read about them in the local paper, how the council had dreamt up the idea for the busy summer season. And he remembered reading a letter of complaint a few days later from a well known local historian and former town councillor, who said that it was a useless idea. Not only did the banana buses look ridiculous, Percy remembered the letter saying, but people had stopped coming to Gorleston on holiday over twenty years ago.

He stopped at the corner shop where Warren Lane met Yallop Avenue and bought some flowers. He wanted to drop them off at Queenie's. He hoped she might be feeling better. He hoped she might even feel like a stroll along the cliff top. She didn't answer her door, however. He stood on the doorstep holding the flowers, another bunch of bright yellow daffodils, for a number of minutes. His heart thumped and his hands started to feel sticky with perspiration. He felt he was crushing the stems of the daffodils. He lent down and put his ear to the letter-box which he pushed open. He heard a voice. A male voice. Though he couldn't make out what he was saying. He then walked round to the side of the bungalow and peered into the sitting room. The television was on but the room was empty. Two coffee cups stood on the table. The gate to the back garden was locked. He knew he wouldn't be able to climb it so he walked back to the front. An old woman wearing a hair net, Queenie's neighbour, was staring at him from her kitchen window. He looked at her. He knew he must have looked helpless.

She opened her window. 'She went out,' she croaked.

Percy asked her if she knew where Queenie had gone or when she might be back.

'Who knows. She does as she pleases.' The old woman shut the window, but continued to stare at him.

He thought she couldn't have gone far. She had left the television on, after all. He tried to convince himself that she had just popped to the chemists. He stood about in her front garden for nearly an hour, the old woman staring at him for much of the time, then he scribbled a note. 'Sorry to have missed you. Hope you're feeling better. Much love, Percy.' He thought about adding an X or two, but he didn't know whether people still did that. He tucked the note into the flowers and left them on her doorstep.

The sun shone for the rest of the day, eventually sinking into the North Sea behind a ship that was registered in Cape Town. Queenie had happy memories of Cape Town. It was her sort of town. She blew the captain a kiss.

10

The Vauxhall Cavalier sped along Marine Parade. Queenie normally insisted on going everywhere in her car, she liked to drive, she liked to be in control, but that day the Metro wouldn't start. The battery was flat again. She agreed to go in Percy's car. And Percy was driving as fast as he could. He knew Queenie wouldn't put up with anything less.

'I'm not very keen on the colour,' she said, extinguishing a cigarette in the clean ashtray. 'What colour is it?' She looked at him and frowned. 'Does it go any faster?' She nudged him hard. 'How about a swerve?' She nudged him again. 'Werr-hay.'

The North Sea was a hazy grey and calm. A ship sat on the horizon. Gulls circled. And people strolled along the cliff top waiting for the sun to break through. They rushed past, past Queenie's old house, the Links, the Gables Nursing Home, St Edmunds, Queenie wrestling the while with the steering wheel. 'Give them a show, Percy. Give them a show.' And on they went, plunging down Cliff Hill, down into Lower Gorleston. 'Coo-ee,' she shouted out of the open window. 'Coo-ee.'

The car rattled along Riverside Road, Percy struggling to keep control. He was driving faster than ever before. So what if I die now, he said to himself, what if I plunge into the river with Queenie. I'm happy. We'll die together.

He looked at her. She was smiling and a cigarette was hanging from the corner of her mouth. Yes, he thought, she is adorable. Across the River Yare the sun had broken through. Great Yarmouth was bathed in sunlight. The docked ships and cranes and factories sparkled. And they were going to Great Yarmouth. It was all so perfect. Percy couldn't remember having ever felt so excited.

'Let's go soon,' she had said on the telephone, after thanking him for the flowers, four days after he left them on her doorstep. 'I'd love to show you Great Yarmouth. There's so much to see, so much to do. Let's go now.' He had quite forgiven her for not getting in touch sooner.

As they passed the harbour pilots' headquarters the road became thick with pot-holes. Queenie pointed out the old wooden ferry jetty, sinking into the mud. She said until recently a man would take you across for a few shillings. At the end of Riverside Road, by a dry dock, they had to leave the river, turn inland, and navigate a one-way system before turning back out to sea on the approach to the Haven Bridge, the old iron bridge that led across the River Yare and into the heart of Great Yarmouth. Percy slowed over the bridge so he could look from side to side, up and down the glinting Yare. Worried about navigating the bridge with its narrow lanes and heavy traffic, he slowed further. A lorry hooted behind. Queenie turned round and shook her small, delicate fist at the lorry driver. 'Wanker,' she whispered.

Percy didn't hear, he was thinking of something he had read in a book belonging to his wife, which had described Great Yarmouth as an island, cut off from the rest of Norfolk by the rivers Yare and Bure, and a great marsh that was once at the north end of the town. He could even visualise the hand-drawn map that appeared in the thin book. But he didn't want to think of the book now. There were too many memories attached to it, to the past. They were too painful. He tried not to think of Elizabeth, but as he caught sight of the Star Hotel he couldn't help remembering once having tea there with her. It was a pretty hotel that overlooked the dockside. It was where the end-of-pier entertainers stayed, their signed photographs hung in the small bar. But Percy and Elizabeth had been there during winter, the last winter they had had together, and the place had been very quiet. They had sat in the lounge by a fire that didn't work, unnoticed for a long while. Elizabeth had told him about Yarmouth, the Yarmouth she used to know, which was a place that was warm and exciting and the people courteous. Percy listened, saying little, as was his way. Eventually a waitress appeared. The waitress was rude because Elizabeth couldn't make up her mind what she wanted, Percy remembered. Elizabeth had always been so decisive, it had shocked him. He ordered for her and then she started to cry, hiding her face behind the stained menu. But he knew then it wasn't because the waitress had been rude or because she had not been able to make up her mind, however. He had thought it might be because it was empty and winter, and she knew that she was dying. Or that the hotel held special memories, perhaps childhood memories that she didn't wish to articulate. But she never explained why she cried. There were many things they never explained fully to each other, more and more as they grew older. Each just assuming the other would understand. At the beginning Percy used to think Elizabeth could read his mind.

The car bounced as it left the steep bridge, running onto the solid, flat ground of Yarmouth. Percy rarely went to Yarmouth. People living in Gorleston rarely did. They just complained about the congestion, about the tourists and how downmarket it had become. Not at all like Gorleston, they would explain, Gorleston was much quieter, much safer. But it was the noise and the life and the danger of Great Yarmouth that Percy wanted now. He found himself quickly tangled in the one-way system. The air was filled with the noise of cars hooting and braking and, as they passed the market place, people shouting. A vibrancy, Percy thought. It seemed a hundred miles from Gorleston. Yet he knew it was barely three. He could see why Queenie liked it so much, why she had insisted they go right away.

'There, turn left there,' Queenie suddenly screamed, 'that's the way to the sea front.' It was too late. 'Oh, Percy. That's where everything happens. Now we'll have to go all the way round again. Oh, turn there, left there.'

This time Percy swung the car left and found himself turning into the Victoria Arcade. 'My God. You can't drive down here.' The narrow Victorian shopping arcade was full of pedestrians.

'Of course you can. I always do.' Queenie looked excited. She sat forward in the seat looking from side to side, window shopping.

The car crawled down the arcade, bemused and angry shoppers getting out of their way. About half-way down Percy began to relax. He thought if Queenie's going to enjoy it then so am I. We can both get arrested. He asked her to light him a cigarette. He noticed two young boys pointing and laughing at him. He smiled back, exhaling a plume of smoke. He felt irreverent, naughty. He felt great.

'Can't we just stop,' she asked. 'I love that shop.' She pointed to a toy shop, its windows full of model trains and planes and a blow-up Mickey Mouse. People were pressed into its doorway, trying to avoid their car.

'Actually I think we'd better get out of here.' He didn't want to disappoint her, he didn't want her to think he was boring, but he could see two policemen's helmets bobbing above the crowd in his rearview mirror. 'I think we're being followed.'

Queenie looked. 'Oh, don't worry about them, I know everyone in Yarmouth, I know everyone everywhere.'

Percy was worried though, he accelerated down the arcade, the daylight at the end getting brighter. He tried to press the horn gently. But it sounded full and resonant in the arcade. Queenie roared with laughter. She leant over and squeezed his arm, smiling. She then thumped the horn, startling more shoppers ahead, many dropping their shopping bags and scooping up their children before leaping into doorways. Percy clipped a few of the discarded bags as he pulled into King Street, by chance the right way into the one-way traffic flow.

He drove to the sea front feeling like an outlaw. Queenie quickly calmed down and held her hand out of the window to see how warm it was. It was not very warm despite the sun, yet Percy noticed that many young men were bare-chested. They arrived at the sea front by Joyland, a group of flashing amusements on the edge of Britannia Pier which stretched out into a calm North Sea. Queenie wanted to drive along the front, she wanted to show Percy all the amusements before they parked. He turned onto the Golden Mile, which she told him was officially called Marine Parade. She laughed. Tinsel-fronted bingo halls, casinos and nightclubs, with their names – Caesar's Palace, Tiffany's, Mint City, Golden Nugget – in bright neon, looked out over different worlds: the Kingdom of the Sea, the Living Jungle, Tropical Butterfly World. Percy drove through the middle, marvelling. He had only been along Great Yarmouth's sea front once before, and that was in winter when everything had been boarded up. It was all so different now. A different world, he thought. Groups of young people bustled along the wide pavements, children eating candy floss. The candy floss reminded Percy of Cassie's hair, blown by a gentle sea breeze.

'What do you think?' Queenie asked, expectantly. 'What do you think?'

Percy caught sight of the Model Village, Hansel and Gretel-like, and Treasure World which had half a pirate's ship protruding above the entrance. 'It's incredible. It's incredible to think Gorleston is just over there.' He pointed ahead. He did think it was incredible, truly, though he wasn't sure how else he felt about it. He wasn't sure whether he liked it even. It was all so, so much. But he was not going to make any judgments that might be contrary to Queenie's.

'Just wait,' she said, 'there's more to come.'

They drove past the Safari Centre, Wally Windmill's Playhouse, Novelty Putting, and numerous shops with colourful buckets and spades and inflatable animals spilling onto the promenade. Percy wound down his window and smelt the salty air of Yarmouth's sea front. It was tinged with the sticky sweetness of rock and candy floss, tomato ketchup.

By the Tyrolean Bier Garden Queenie pointed ahead. 'Look,' she said in a hushed tone, 'look.' He leaned forward and there rising in front of them was the rollercoaster, set in an Alpine landscape, a giant mural of forests and meadows and snowy peaks. 'My favourite,' she said, leaning forward further still and looking up in wonder.

Percy thought it looked terrifying. He had never been on a rollercoaster before. He wasn't sure whether Queenie intended to just look at it or go on it. But it wasn't long before he realised she had every intention of going on it.

'Stop,' she said, 'let's park.'

He continued for a while looking for a parking place. The Golden Mile ended abruptly after the rollercoaster, as if nothing could compete with it. There was a caravan park, then a low warehouse with a sign that said Offshore Portable Foam. He turned the car round and managed to find a shady spot near the icy wonder of the rollercoaster.

Queenie took his hand as they entered the Pleasure Beach, trotting ahead, pulling him along, pretending to be Peggy the donkey. 'Thank you for bringing me here.' She said she knew the sun would shine this afternoon and added softly, 'I think you're absolutely marvellous.'

Percy felt himself tingle all over. Nothing would have stopped him from joining her on the rollercoaster. They headed straight for it. Percy having trouble avoiding the half-eaten hot dogs, burger wrappers, chewing gum, pools of tomato ketchup, that littered the ground. As they neared he heard a terrible rumbling and screaming. A train clattered nearby, shaking everything. Percy felt slightly ridiculous queuing with the teenagers and the few scared-looking parents. He felt far too old. But Queenie didn't look old, not to him. She looked young and full of life. She was pushing her way along the queue faster than anyone else, pulling him behind her. 'Watch out, gran,' a kid shouted angrily. Percy thought about punching the boy but he hadn't punched anyone in his life so he just glared at him.

'We've got to get the back seat,' Queenie said. 'We've got to get the back seat. That's the best place.' She sounded breathless with excitement, and she knew exactly where to line up on the pretty Alpine platform, with flowers in boxes and signs in Gothic script. A train rumbled in. The station shook. As the ruffled-haired passengers climbed out there was a mad scramble between those waiting to board. Percy noticed Queenie elbowing a small boy out of her way. But she made it and sat down on the very back seat of the last coach. No one was going to sit next to her apart from Percy. No one.

After everyone settled down the train jerked into motion and slowly rattled into a tunnel. Light seeped through gaps and cracks and Percy could see that the mountains were built around a flimsy wooden frame. 'Are you sure it's safe?' he said loudly, above the creaking and groaning. 'I don't feel very safe.' He was clutching the safety bar across his lap.

Queenie was brushing her hair back with her fingers. 'Of course it's safe, safe as anything. I've been riding this thing since I was a child. Don't you just love the way it creaks and groans?'

Percy didn't answer and the train rolled out of the tunnel and into the bright sunlight. Then it started a slow, steep climb, clinking and clanking away. He reached under the safety bar for Queenie's hand. He found it and held it firmly. As the train carried on climbing, Yarmouth Beach spread out below them, wide and golden and lovely. He thought it much grander than Gorleston Beach. Yet it was deserted.

'They're all playing on the amusements,' Queenie said as if reading his thoughts. 'Much more fun than sitting on the beach all day.'

Percy wasn't going to say he didn't think so or that he would have much rather been on the beach with Queenie, holding her hand, walking by the shore, paddling even, than be on a rollercoaster that carried on going up and up. He wasn't going to contradict her. He tried not to think about being on a rollercoaster. He saw Yarmouth's two piers stretch far into the calm North Sea. He thought they looked like large groynes. Three oil rigs sat on the horizon. He thought of Burt, and Linda. Then he thought of Queenie. He wanted to tell her he loved her but his stomach left him as he felt the train drop. He couldn't catch his breath and his eyes began to water in the rushing wind. He tried to look at Queenie. All he could see was an orange blur.

The second descent was the worst. Barely had Percy time to get his breath when the train dropped down a far steeper slope, plunging into darkness through a timber gap, the top of which he was sure was going to slice his head off. And in that split second he had thought of Linda's dead husband, his headless body slumped in a train. But Queenie, he had noticed, was holding her arms aloft, as if reaching for the sky. 'Whoo-ee,' she screamed. He thought he was going to be sick.

Queenie was laughing and laughing. 'My, you look a little pale.' Her wrinkled cheeks were flushed. She was eager to move on to the next ride, the next thing. She always was. 'Come on Percy.' He held out his hand, pathetically, hoping she would take it and pull him along. His legs had turned to jelly. He was having difficulty walking. He really needed to sit down. 'You can sit down in the dodgems,' she shouted, trotting ahead.

In 1929 the ferryman Robert Maystone died. He had rowed over 140,000 miles, backwards and forwards, across the River Yare.

In 1908 he left his employment with the Ferry Company and started up his own service near the Fishwharf. Maystone was a proud Gorleston man, as were all the ferrymen. He ferried policemen for free, changed his landing points to order, and made no charge, relying instead on the generosity of his customers.

However, his old employees took him to court. The Ferry Company produced a number of historical documents that showed that they held the charter, first obtained in 1509 by Sir Henry Jernigham, Lord of the Manor of Lothingland, which claimed the sole right of ferriage over the Yare. The case went to appeal, but the Ferry Company eventually won, re-establishing their right to the water crossing of the Yare, as inherited from the Lord of the Manor of Lothingland.

Maystone never rowed again.

In 1954 a motor boat which could take 40 people replaced the rowing boat and the fare was raised from half a penny to three pence.

* * *

'That's where we used to live,' Queenie said, pointing at the Carlton Park Hotel across the road. 'Of course it wasn't a hotel when we used to live there.'

Percy studied the building. It was huge and white, with balconies leading out of the first-floor rooms. It was by far the smartest building along the Golden Mile. It looked quite out of place amid the gaudiness of the bingo halls and flashing amusement arcades. He wasn't sure what to say. The place was so large and smart that he began to feel inadequate. 'What was it like?' he said at last.

'It was bloody draughty. But we had some great parties, especially during the war. They were great times.' She sighed. 'Things were never the same after that.'

He looked at her. She looked sad. He had never seen her look sad before. He found it quite, quite moving, and felt tears in his own eyes well up. 'I'm sorry. Should we move on?' He stepped closer to her. He reached for her arm.

'Yes,' she said briskly, turning away. 'One's got to move on. There's no point dwelling on the past. No point at all.' She started to hurry down the promenade, towards the glittering lights and weird electronic noises.

Before Percy caught up with her she disappeared into the Living Jungle. He paid and hesitantly stepped forward. Squeaks and squawks emanated from the darkness ahead. He couldn't understand why it had to be so dark. It was hot and the air was thick and sticky. The noises, the jungle noises, grew louder and louder. He felt something brush his arm. 'Coo-ee,' he heard faintly. 'Coo-ee.' But he wasn't sure it was Queenie calling him from the dark, slimy depths of the jungle. His eyes became more and more accustomed to the faint light. He saw a monkey stuck lifelessly halfway up a palm tree. Condensation, like rain, dropped from the ceiling. Thunder rumbled in the distance. It seemed to Percy that a storm was about to break.

'Queenie,' he yelled. 'Queenie, come back.' He began

to panic. 'Queenie.' His voiced barely audible above the squeaking and squawking and thunder. He felt alone. He felt lost. He brushed frantically through the clamorous jungle, catching his jacket sleeves and trousers on the thick, damp plastic vegetation. The ground was slippery with fake leaves and roots. He lurched into two boys trying to pull something off a tree.

'Watch out, granddad,' one of the boys shouted.

'Yerr, watch where you're going,' the other said.

Percy staggered on. Drops of water were landing on his head more regularly now. Lightning broke and there, sitting serenely under a palm tree, was Queenie. He rushed to her. He bent down and wrapped his arms around her. 'Oh, darling,' he said, 'I thought I had lost you.' He kissed her warm, wet cheek. Thunder cracked overhead.

'Calm down,' she said, pushing him away. 'Calm down. People will see. Really now.' The jungle lit up again, turning her hair fluorescent. Percy joined her on the bench and she allowed him to hold her hand. 'If only this was real,' she said. 'I'd love to be in a proper jungle. Just think of the real heat and the humidity. The stickiness. Oooh, you would just have to take all your clothes off. Just imagine.' She wriggled on the bench, which was meant to look like an uprooted tree trunk. 'And just imagine the noise. Coo-ee.'

The two boys Percy had bumped into earlier walked past. They turned to look at what had made the noise. 'Coo-ee,' they imitated, before giggling and rushing off.

Queenie lit a cigarette and Percy followed, though he was sure he had seen a No Smoking sign on the way in. For the first time he felt he really needed a cigarette. They puffed away on the bench not saying anything. He thought she seemed distant. And he was worried. He was worried that he had let her down on the rollercoaster, that he had failed some sort of test. He thought she might think he was timid, pathetic even. But he knew he wasn't. He vowed to himself that he would prove it to her. He wasn't sure how, but he knew he would. He would do anything for her. Smoke curled up into the damp atmosphere. The storm had subsided. The animals began to chirp away with fresh vigour. The jungle became brighter, more friendly.

'Out, you two.' A man in green overalls was pointing at them. 'Come on, you saw the signs. You should know better than to pollute our environment. Come on, out.'

'I say,' Queenie said, 'do you work here?' Percy looked at her. She was calmly exhaling. Then he looked at the man. His face was scarlet and mean.

'Come on, out,' he repeated, not answering Queenie's question. 'And you too,' he nodded at Percy. Percy was trying to conceal his cigarette behind his back. He felt the smoke rising up his arm, seeping up his sleeve.

'Have we done something wrong?' Queenie asked politely.

'There's no smoking in here and if you don't leave now I'll call the police,' the man spluttered.

'Now wait a minute, little man, we've paid to come in here.' Queenie shuffled on the bench. She inhaled deeply and sent a cloud of smoke billowing into his face.

'Right, that's it.' The man moved closer, towards Queenie.

Percy thought he might grab her. She looked so delicate, fragile even, perched beside him on the plastic tree. He then stood up, amazed with himself. But he couldn't help it. Something inside him brought him to his feet. He blocked her from the man, whom he thankfully noticed was shorter than himself. He knew he had to protect her. He would protect her if it was the last thing he ever did. His heart was pulsating heavily, the whole jungle seemed to be pulsating heavily. He dropped his cigarette on the jungle bed, in front of the man, and squashed it under his foot. The man raised his fist at Percy, shook it, then turned and hurried off into a nearby thicket.

Queenie laughed and laughed. 'You saw him off. You saw him off. You're my kind of man.' She stood up, on tip-toes, and kissed him on the cheek. 'My Tarzan,' she laughed. 'I never thought you had it in you.'

Percy knew his cheeks were flushed. And he knew he was grinning from ear to ear. He felt so proud of himself. He felt more proud of himself than ever before. He felt, in a way, like a new man, younger, stronger, bolder. I've done it, I've actually done something, he said to himself, as they headed back through the jungle, in search of Great Yarmouth, in search of the real world. Percy clutched Queenie's hand. He wasn't going to let her out of his sight. He was going to protect her always. They strode out of the exit into the brightness and sweet sea air.

They had a cup of tea and a cake each in a smoky cafe by the Silver Slipper amusement arcade. Percy's cake had white icing and Queenie's had pink icing and a dollop of whipped cream on top. 'Urrgh,' she said when she bit into it. 'Urrgh. How disgusting.' The woman who served them was enormous and tightly wrapped in a huge, dirty apron. Percy couldn't help noticing the odd bulges that protruded here and there and the great folds of skin that flopped down from her chin. In comparison he knew Queenie looked quite stunning. She always did. He loved her face, her figure.

'That woman's a disgrace,' Queenie said loudly as they walked out of the cafe. 'She shouldn't be allowed to work in a place like that. It's disgusting. It puts you off your food. She should get a job in the Living Jungle. I should think the Living Jungle's crying out for things like that.'

Percy bought Queenie a stick of rock from the Rock Emporium, where everything was pink and chrome. Smudged, sticky chrome, he noticed. Queenie played on the lucky dip machine outside. 'Here,' she said to Percy as he emerged from the shop. She handed him a plastic egg. 'It's a present for you. I won it.' He took the plastic egg and twisted it in half. They began to walk down the promenade. He fished the little package out of the plastic shell and held it up. It was not until they had passed Ripley's Believe It Or Not that he realised what it was. He felt his cheeks flush again. 'Here, let me see,' she demanded. 'Let me see. What is it?' She snatched the condom from him. 'My,' she gasped. 'I haven't seen one of those for a long while.'

Percy hadn't either, but he didn't say anything. He was far too embarrassed.

Queenie suggested they call in to see her dear sister Doris on the way home. 'She would be so pleased,' she told Percy in the car. 'She doesn't have many visitors.' Percy had wound down his window and was trying to rest his elbow comfortably on the ledge. 'She's not at all like my other sisters. Doris is the serious one. She'll like you.'

He was surprised and pleased she suggested calling in to see Doris. He wanted to meet Doris. He wanted to meet all Queenie's family. He wanted to feel part of her family. They passed the boating lake with its bridges and houses, a harbour. And there were a few small boats chugging slowly about. He thought of Gorleston's model yacht pond and the boat that crashed when Queenie was at the controls. He now thought that perhaps she had done it on purpose. He now knew that that was the sort of thing she was capable of doing. But he loved her all the more for it. She did things that he knew no one else would dare do. They passed Britannia Pier, swarming with people in the dying afternoon sunshine. He then remembered the story of Queenie stripping on the pier during the war. He didn't mind. He thought about what she had said earlier that afternoon, that one's got to move on. That there's no point in dwelling on the past. No point at all. He knew that, of course.

The amusements came to an end by a pub called The Iron Duke. The pub looked closed down. Its windows were covered with whitewash and the forecourt was empty. Weeds sprung up here and there. The sun was sinking behind the pub. They carried on, on towards Doris's home, with sunbeams streaking across the road and over the sand dunes which were covered with marram grass, and out over the North Sea. The sea was streaked gold. Great fans of gold. Queenie was laughing, chortling in the Cavalier. She was thinking about French letters. She hated the things.

15

It took Queenie and Percy some time to find Doris's house. Queenie said she knew where her sister lived, on the outskirts of Great Yarmouth, not far from the River Bure. But Percy, who had a good sense of direction, found her directions illogical and confusing. And sometimes dangerous. He soon realised she didn't know where her sister lived. 'Turn here,' she'd suddenly say, often too late. But he didn't mind. They joked and laughed as they drove round and round the rows of small terraced houses. They drove down to the river and out by the race course. At one point they got as far as the golf course, the sun sinking as they went. Then they chanced upon the Pavilion Dance Hall. Like The Iron Duke, the Pavilion looked closed down. Faded bill stickers fluttered on a large notice-board tacked to a side wall. A number of first-floor windows had been smashed. Percy wondered about Yarmouth, whether it had seen better days. It had seemed so vibrant, so full of life earlier in the day. Now all he saw were closed-down pubs and dance halls. But it was not the height of the season, he reasoned. Perhaps the Pavilion was to open up for the summer yet. He wondered whether Queenie had ever been there. And he wondered with whom. For she suddenly knew where she was and directed him effortlessly to Doris's small road.

Doris opened her front door wearing a blue nylon house-coat. She was delighted to see Queenie, which made Percy smile. He wanted Queenie to get on with her family. Families were important. But he thought Doris looked at him suspiciously and it was not until she had led them into the front room that Queenie introduced him. He thought for an instant that Queenie might be embarrassed about him.

'I found him in Gorleston,' Queenie told her sister as she sat down. Percy sat on the sofa next to her.

'How unfortunate,' Doris said. 'You poor man, living in Gorleston with all my sisters. How do you cope?'

Percy laughed, nervously. Queenie said he loved Gorleston. She said he was completely spoilt with people fussing over him. 'Spoilt rotten,' she said.

'You could say that,' he smiled at Queenie. He felt too smug to look at Doris.

'Well,' said Doris, 'there's being spoilt and being spoilt.'

He immediately warmed to her. She seemed to command respect and he had a feeling he would get to know her well. That she would become a friend. Not a friend in the way Queenie was, but a friend, an older friend he could trust, someone he could confide in. She was nothing like the other sisters. Though he didn't think she seemed as serious as Queenie had made out. She had taken her house-coat off and she was wearing a comfortable wool dress, not one of the tight suits favoured by Queenie or Toots. She was not as attractive as her younger sisters, Percy thought. She certainly didn't have Queenie's looks. He thought Queenie was the most attractive woman he knew. Doris looked much older. Percy presumed she didn't take as much trouble to disguise her age as her sisters, certainly Toots, did. She seemed to have come to terms with age. Her hair was thin and grey. She moved slowly, carefully. She seemed of another generation.

She poured Percy and Queenie tea, adding the milk after,

in fine, bone china cups with saucers. Queenie lit a cigarette. 'I suppose you'll never stop. I suppose there's little point now,' Doris remarked. 'You've been lucky, you know.'

Percy decided not to have a cigarette, it didn't seem right. He felt as if he had to be on his best behaviour. He felt as if he was being assessed. As if he had been brought here to gain Doris's approval. He looked around the room as the two sisters chatted, Doris poised on the edge of her armchair, Queenie reclining on the sofa next to him, her leg just touching his. The room was small but tastefully decorated. Framed photographs stood on the mantelpiece. They were too far away for Percy to discern clearly. The images were blurred. A number of china plates hung on the walls together with a few prints depicting maritime scenes. Doris's husband had been killed in the war, Queenie had told Percy earlier. He had been in the navy and Doris never remarried. Queenie said she didn't know what made Doris go on. That she just couldn't understand it, after all these years, all on her own. 'She's never even seen other men. You would have thought she would have died of boredom if not loneliness.' Doris had two sons, but Queenie said she rarely saw them now, now they were both married and living abroad. But she told Percy that, though she might not understand Doris, she respected her. 'She's my oldest sister after all. In a way she's been like a mother to me.'

He tried to listen to the sisters' conversation. He didn't want to appear rude, or shy. He wanted to take part. He wanted to impress. He wanted to gain Doris's approval. But Queenie's lovely leg was pressing against his, quite forcibly now. He found it hard to concentrate on anything else. And her breathing seemed uneven, excited. She smoked quickly.

'So why exactly have you ended up in Gorleston?' Doris asked Percy.

He was looking at the coal-effect gas fire that hissed

hypnotically in the warm, stale early summer evening air. Trying not to think about Queenie's leg. But it was hopeless. He was having feelings that seemed quite new, quite uncontrollable. Urges. Sensations. 'Urrgh, it was my wife's idea, actually.' He didn't like talking about Elizabeth, not in front of Queenie. It made him feel uncomfortable. He thought it was disloyal to both his wife and to Queenie. But Doris urged him on. She wanted to know more. 'She used to come here, oh, years ago. And I suppose she just fell for the place. She had friends, distant relatives in fact, in Gorleston. They're all dead now or have moved away, as far as I know.' He wasn't totally sure. 'I don't see them.'

By the time they moved to Gorleston Percy found Elizabeth didn't seem that concerned with keeping in contact with whoever remained here. As her illness slowly wore her out she seemed more than happy with just seeing him. And he was not going to make any more effort to see these other people than Elizabeth wished. They were her friends. On the few occasions he had met them he had never felt comfortable with them. He found them clever, perhaps too clever, and conceited. He couldn't keep up with them, their talk. And he was sure they had never felt comfortable with him. In a way he felt his wife had wanted to keep them separate, out of the way. She had always compartmentalised her life. He was not part of that particular compartment, never had been. Yet he felt very much that he had been the one constant thing in her life, which existed outside and above all the compartments, or finer chapters. He felt he was the thread that had bound her life together, strong, uncomplicated. He liked to think these things anyway. He liked to think she had needed him as much as he had needed her. He had needed to think things like that. It was, perhaps, why their marriage survived. Why they had survived together for so long.

Doris asked Percy what his wife's name was.

'Elizabeth,' he said, quietly. 'Elizabeth.' He repeated the name. It felt strange saying it, thinking of her, here, with another Elizabeth. But he could never think of Queenie as Elizabeth. He realised Queenie was no longer pressing her leg against his. She sat up, arched her back, and smiled at Percy pertly.

'What a coincidence,' Doris said, smiling. The smile then dropped from her face, as if something had suddenly registered. Her face seemed to collapse. She looked, in a way, frightened.

Queenie noticed. 'Is something the matter dear?'

Doris said nothing for a while and Percy could clearly hear the hiss of the gas fire. The faint evening sun glowed outside, tired shafts trickled over the terraces and into the warm living room. He looked at Queenie, as if for an explanation, then at Doris, her sad, crumpled face. Doris shook her head. She shook her head again, this time as if trying to shake a headache clear. 'I'm sorry,' she said. 'It must be my age. I don't know what the matter is. How very strange.' She shook her head yet again and sipped her tea, loudly. Percy could see her hand shake as she tried to replace the cup on the saucer. It clinked terribly. 'I feel better now.'

He looked at Queenie, and she said perhaps they should be going.

'I feel better now, really.' Doris's voice wavered and she held out her shaking hands. 'Another cup of tea?' It was if she didn't want them to go. As if she didn't want to be left alone.

'No dear, really,' Queenie said. 'We should be going.' She patted Percy on the knee. 'Come on, dear.'

Doris stood waving and shaking on her front doorstep. 'Call again. Oh, Queenie, did you hear Poppy went out the other day? First time in five years. Keith drove her to the sea front. She loved it. The doctor says she's getting better.' She then looked at Percy.

But Percy didn't notice the smile leave her face again as

he climbed into his car. 'Is Doris feeling alright?' he asked as they pulled off. He felt troubled.

'Oh yes.' They passed the Pavilion again. 'How sad. You will take me dancing one day, won't you?' She patted his knee again.

Of course he would take her dancing. He would love to. He would take her anywhere she wanted to go. He suddenly didn't feel troubled any more. He felt aroused.

The Cavalier charged over the Haven Bridge. The sun all but gone, leaving the Yare a pale ochre. They both had butterflies as the car lurched down the bridge, the exhaust sparking on the tarmac. 'Coo-ee,' they both yelled. Queenie slid her hand over the gear stick and started to caress Percy's thigh. And Percy had butterflies all the way to Gorleston, along Riverside Road, Cliff Hill, and along a calm and deserted Marine Parade. Never had he seen the North Sea look so beautiful. Never had he been so delighted to be back in Gorleston. 'Look,' he said to Queenie, slowing down. 'Look.'

'Come on, Percy,' she said, looking at him and not the soft sea. 'We haven't got all night. Put your foot down.'

She knew where she wanted to be and what she wanted to be doing. She always did.

On 8th June, 1891, a lesser rorqual whale, bemused by Scroby Sand, lost its way and swam into the harbour mouth. Its arrival caused much confusion and excitement. The whale was 30 feet long and eight feet in girth. The lifeboatmen and longshoremen organised a whale hunt and for many hours the harbour was the scene of a most extraordinary chase. Huge crowds gathered quickly along the quays and the old pier.

In a frenzy the whale broke its jaw on the South Pier. Injured, it was then attacked with boat hooks and other weapons. Eventually they fastened ropes around it and moored it to the capstans where they set upon it with fresh vigour. The whale took two hours to die and the Yare became scarlet with blood.

The dead whale was then towed to the lifeboat shed, which had been vacated by the Elizabeth Simpson. *There it was drawn up, tail first. It weighed six tons. The lifeboatmen and longshoremen, the heroes of the day, had their photograph taken beside it, then it was put on public show. People travelled many miles to see the whale, some 2000 came in two days. The vicar of Gorleston, the Reverend Forbes Phillips, was so intrigued when he went down to the lifeboat shed that he forgot he had a wedding to attend to.*

Tar was burnt to suppress the smell as the carcass began to rot, before a local taxidermist took on the job of stuffing and preserving the whale. He filled it with straw and the whale was taken to London, Norwich and Great Yarmouth, where it spent many years before it gradually disintegrated and was destroyed.

Arthur Patterson, the Gorleston naturalist, was offered the management of the Gorleston whale. 'I lived on that whale all the summer of 1891,' he later wrote. He eventually became a school attendance officer.

Moonlight flooded into Queenie's cold bedroom. The room was still, blue. Silent. It smelt sweet. It smelt of her. She didn't put the light on. She took her jacket off and went to sit on the double bed. She proceeded to slip her shoes off. Percy walked over to the window, trembling. He looked out of the window, and with his back to her, struggled to get his jacket off, which he then let drop to the floor. At home he would have carefully hung it up, but he didn't want to appear fussy. He could see a neighbour moving around her bungalow. He wanted to shut the curtains, but felt he shouldn't. He removed his tie and pullover. The pullover caught on an ear and he had to tug at it. He was glad it was dim. His face was hot. He knew he would be blushing. He turned to see that Queenie had reclined on the bed. An arm spread out, casually inviting him to lie down beside her. Despite the dimness he could see she was smiling. Her eyes wide open. Her hair, luxuriant, fell in loose curls onto the pillow. He could hear himself breathe. An uneven, troubled breath. Strange, abstract thoughts flashed into his head. He shut his eyes and for a split-second he thought he was still on the Golden Mile. The sweetness, the flashing lights. The stomach-tingling terror. He moved over to the bed. Not knowing what would happen, not knowing whether he would be able to do anything. Oh, but he wanted to, more than anything. He felt passionate, physical. He longed for her. He longed for her like he had never longed for anything in his life. He was experiencing feelings, sensations, he had forgotten existed. As he leant over her she reached up and pulled him to her. He felt his face being smothered with kisses, his cheeks become moist with her saliva, as he collapsed on top of her. She felt harder than he had imagined. Bony. Her small, delicate hands ran frantically over his back, her fingers running down his spine, pulling and tugging at his shirt. He felt he was squashing her. He tried to loosen her grip and roll to her side. He kissed her on the mouth. Her tongue darted out and curled round his two good front teeth. Still kissing, he rolled to the side. Her teeth were perfect, porcelain smooth. She untucked his shirt and slipped her hands underneath. He felt her hands on his bare back. Her hands were warm, sticky even. He felt her nails scratching his skin. He ran his hand down her side and up and underneath her blouse and corset. Her skin felt loose. He didn't mind. He didn't know any better. He started fumbling with the buttons on her blouse. The blouse was soft, silky. He couldn't get a grip properly. His hands were shaking. She helped him. She then placed his hand on her left breast, still captured in the corset. The breast was small, soft. Too small for the corset. He kissed her mouth, her nose, her cheeks, her neck, the while cupping her breast. He began to rub the breast, moving his hand in circles. The corset started to wrinkle up and get in the way. She grabbed his hand firmly and guided it down, over her flat stomach, down to the bottom of her woollen, itchy skirt, which was also wrinkling up, up her thin thighs. He felt awkward and clumsy as his hand was moved to the top of her stockings. His fingers touched her flesh, the thin flesh of her thin thighs. Her breathing was heavy, irregular. She was groaning, almost grunting. She pushed his hand further, further until he felt her warm, damp panties. She spread her legs and his hand fell into the gap. She groaned and began to move her hips. Percy began to get an erection.

He maintained the erection until they were both completely naked in the blue dusk. He didn't let his mind waver, he just thought of her, how much he wanted her, how much he longed for her. How much he loved her. She lay back and pulled him on top of her. Her hands searched him out and she pulled him into her. He shut his eyes and thought he was in heaven. He licked and kissed her ear, fighting for breath. She started to moan and groan. 'I love, I love you,' he whispered as the constellations twinkled above 16 Yallop Avenue, Gorleston-on-Sea.

Queenie lit a cigarette, exhaling a perfect plume in the still air. Percy thought it looked beautiful, floating into the night. It was beautiful. Everything was beautiful. Queenie, the stars, the fact that they had made love. They were under the covers, between the sheets, which smelt damp, but clean. Unused. He tried to put his arm under her, to pull her to his chest, but she hadn't realised what he wanted to do and his arm rested awkwardly on the top of her pillow, above her head. He looked at her. She was staring out of the window. The moon had disappeared behind her neighbour's chimney stack, which rose far above the bungalow's roof. He moved closer to her and kissed her gently, tenderly, on the cheek. She exhaled another great plume. The smoke slowly dissipated. The air was now misty. He wasn't sure what to say. He wasn't sure he should say anything. It wasn't that he didn't feel close to her, he did in every way. He felt part of her. He just didn't want to spoil the moment. It was perfect. And he hadn't felt guilty. He hadn't thought of his wife at all. Not until now. This was different. A new experience. This was passion. He hadn't known passion with Elizabeth. Not that he could remember, anyway. Not that he wanted to remember.

Queenie sighed. She sighed again. She was thinking of an old lover. 'Did I tell you about the whale?'

'What, the whale? No, I don't think so.' He was short of breath and his voice was faint. He thought it sounded strange here, in this room, Queenie's room. He was quite uncertain of it. He didn't want to speak.

'Before I was born, a long time before I was born, a great whale swam into the harbour. Can you believe it, here in Gorleston? It was completely wild of course, and huge, forty, fifty foot long. Much longer than the old fishing smacks. And it was covered in barnacles. Urrgh.' She moved up in the bed a little, squashing Percy's arm. She lit another cigarette excitedly. 'A number of boats set out to capture it and the whole town came out to watch.'

Percy found himself enjoying the story. The way she was so excited, so animated. She didn't often tell stories. She didn't often talk about the past. He sometimes wondered why. He wondered why she didn't like reflecting, why she had to move on to the next thing all the time. But it was just the way she was, he supposed. He could respect that. Understand it even. Of course he could. Besides, he thought, in many ways it was very healthy to listen to someone who didn't talk about the past all the time, particularly around here. The more he thought about it the more he realised that it was one of the reasons why he found her so appealing. Why he loved her so much. He had long tried to distance himself from his own memories and he was fed up with other people's. Sometimes it seemed that that was all people had in Gorleston, memories.

'A number of lifeboatmen were killed trying to capture it, including two of my great uncles. They were eaten alive as the crowd watched in horror.' She looked at him, raised her pencil thin eyebrows and smacked her lips. 'Eventually they caught the beast and killed it. Later it was stuffed and put on show.' Her voice became hushed. 'After many years the whale fell to pieces and they had to burn it. Though my grandfather was given one of the whale's teeth. He used to show it to me. I've never forgotten that story or that tooth. It was huge.' She shut her eyes dreamily.

'What a story,' Percy said enthusiastically, perhaps over-enthusiastically. He had heard a similar story about a whale before. Elizabeth was fond of local history. She used to read books about it, and she used to know a local historian, who was at one time married to one of her Gorleston relatives. But he did not encourage her when she was recounting various stories or theories. For he had felt intimidated by the historian and his stories, the way he captured his wife's imagination. He saw it in her eyes. He could never do that, not in the same way. Sometimes he even tried to ignore her when she was going on. But he remembered a story about a whale, he remembered much more than he thought. He remembered how the Yare went scarlet with blood. Though he couldn't remember anybody being eaten alive. He thought most whales lived off plankton or shoals of small fish they swallowed whole. But he wasn't going to worry about the small details of Queenie's story. If she said her great uncles were eaten alive by a whale, then they were.

Still, he couldn't help wondering what Elizabeth would have made of Queenie's story. She would have laughed, and said what nonsense. She had hated it when people obviously elaborated stories or incidents. Percy had found her particular about the truth, the facts. He had learnt not to embellish anything. He found it difficult thinking of her now, haunting. Then he saw her drifting round and round a smoke ring. She looked how she looked when she was reading, serious and slightly pained.

He suddenly realised he could no longer feel his arm beneath Queenie's back. 'I'm sorry dear, I think my arm's gone numb.' Queenie was far away, her eyes wide open, staring into the night. 'I'm sorry dear,' he tried again, 'my arm's numb.' He pulled his dead arm clear, trying desperately not to unsettle her.

'What? What's going on?' She looked startled.

'Nothing, nothing,' he reassured. He shook his left arm with his right, trying to get the blood circulating, the feeling back. His arm felt heavy. He was tired. Exhausted. He wanted to curl up with her and go to sleep, to dream of the rest of their lives together.

She sat up and sighed. 'I'm gasping for a cup of tea.' She resisted his feeble attempts to hold onto her and shot out of bed. Her small, naked body skipped across the bedroom and out into the corridor.

'Do I get a cup?' he shouted after her, desperate for her to come back. 'Two sugars please,' he added when no reply came. He heard her rustling about in the kitchen. He heard cups and saucers clinking, the fridge door opening and shutting, water pouring into a kettle. Then he heard her move down the corridor, turning on lights, and into the living room. He heard the television come to life, a male commentator, great roars, chanting. The bungalow bubbled with noise and light and activity.

Queenie appeared at the bedroom doorway bathed in

light. Her hair was standing up and wild and orange. 'Get up old man. The night is young.' And then she hurried back down the corridor, still completely naked.

He heard her footsteps, light and fast. The last thing he felt like doing was getting up. All his limbs ached. 'Darling, darling, can you bring me tea in bed? Please.' He pleaded loudly. There was no answer. The bungalow continued to reverberate with activity and eventually he pulled back the bed clothes and gingerly climbed out of bed. He felt wobbly, for the second time in the day. He was shaking slightly all over. He needed some sugar. He stood by the bed for a while, naked, getting cold, wondering what to put on. He didn't want to get dressed because he wanted to get back into bed with Queenie as soon as possible and he thought that if he appeared dressed it might give her the wrong impression. She might even think he wanted to go home. He walked around the room, flooded with light from the corridor. He noticed Queenie's underwear, her corset, her panties, her stockings, heaped in a fluffy cream pile at the bottom of the bed. He picked up his trousers then let them drop back onto the floor. He did the same with his shirt. He moved over to the window and contemplated putting on just his jacket. He kept his hands over his genitals, fearing a neighbour might be looking in. He then saw a dressing gown hanging on the back of the door. It was a maroon silk dressing gown. A man's dressing gown, not dissimilar to the one he had tried on in Marks & Spencer. The sort of dressing gown he had once imagined he had wanted. He pulled it off the hook and put it on. It was a little short and clung to his body. It felt sticky, salty. It smelt of aftershave. His white legs, streaked with thick, bulging blue veins, protruded in an ungainly way. He smoothed the thin strands of his hair over his head, mustered all his energy, and launched himself into the bright corridor.

Queenie was watching football so intently she didn't

notice him enter. On the coffee table was a tray containing the tea. 'Hello,' he said, hopefully. She looked round and let out a scream of laughter. 'I hope you don't mind, I wasn't sure what to put on.'

'You look ridiculous. It's far too small for you. Look at your legs. Urrgh.'

He hovered by the sofa, not sure whether to sit down next to her, not sure whether she wanted him to sit down next to her. 'Can I get you something to put on? You must be cold.' She was still naked and the living room curtains were not drawn. A yellow street lamp reflected in the mirror above the mantelpiece. A terrific roar came from the television.

'You've made me miss the goal,' she said angrily. 'Sit down and be quiet or go home.'

Percy laughed. She was joking, he was sure of that. He sat down next to her. But he felt uncomfortable with her being naked, the curtains not drawn. 'Are you sure I can't get you anything to put on.'

'Oh very well then, if that'll shut you up. There's a coat in the hall, just fetch that.'

He fetched the coat, the fur coat that had once lain on his bed. He buried his face in it and inhaled deeply as he walked back into the living room. It smelt faintly of pipe tobacco. Pipe tobacco, there was no mistaking it. She wrapped the coat around her, lit a cigarette and stared at the television again. He was not interested in football. He had never been interested in football, nor sport in general. He poured the tea and slurped his loudly. He put his hand tenderly on her knee and began to gently caress it with his fingers.

'It tickles, don't.' She moved his hand away.

He smoked a cigarette and practised blowing plumes and smoke rings. Occasionally a car would sweep along Yallop Avenue, its headlights tracing across the room. But he soon became drowsy. After a while he had difficulty keeping his eyes open, shaking his head, shaking himself awake.

Queenie was still glued to the television. Snooker had followed the football. 'It's the beginning of the Skoda Grand Prix,' she informed him.

He stayed up for as long as he could, but he knew he had to sleep. He didn't want to fall asleep on the sofa, it was cold and he thought it would bring back his rheumatism, arthritis, everything. He desperately wanted to get back into bed with Queenie, but she didn't look like she had any intention of doing that, not for a long while anyway. 'Do you mind if I go to bed?' She looked at him oddly. He thought she looked disappointed. 'Is it all right if I stay, I sort of presumed?'

'Oh, yes, yes. Fine, fine.'

'It's been such a busy day hasn't it? But a wonderful day.' He would remember it forever. He stood up, stretching the dressing gown as far down his legs as possible. 'Thank you.' He lent over and kissed her forehead. 'Come to bed soon,' he whispered. I love you, he mouthed. She looked at him blankly, then turned back to the television.

He gargled some Listerine he found in the bathroom. His throat felt tight, sore. And he climbed into bed. He carefully kept to one side, making sure to leave plenty of room for her. He patted her pillow. He longed for her to get into bed. He wanted to hold onto her. He thought of her watching television, naked under the fur coat. He loved the way she was so original. The way she reminded him of no one. He shut his eyes and felt as if he were back on the rollercoaster, climbing the first mountain, holding her hand, looking down over the deserted sands of Great Yarmouth. He then plunged into a deep sleep.

Sun streamed through the windows, hitting Percy's eyelids with a blast of orange. The curtains hadn't been closed. The sun had warmed the room. He blindly reached out for Queenie, his arm stretching across the bed. She was not there. He opened his eyes, blinked a few times, and then sat up in the brightness. Her side of the bed was cold and empty. He could tell she hadn't been there for some time, if at all. 'Queenie,' he shouted. 'Queenie.' He leapt out of bed, stepping over the piles of clothes and undergarments. His back ached. His head ached. He found his watch in his jacket pocket. It was eight-thirty. He never slept this late. He couldn't believe how late it was. He hurriedly got dressed and then rushed about the bungalow hoping he might come across her. He even opened cupboard doors. The fur coat was gone and he looked outside and saw the Mini Metro was gone too. But it couldn't have, he said to himself. It couldn't have. It had a flat battery.

On the kitchen table he found the note. 'P. Something has come up, let yourself out. Q.' His heart sank. Something has come up. 'What?' he said aloud. 'What does she mean?' What's happened to her? Thoughts raced through his mind, foggy from too much sleep. Surely if there had been trouble or something awful had happened she would have woken me, asked me to help in some way. He read the note again. The writing was barely legible. A scrawl of small black letters. Not even a love Q, just Q. It was the first letter he had ever received from her. He rushed outside, into the brilliant day. He looked up and down Yallop Avenue. He didn't know what else to do. He noticed her neighbour's miniature windmill. There was not even a sea breeze to turn the tiny red plastic sails, so calm was the day. So perfect.

He went home eventually, and rang Queenie on the hour, every hour, for the whole day. She didn't answer. She wasn't in Gorleston. She was far away.

12

Days drifted along with the tankers on the horizon. Those people who rose early caught the slow mists that blanketed the North Sea, and then quietly evaporated with the rising summer sun. It was a peaceful, thought-provoking time of day. People would watch from the carpark and as they ambled along the cliff top, gulls cracking the silence, memories distilling into regrets. Or longing.

Percy couldn't help but feel the great depth of things. The southern North Sea is no more than 130 feet deep, he heard his wife saying. Her voice, as clear as a gull, rang in his head. She liked to contradict. She liked to put him right. Anywhere. He turned. There was no one behind him. 'Elizabeth,' he said softly, into the warming air. 'Elizabeth.' He felt compelled to walk along the cliff top every morning. He couldn't explain it. He had been up early with the mists shortly after his night with Queenie. The night he would remember for the rest of his life. He had eventually spoken to her two days later.

'Hello, Percy,' she had said on the telephone, casually, 'I've been away.'

'Yes, I gathered.'

'Sorry, didn't think to ring sooner. I hope you didn't worry. Uhmm. Doris had one of her attacks. She rang in a panic and I had to rush over to be with her.'

'But why didn't you wake me?'

'It was the middle of the night. Besides, she has them all the time. It's nothing to worry about really. In fact she's probably forgotten all about it herself by now. That's what tends to happen. One minute she feels she just can't cope. She panics. Then the next minute she calms down. Forgets all about it. I think perhaps our visit unsettled her. She kept calling me Elizabeth. Only Ruby calls me that.'

Percy hadn't asked her why she had to stay with Doris in Great Yarmouth for so long if Doris's panic attacks only lasted a minute. And he hadn't asked her about the car, how she managed to start it. He was just glad to hear from her. He was just glad she had rung him, for he had thought she had left him. He thought she had left him for another man. And mad with jealousy, he had pored over everything, why she had not woken him, why she had not explained where she was going, why she hadn't returned. He had not been able to comprehend it. He had not been able to comprehend the fact that Queenie was an independent woman, a widow. For he had thought their lives were entwined.

And now he kept thinking of Doris, having a panic attack, and Queenie rushing to help her. How thoughtful she had been and how selfish and demanding and dependent he had been. He felt he was just entrapped with love, with passion. He felt obsessed with Queenie. Though he knew there was little he could do about it.

He looked forward to his early morning walks more and more. He loved the laziness, the gentle, rhythmic quietness. The gulls and the waves. He found it was the only time he could really think. And he began to think of the future and of the past, the past he had tried not to think about for so long. Memories, not even important memories, would pop into his head. Odd details, notes, shapes, colours. And now voices. But the voices did not unnerve him. He regarded them as a further development. Something that was trying to help him, something that was looking after him. Something that was trying to help him find himself. For he felt quite lost.

One morning he thought he saw Poppy out along the cliff top, her tiny frame supported by a short fat man. He didn't say anything, but as she passed he smelt her bungalow. It was as if a cloud of warm roast dinners was trailing behind her. It surprised him. He remembered the smell so well. It made him feel claustrophobic. But he was pleased, genuinely pleased she had overcome her agoraphobia. He was pleased she was able to enjoy the beautiful, still, summer mornings. The lazy, shallow North Sea.

Queenie arrived shortly after lunch. The letter-box fluttered.

'Coo-ee.'

Percy kissed her hello on the mouth. She tasted of cigarettes and lipstick.

'Hello, old boy. You are frisky.'

Since they had made love, whenever he saw her, he found himself unable to refrain from touching her, caressing her, kissing her. He was continually searching for a reciprocal sign. He blushed. He was just pleased to see her. He didn't see her every day. He didn't see her half as much as he wanted to. He wanted to see her all the time. But much to his concern she had different ideas. She didn't want to be tied down, she had recently told him. She did as she pleased, she had said. She always had done and there was no reason why she shouldn't always do so, now in fact more than ever, now that she was getting on, even though she didn't feel it. He had protested, saying she could hardly call herself old. Not paying any attention though, she had carried on, saying it was her life. And she could do what she pleased with it, now it was fast running out. Though she did say that he shouldn't take it to mean that she didn't want to see him, because she did. He would just have to be understanding. And that was just enough to keep Percy going.

'I thought we could take Poppy for a walk.' Queenie was still standing on the doorstep and she didn't look as if she was going to enter. 'She loves to get out and about now. She's expecting us.'

Percy's heart sank. He didn't want to go for a walk with Poppy. He didn't think Queenie spoke to her. Just thinking of her he could smell that terrible smell. He wanted to spend the afternoon with Queenie, alone. He wanted to go to the High Street with her, or take her for a romantic stroll along the pier as the sun started to slip in the sky. As orange sunbeams danced across the North Sea.

'Oh, come on Percy, don't be spoilt.'

He felt like a rejected child and he knew his tired, old face must have looked utterly disappointed.

'It's as if she's embarking on a new life. She's quite a scream. And she wants to see everyone and do everything.'

She knew he would go and he knew he would go. He always did what she wanted him to do. He would have followed her anywhere. He went to get his jacket.

It was just a short trot to Poppy's, at the end of Bately Avenue. They set off briskly, Queenie even taking Percy's arm. She hummed with happiness. Smoke, from the cigarette clamped in the corner of her mouth, drifted into his face. But he soon cheered up. When Queenie was happy, so was he. His eyes started to water. Ahead, the bungalow's tiny window panes refracted the sun. Poppy's garden was filled with rose bushes. Bees buzzed in the warm haze. Percy felt himself drawn into the garden and up the path, with Queenie close beside him, hanging onto his arm. As they knocked loudly the door swung open. The smell in the electric heat was unmistakable. He could hear the television. They proceeded to the lounge. Just as before Poppy was slumped in a huge armchair watching television, the sound distorted by the volume. He thought she looked as if she had been hypnotised by the television. Her head nodded with the sound, the television flickering on her eyes, like flowers in a breeze. She hadn't heard or seen them enter. Queenie leant down and coo-eed in her ear. She sat bolt upright.

'Oh, it's you.' A smile crept along her lined face. 'Ha, ha.'

Percy couldn't understand why she laughed. Shock, he thought.

'Let yourselves in then, did you?'

The room was hotter than it had been at Christmas. The gas fire glimmering dimly in the brightness. Sun poured in, through the small panes, fretting the room with shadow. The air was thick and lifeless.

'Oh, I am pleased to see you.' Her voice was thin and wavered. She was looking at Queenie, then she looked at Percy. 'And you, young man. I never can keep up. Still, what a treat. And what a lovely day.'

Percy wasn't sure how Poppy knew it was a lovely day. He didn't think she could have been out in it, so sunk into the armchair was she. She looked attached to the chair, part of it even. A minor growth.

'I'm dying to get out. I haven't been out yet today. I didn't want to exhaust myself. But I'm all ready, I put my teeth in specially. I'm raring to go.' She moved her jaw around, as if she were munching on some grass. 'It's really quite extraordinary. I love going out now. My doctor says there's nothing better for me. It's a miracle. I put it all down to him, though. He's been marvellous. And he still says he'll visit me every day. You know, just to check things are working properly. I could still have a relapse. I'm still worried about that. And what if it happens when I'm out? I fear it would kill me. I'd die of fright.'

Percy had forgotten how much and how quickly Poppy talked. It was as if her agoraphobia, over the years, had intensified her need to communicate.

'No point sitting around any longer then,' she said and struggled to get up. She was even smaller than Queenie. Percy held out his hands for her to clasp and steady herself on. Her bony fingers latched onto his. He shivered. She smiled at him. A wily smile. He led her slowly into the hall, while Queenie fished around in the hall cupboard for her coat. 'The thick brown one, dear,' Poppy directed. The smell of stale air and mothballs flooded out of the cupboard and into the hall. Percy noticed the coats, hanging in neat rows, were pristine. Coats that had hung idle for years. Poppy seemed to become more excited as he helped her with a thick camel-hair one. 'I can't wait,' she said. 'I just can't wait.' She started to shuffle her feet and salivate. He led her into the sunshine. He was glad to be back outside, in the fresh air and coolness of a Gorleston summer day. She looked up at the sky, squinting. 'My, what a day.' She remained looking up, squinting, for some time. He was unable to move her on.

'Come on, dear,' Queenie said at last, grabbing her other arm. 'We haven't got all day, you know.' She started to pull Poppy and Percy down the hazy path buzzing with bees.

'I'm frightened of bees,' Poppy said anxiously. 'Don't let them get close.' She detached her hand from Percy's arm and tried to wave it about, in front of her. 'Bloody bees.'

Queenie asked Poppy if she thought she could make it to the sea front. She said of course she could, she had been walking there for weeks. It was slow going, though. Percy ambled behind the two sisters, catching snippets of their conversation, and that smell of stale air, roast dinners, urine too.

Queenie spoke louder than usual. 'Nothing special, dear. I think I'm past all that. But I suppose you never know.' He didn't catch the next sentence.

'Well I never,' Poppy's voice fluttered. 'You'd better be careful. You're not getting any younger.'

'Don't you start that.'

They reached Arnott Avenue and turned towards the sea. Poppy shivered and pulled the neck of her coat closer together. Gulls played noisily in the blue sky and a yellow banana bus floated down Marine Parade. They crossed the road by the Gables Nursing Home.

'I expect Keith will put me in there one day. I don't mind. I'm quite looking forward to the company. They say it's a wonderful place to meet new friends. I might even meet a nice young man.'

'It's not for me. Never. I'd rather die.' Queenie skipped across the grass, covered with the odd mound, leaving Percy to lead Poppy.

He felt awkward, shy. She grasped his arm. 'Life,' she said, looking down at the grassed-over crazy-golf course, 'sometimes I wonder if it goes on for too long. Doris tells me she's had enough. And she's as fit as a fiddle. Nothing's ever wrong with her. She says she's just seen enough and heard enough. Toots will die frustrated. Though she'll keep trying until the end. She's not one to give up. Cassie will drop off in her sleep, happy, though.' A small dog, a terrier, ran up and started to sniff at Percy's trouser bottoms. 'I thought I'd had enough, but recently I've changed my mind. I like life. There's still some of it left in me. No one should give up on me yet. I feel younger than I have for years.' She breathed in loudly. The dog scampered off. They walked round a long, thin mound. Percy thought it an odd shape for a bunker. 'Queenie will go on and on. You can be sure of that. She'll always be around. I can't imagine Gorleston without her. Can you?' He couldn't.

They reached the cliff top, the sticky tarmac of the upper esplanade. Queenie had disappeared. They both peered over the edge. The huts looked splendid and freshly painted in a multi-coloured row below. Some were open, their doors pinned back, with people sitting on deck-chairs in front of them. A few children, even, were running about. There was no sign of Queenie, though, no sign of her leaping between the huts, no flash of orange.

'She's always disappearing,' Poppy wavered. 'She's an enigma. Yes, I think that's the word. She likes to have secrets. She's full of them. You can never get anything out her. She'll never tell you anything. Well I'll tell you something.'

Percy looked at the small, frail woman, Queenie's sister, older and probably wiser. He then looked out to sea, the great glare.

'Her husband died in that hut.' She pointed vaguely at the timber row. Her hand shook. 'That one, that smart blue one. Of course it wasn't always so smart.'

Percy knew instantly which one she meant. It was the hut Queenie had got stuck behind. It was where he had first held Queenie in his arms. He looked at Poppy, she was still pointing, her finger still shaking in the fine, sea air.

'He was found one morning, frozen solid with an empty bottle of whisky beside him. They used to own that hut, but after his death Queenie gave it away, to the Harbour Pilots Association I think.'

A gull swooped close by. Percy ducked instinctively. He remained cowered, looking at his feet. He wanted to curl up. 'How tragic.' He felt his voice tremble. 'How awful. How awful for Queenie.' He didn't want to look at the hut. He didn't want to think about it. But his mind filled with the image of a man lying stiff on a sandy wooden floor, an empty bottle of whisky beside him, in the frozen blue twilight. He shuddered. He felt so sorry for Queenie.

He had had no idea. He then thought about the time he had held her in his arms, right by the hut. He wanted to hold her now. Tell her he understood. Comfort her.

'It depends how you look at it,' Poppy was saying, her voice no longer wavering, clear, excited. 'A number of people didn't speak to her at the funeral.' But Percy wasn't listening properly, he was staring at his feet, thinking of the game of hide and seek, why Queenie had hidden behind that hut, why she had lured him there. He didn't know why. He didn't understand. 'They blamed her, you know. And I know what I think. Doris thinks the same. I suppose, though, you can't blame Queenie for everything.'

'Coo-ee.' They both turned to see Queenie cantering up behind them. She was carrying three enormous, fluffy white ice creams. Her orange hair as fluffy, as vivid. 'A special treat for Poppy, seeing as she has decided to rejoin the living world. Besides I love ice cream.' They sat on a bench nearby. The model yacht pond, round and brilliant, shone like a coin in the distance.

'Mr Whippy,' Poppy said. 'My favourite.' She licked frantically away. As did Queenie. Percy didn't feel like his ice cream. It started to drip down the cone and onto his hand in the hot sun. He couldn't get the frozen man out of his mind. And the ice cream made it worse. He stood up, pretending to lick the great cone. He walked a few yards along the upper esplanade, his back to the two sisters. He had an urge to lob the ice cream far away. The terrier suddenly returned, and resumed its mad sniffing about his ankles. He tried to shake the dog away, but it persisted. He looked out to the glinting sea again, trying not to look at the beach huts as he turned his head. He dropped the ice cream on the tarmac. It collapsed into a pool, the cone sticking up like a rocket. The dog started to lap up the cream, its nose and whiskers quickly whitening. He watched until it had crunched the cone as well, then ran off, across the grass covered with funereal mounds. He knew now that's what they were, and not long-buried bunkers from a crazy-golf course. He saw the dog in the distance searching for more treats, more ankles. If only life could be so easy, so determined, he thought. He turned and walked back to the bench. Queenie was wiping her mouth with a tissue. Poppy sat quite still staring out to sea, her faced smudged with ice cream.

'Here dear,' Queenie lent over and handed Poppy the tissue, 'wipe your face with this. You're covered in ice cream. You messy girl.'

There was a time at the beginning of this century when long lines of tents stretched from the sea wall to the water's edge. Both bell tents and square tents were pitched on the powdery sand of Gorleston beach, often as many as two thousand on fine days. Alfred Dye, George Austin, Peter Adams, Gordon Burgess, were the chief tent operators in those crowded summers before the First World War.

It was custom to drop the tents in the late afternoon should a strong wind spring up. But the tents were back up by five in the morning, for they did good business with early morning bathers. The best pitch was near the pier, where most men swam, whilst the ladies, more shy of bathing in public, tended to use the south end of the beach.

After the Great War the Tomlins family took over the beach with their wooden huts. At the end of each season the huts were lovingly taken down for winter storage and repainted. Finally, though, the Tomlinses were beaten by the sea. With much of the beach gone the town council ruled that all beach huts must go on the promenade and the owners pay rent.

The huts on the promenade were never as popular and with fewer and fewer holidaymakers coming to Gorleston, Kathleen Tomlins found she could not afford to pay the council rent at the end of her first season on the promenade. She was forced to retire at the age of sixty-nine, having spent fifty-three years making a living off the beach. Some huts were sold, others were eventually broken up by the wind and the waves and the vandals.

Poppy said she thought she could go on a little further. The sun, slipping now, shone across Gorleston, across the tops of the fancy chimney stacks and satellite dishes, and out over the sea. The shadow of the cliff crept further out along the beach, having overtaken the huts' shadows. Shortly it too would seep into the sea. Queenie lit a cigarette as they strolled, the sun giving the smoke a coppery hue. Percy couldn't even bring himself to smoke. So stunned was he.

'You are doing well,' Queenie shouted in Poppy's ear. Poppy smiled, smugly. 'Isn't she doing well?' She nudged Percy with her elbow, then raised her eyebrows. They kept to the upper esplanade, congested with afternoon strollers and dogs. 'I wouldn't like to make a habit of this. It's fine taking the old girl out once in a while, but I wouldn't want to do it every day. Hopefully her son will do that. Keith needs the exercise. He's so fat he can't see his own feet.'

'Do you find it sad?' Percy mumbled. He felt he had to say something.

'What?'

'Do you find it sad, walking along here?'

'What are you talking about? Do I find it sad? Don't be so daft, Percy. Are you sure you're feeling all right?' She looked puzzled, amused even.

'No, you don't understand. What I mean is here, near the huts. The beach huts.' Percy noticed Poppy was looking at her feet. He thought she might possibly have been studying the surface of the path, watching out for cracks and bumps that might unsettle her, topple her even. Queenie didn't say anything. 'And how can you bring yourself to play by the huts, that hut?' He looked over his shoulder, and saw down below the blue hut, sunk in shadow.

Queenie looked over her shoulder, too. 'Has Poppy been telling you stories?'

'I just never knew. I'm so sorry. It must have been awful.' He had been thinking. And he thought he was beginning to understand. He was beginning to understand that the huts were of some special significance to her. Of course they were. It was all part of her mourning. She had to go down there. It was a spiritual place, a tomb almost. A place where she took her most treasured, her most important friends. Her lovers. Yes. He suddenly understood. And he felt deeply touched and honoured to be part of her grief, to be part of something of such importance. To have been taken down there, lured to the very back of the hut, encouraged to embrace her there. It all made sense now. No, he wasn't the most important person in her life, how could he ever hope to be? But she had let him in on her most sacred ritual. He played an important part. That was enough.

'I wouldn't believe everything Poppy says.' She sounded almost threatening. 'She watches too much television. Her mind's going.' She pointed to her sister's head and twisted her finger.

They walked Poppy slowly home, through the lazy roads and avenues, bungalow after bungalow. Net curtains parted and faces peered out at them, some wishful, some disdainful. Someone was mowing their small front lawn. The hum of the motor filled the sweet air.

Poppy said she wanted to spend a while in her garden and that there was no need to see her inside. She said she was quite capable of letting herself in. They said goodbye by her gate. Percy shook her limp, bony hand. 'You don't drink, do you?' she asked as he turned to walk away. He didn't answer. Queenie had raced ahead, as usual. He wasn't sure where to go, so he trotted after her. He turned once to look at Poppy's bungalow with its wooden beams and fretted windows. Oddly it didn't look out of place on the corner of Bately Avenue and Brett Avenue. Poppy was bending over a rose bush.

13

'Oh, by the way, Poppy's gone.'

'Where?'

'Gone, gone for good. She's passed away.'

Percy took a deep breath and sat on the hall stool by the telephone.

'First one down.' Queenie laughed.

He felt terrible, faint. 'But she seemed so well only the other day. What happened?' He had an image of Poppy suddenly gripped with fear out walking along the cliff top. Her agoraphobia abruptly and fatally returning. Poppy suffering a massive stroke, falling onto the upper esplanade, the little terrier coming up and sniffing her, licking her cold blue face.

'Keith, you know her son who can't see his own feet I was telling you about, found her slumped in her armchair in front of the television. He thinks she'd been watching *Gladiators.* She loved the programme. He thinks she had a stroke.' Percy heard Queenie light a cigarette. 'Still, it's a blessing in many ways,' she exhaled. 'She would have tripped up sooner or later. I don't think she would ever have got used to going out, not after all those years indoors. Something terrible would have happened to her. Some awful accident.' He heard her drawing on her cigarette. 'Keith's rather grateful, not that he would admit it, but I can tell. He had her booked into the Gables for the coming winter. He thought she wouldn't have been able to cope on her own. He hadn't told her, thankfully. I know she was looking forward to being put away, but it wouldn't have been very nice. I just can't believe anyone would want to go into one of those places, certainly not a member of my family. Besides it's very pricey, the Gables, you know.'

'Well, I'm very sorry.' And he was sorry, and sad. Even in Gorleston where people were dying all the time, he still couldn't get used to it. He hated it when people died. 'It must be very sad for you, to lose a sister.' He felt the loss himself. For he felt as if Poppy had been his sister too, sister-in-law anyway.

'Well, it was always going to be a toss-up between Poppy and Doris, who went first. I shouldn't think Doris will last much longer, not now. She's been looking forward to going for ages.'

'I feel quite shocked. And she was just beginning to enjoy herself.'

'Well, maybe that's what really killed her. I wouldn't be surprised. She should have stayed indoors.'

'I always find deaths sad,' Percy heard himself saying down the telephone line to the woman whom he thought he loved.

'Of course they're sad,' she said briskly, as if she wanted to talk about something else.

Percy looked at the sandy-coloured wall a few inches in front of him. His mind started to drift. He thought of Gorleston beach, not the real beach, but a beach that stretched far into the distance, as far as the eye could see, flat and shimmering. A small figure came running towards him. At first he thought it was Queenie, but then he realised it was Elizabeth, his wife.

'The funeral's the day after tomorrow.'

'When?' Percy shook his head. He was trying to dislodge the image of his wife.

'Thursday.'

'I would like to go. It would be appropriate, wouldn't it?'

'Oh, of course. Everyone goes to funerals all the time here. I have friends who have dresses made specially. Look on it as a party. The more the merrier. Thursday, ten o'clock. See you at the crematorium.' She hung up.

He immediately wanted to see her, to comfort her. To be comforted by her. Though he realised she would have all manner of things to do and sort out. And slowly he realised that perhaps he wanted to be on his own, to think things through.

Percy heard Sandy scrapping around in the next-door garden. Shortly he heard Mrs Yarren join the dog, pat him, encourage him. Lying still on his bed he could imagine Sandy and Mrs Yarren chasing each other around the small lot, the dog growling and the old woman yelping. The sun was not yet up but the thick air was quickly brightening, lightening his airless bedroom.

He drove to the carpark. Lately he would have walked to the cliff top, but he was in a hurry to get there. He was in a hurry for the view, the quietness, some answers. The carpark was already quite full; blank faces watched him manoeuvre his car. He left it and headed the only way he could, towards the pier and Yarmouth Power Station, the great chimney looming pale pink above the mist, its tip blackened with soot, years and years of soot. He took deep breaths of the damp air, opening his dry mouth wide. Groynes pierced the mist blanketing the North Sea. Warped and twisted, the irregular rows looked defeated. He shut his eyes and then opened them, trying to conjure up the voice, Elizabeth's voice. But he heard nothing except the gentle lapping of the sea, the occasional bark and squawk, muffled by the slow morning. 'The southern North Sea is no more than 130 feet deep,' he said aloud. He thought of an afternoon shortly before his wife had died. 'They think the erosion is caused by littoral drift. They've never been able to stop the beach erosion here, the groynes have been useless,' she said, looking up from some pamphlet she was reading. 'Though sometimes the drift works oppositely and deposits sand. No one's ever understood why it does that. It's just a matter of time. It's cyclical, apparently.'

He started to descend the cliff, taking a path wet with dew glinting in the first rays of sun which now floated over the mist. He hadn't intended to take the path, he hadn't intended to leave the familiarity, the friendliness of the upper esplanade, where the view was embalmed forever on his mind. It was cooler the lower he went. He took care not to slip on the dampness, at times reaching out to steady himself on the grassy bank. His heart thumped. Mounds of moist sand littered the lower esplanade. The blackness of the tarmac diffused, greyed, by the quartz. He wondered about the littoral drift, how powerful it was, how it had shifted all this sand. On the lower esplanade, promenade as Queenie liked to call it, sand was everywhere. He walked over to the railing running along the edge. It was not a big drop to the beach. He felt he could have jumped it. He looked out to sea, now beginning to sparkle in its nakedness. Then he turned and headed for the huts. It was almost as though he were being drawn there.

No one else was walking along the promenade. It seemed to him that everyone kept to the top at this hour, as if they were afraid of what they might find down here. He shivered. He felt lonely, almost frightened. The huts were all closed up and shuttered. He thought they looked unbelievably sad, their fresh pastel shades muted by the low sun and the dampness. And there amid the last row the Pilots hut stood solemnly, conspicuously. It was dark, just dark blue.

He stopped and stared at it. He didn't know what he was looking for, he didn't know what he was doing. He then inched his way down the side to the back of the hut. It smelt of stale tobacco. And a sweeter smell. Queenie's smell, her perfume, he was sure of it. The gap between the hut and the grass bank was tight. The grass had been worn in many places, leaving large patches of dirt. He leant against the bank, wondering exactly where it was that Queenie had got stuck. He reached out and ran his fingers along the hut's wooden planks. The wood was rough, splintered where planks were grooved into one another. His fingers then made out an odd-shaped indentation. He shifted along a little. And there, scratched into the wood, was a crude heart. Below it was scratched Q LOVES CHARLIE.

Percy laughed. He couldn't help it. It was a spontaneous, nervous reaction. He squeezed back between the huts and out into the overwhelming brightness of the promenade. In the distance two figures were running. He squinted. It looked as if they were running towards the pier. Running away from him.

Percy loathed the suit. He had last worn it at Elizabeth's funeral, which was the last time he had been to Gorleston Crematorium. It was a dank November day. Not many people were there, most of their relations were too distant, too old or lived too far away. He was so distressed he hadn't really noticed who was there anyway. Though, he remembered, there were one or two people he thought he hadn't seen before. He was never very good at putting names to faces, particularly faces that had changed with age. But he thought of them now, wondering who they were. These people mourning his wife.

He bought a plot for her ashes in the churchyard of St Andrew's. It was a fine church in a lovely setting. It overlooked the site of the Augustinian Priory. Elizabeth had told him about the priory on numerous occasions. That it was built in the reign of Edward I, and that the one hundred foot tower survived until 1813 when it was blown down in a gale. He couldn't have ignored the fact that Gorleston once had an Augustinian Priory. And he supposed it meant something special to her. A fascinating chapter of the past? He wanted her to be left in a special place, a place dear to her. He could not have left her in the crematorium's Garden of Remembrance. Somewhere so appallingly anonymous, and sad, a place he knew he would have to visit today.

The suit smelt damp. It was thick and uncomfortable and sticky. The day was still, cloudy, warm. Too warm for the suit. He reached round, trying to brush the dust and dried skin off the shoulders. He was tired, his eyes felt sore. He suddenly didn't want to go. He didn't really feel up to going. His stomach began to ache with nervousness and apprehension. He smoked a cigarette, his first in quite a while, with a cup of coffee. He kept looking at the clock. And his mind kept drifting back to Gorleston Crematorium, the awfulness of his wife's funeral. He tried to cheer himself up by thinking of Queenie, their time at Great Yarmouth Pleasure Beach. He thought about calling her to find out how she was coping, whether she needed anything. Just to hear her voice, her laugh. She could always laugh. But he thought better of it. He knew he shouldn't call her now, just before her sister's funeral.

He set off in good time. The crematorium was on the other side of Gorleston and he thought the traffic might be bad. It was always bad by the crematorium. He drove out along Links Road, past the Mariner's Compass housing estate, its television aerials and satellite dishes crowding the cloudy sky, and turned onto Lowestoft Road. The traffic was thick by the James Paget Hospital, cars flooding in and out of the huge carpark. The hospital was relatively new and since the last holiday camp closed down it was one of Gorleston's major attractions. Many people moved to Gorleston just because of the hospital. Percy often heard people extolling its virtues, that if it wasn't for the Paget they would be long dead. The hospital eventually gave way to fields and fields of allotments, like a shanty town he had seen in a geographical magazine. He could see a number of men working their small patches of land, others ambling in and out of their shabby sheds. Makeshift fences and scarecrows were everywhere. He had never wanted to have an allotment. He didn't see the point. He had wanted to be with his wife too much.

Increasingly anxious, he turned into Brasenose Avenue for the final wind through a road of small houses, council houses. He thought it sorrowful they were so neglected, the front gardens dirty, unkempt. Battered cars sat in the road. Grubby children scrambled around them, over them, kicking balls, shouting. This was only the third time he had driven along this road, through this part of Gorleston. It could have been another town, so far removed was it from Bately Avenue. Just before the turning for the crematorium he passed a school. The playground was empty, silent. He realised the children must have been well into their summer holidays. As he turned into the Garden of Remembrance, he thought it an odd juxtaposition. A school next to a crematorium.

The Garden of Remembrance was neat and tidy. Small plaques were lined up, row after row, in the striped grass. A number of people were tending the plots of their dear dead ones, quietly crouching, laying flowers, polishing the marble and plastic plaques. Percy progressed slowly down the smooth drive which, like the upper esplanade, had no markings, no signs. There were a number of small rectangular flower beds, in which were planted young trees and yet more plaques. He wound his window down and immediately felt better for the rush of air. Then the crematorium came into view, its steep roof, fashioned, he thought, to look churchy. And next to it was the chimney, a fancy Yallop Avenue style chimney, covered in a white trellis. Smoke was curling lazily up into the sky, which was solid with cloud.

He heard voices, laughing. As he swung into the carpark he saw a group of people standing in front of the Cooperative Chapel of Rest. They were gaily clothed. Some were smoking. Some wore hats, broad, outlandish, others carried great garlands of flowers. Amid the group he made out Linda. She was wearing dark glasses and the purple dress that hugged her so tightly. She was standing next to Burt, big and unkempt. Both were smiling, laughing. They looked as if they were sharing a joke. Percy slunk in his seat. He had forgotten about the rest of the family, he had forgotten they would be here as well as Queenie. Linda, Burt, Toots, Charlie, Cassie, and Doris, whose funeral it might have been. Toots, he thought, anxiously tapping the steering wheel. Toots. He had last seen her tottering down her driveway, drunk. And that was after she had propositioned him. He parked the car behind a low hedge at the far end of the carpark and sat quite still in the car for a number of minutes, for as long as he thought he possibly could. Other cars parked nearby, their occupants noisily clambering out, rearranging their dresses and suits, hats and ties. All behind the manicured hedge.

When he felt he couldn't wait, hidden, any longer, he climbed out. His suit felt even heavier and hotter. It was a winter suit. He wiped the dampness from his forehead. He didn't feel mournful, or particularly moved now, just apprehensive. He rounded the hedge. Trying to look discreet, he headed for Linda and Burt, who were still smiling, still laughing, in the thick of the swelling, merry crowd.

'Percy,' Linda shouted. 'Percy, over here.' She waved. The crowd turned and looked at him. Stooped and old, he felt himself hobble across the forecourt. His head down, he studied the surface, looking for sand, specks of quartz. 'Percy,' she giggled, 'I say, you do look hot. Your suit looks rather thick for this weather. Lovely to see you.' She bent down, he looked up, and she kissed him on the cheek.

Her lipstick was thick and mauve. He felt it on his cheek. His right cheek. He knew he couldn't go into Poppy's funeral with Linda's lipstick on his cheek, and what if Queenie saw it? He wanted to wipe his face with his handkerchief, but thought that might look rude. He coughed and as he cupped his hand over his mouth he tried to wipe his face with his sleeve, the thick, rough, woollen sleeve of his dark suit.

'Burt, Percy looks like an undertaker, don't you think?'

Burt laughed and thrust out his large hand for Percy to shake. 'Right place for it.' The youngish couple smiled again and started to giggle.

Linda calmed down after a while. 'Good of you to turn up for the old girl. Of course, she should have gone ages ago. Still, not a bad turn-out. I think it's the party afterwards that everyone's really come for. Keith and Susie always lay on a good spread. Mother's been advising them. She's in terrific form. They all are.'

The chatter among the group died down as heads started to drift out along the drive. The hearse had swept into view, bedecked with flowers, inside and out. It was followed by two black limousines. Percy thought it took forever for the cortege to come to a stop by the Chapel of Rest, the limousines bumper to bumper behind the hearse. Keith struggled to get out of the first limousine. Percy recognised him as as the man who had been with Poppy the morning he had seen them out walking along the cliff top. He was followed by a trim little woman, with tight, curly blonde hair. She was wearing bright red lipstick and a short black dress. A black shawl draped over her shoulders. He presumed it was Keith's wife, Susie. He thought she looked too old to be wearing such a short dress. And he thought it rather disrespectful. Two other people got out, a thin, pale young man, who reminded Percy of Poppy, and a large boy with a fat red face and curly hair. Keith buttoned up his jacket with some difficulty and walked over to the hearse, leaving his family to look at each other.

Everyone was watching the occupants of the second limousine, the remaining sisters, spill out onto the warm forecourt. They were clamouring and shrieking and the crowd began to swarm around them, as if it were they, and not the sisters' dead sister, they had come to see off. Percy stayed where he was. He didn't want to rush over with everyone else. But from where he was he could see they were all there. Doris, Toots, Cassie and Queenie. And they were all resplendent in their own way. Each had made a great effort with their hair, even Doris, if in a quiet fashion. The colours were enhanced by the grey sky which was becoming greyer by the minute, Doris grey. Cassie's hair was fluffed-up white and bright, Toots's a rich purple piled high, and Queenie's was almost fluorescent, the luxuriant curls swept back. No one was wearing black, just bits of black. Queenie was carrying a black handbag, Cassie had a black silk scarf wound round her neck, Doris was wearing sensible black shoes, Toots made do with black-framed glasses. Percy could not help but think it was as if they were all going to a party, not a funeral. And he thought it seemed as if now one of them was gone they had to make more of a show and stick together. Forget old grievances, perhaps. They had arrived together after all.

Percy noticed Charlie slip out of the limousine's front door. He thought he must have accompanied the driver in the quiet up front, partitioned off from the remaining sisters. And he looked at Queenie, waiting for her to glance his way. He wanted to wave, to let her know he was here. But she was talking to a group of people he didn't know. He watched a man light her cigarette. He was about to walk over when John Conway, dressed much like himself, in a thick black suit, walked up.

'What a do.' His face was red and sweaty as usual. 'They certainly know how to put on a show.' Percy smiled. He was pleased John had found him. He was an ally of sorts.

The air was becoming more and more oppressive. Suddenly people started talking in whispers and shuffling towards the chapel. The coffin had been taken out of the hearse and was being pushed into the chapel on a trolley and everybody was following. Keith, his wife and the two boys were first inside after the coffin, the sisters next, having shuffled faster than anyone else to the entrance. Lipstick-stained cigarette butts were piling up on the small step by the double doors. Percy wondered which one was Queenie's.

Hopton Holiday Camp, sited on top of Gorleston's southern cliffs, was never derequisitioned from the War Office after the Second World War. The two large guns, covered with preserving grease, were never dismantled. Tufts of grass sprouted through the surface of the tennis courts. For years doors and windows banged eerily in the dilapidated bungalows. Surrounded by high walls and rusting barbed wire, the camp slowly crumbled into the sea as the cliffs were eroded and collapsed.

After 36 years Elmhurst Court Holiday Camp, once the pride of Gorleston with a ballroom and swimming pool, was closed, too. In September 1975 the bulldozers moved in, flattening the chalets and dining hall, the shops and washing facilities, to make way for two hundred and fifty homes. The ballroom's wooden floor was divided up between Hethersett Social Club and a large house in Hatfield, Hertfordshire.

Once, to this quite resort, on the far side of Yarmouth harbour, hundreds of families came summer after summer from London, the Midlands and from East Anglia. Elmhurst Court was the last holiday camp to close. No one came here on holiday any more.

Thunder rumbled in the distance, miles away, as the coffin slid behind the purple velvet curtain and into the furnace. The assembled mourners, subdued by having to be quiet for the short service, shuddered together. John Conway, whom Percy found himself sitting next to, lurched forward, as if he had been asleep. Once the thunder died down Percy was sure he could hear the roar of the flames over the piped organ music. The sisters on the front row dabbed at their eyes with handkerchiefs. It was the first sign of sorrow he had seen them express. And he, too, began to feel mournful for the frail old woman who was for so long frightened of going outside. She was not like the other sisters. He began to wonder why. He began to wonder what might have happened to her.

There was some confusion getting outside. Fat drops of rain had started to fall. Some of the sisters, Toots and Cassie, hesitated by the chapel entrance, not wishing to get their hair wet. Queenie emerged, looked at the sky, her huddled sisters, then stepped into the rain. A man ran over with an umbrella and held it over her. She smiled sweetly, coyly, as if she had known he would do just that. Percy wasn't sure what to do next. He hadn't exchanged a word with Queenie yet. He didn't know whether he should go on to the party, for drinks and the great spread. He didn't know where Keith and his family lived.

'I wonder who that is talking to Queenie?' It was Toots. She had found an umbrella and she had found Percy. 'He looks a bit young, still if it cheers her up.' She said it in a pleasant enough way, as if she really meant it. And Percy was surprised she had called Queenie Queenie and not Elizabeth. It was as if they had patched up their differences.

As if she were accepting her younger sister, the way her younger sister behaved. Toots looked around. 'There hasn't been such a large turn-out since the old boy went.'

'Who?'

'Oh, Neville, Queenie's husband. That was a truly black day.' She blinked. 'We all wore black, even Queenie, nothing but black. It didn't do much good. It was all too late, I suppose.' The rain began to come down harder and Percy found himself sharing Toots's umbrella. 'I miss the old boy. He had a time of it. And then the end. It was terrible. You see I never realised. I never realised quite how much I meant to him.'

Meant to him, Percy repeated her words to himself. How much I meant to him. Surely she didn't mean it. 'What?' he almost shouted. They both had a hand clasped to the thin metal stem of the umbrella. He could feel her little finger rubbing against his thumb. He looked at her and saw a tear rolling down her cheek, though it could have been a drop of rain. 'What did you say?'

But Toots changed the subject. 'Poppy, God bless her, she was a wise old bird. Though she was never the same after her breakdown. I'm not going to blame that on Queenie. There's no point in dwelling on the past.' Percy was reminded of Queenie, Queenie's favourite saying. The rain was cascading off the umbrella, and he felt Toots press against him. 'Well, we've found Poppy a nice spot among some young pine trees, over there.' She pointed to the Garden of Remembrance, thick with rain. 'I must say it was very reasonable. I expect I'll see you at Keith's.' She hurried off towards a large group of people sheltering by the chimney.

Feeling suddenly very lonely but determined, Percy walked over to Queenie. She was still chatting to the man who had rushed across with the umbrella. They were now sharing the umbrella. 'Hello,' he said, touching her elbow.

She turned and looked at him quizzically. He thought for a moment that she wasn't sure who he was. That she didn't recognise him.

'Excuse me,' she said to the man, stepping away from him and the umbrella. She then smiled at Percy. He could have kissed her, then and there, in the rain, by the crematorium's fancy chimney. Puddles were forming on the blackening forecourt. 'Well,' she said, 'what a surprise.' Her smile disappeared from her face and she dabbed her bright eyes with a crumpled white handkerchief she must have been holding in her hand. 'Nice to see you, dear.' The man, who had been hovering in the background, perhaps waiting to be introduced, wandered off.

'I'm so very sorry,' Percy said. He couldn't think of anything else to say.

'Sorry about what, dear?'

'Poppy.'

'Oh, yes, yes. Well, there you go. It can't be helped.' She looked over her shoulder, Percy was sure, to see if the man was still there. She quickly turned back. 'We're going to bury Poppy's remains. We've bought a lovely little spot for her. It was very reasonable, you know. Are you coming to watch?'

The group clustered around a small hole in the wet grass. Percy watched as Keith struggled to drop the pale wood or plastic casket, he couldn't tell which, into the hole. There was a squelch as it hit the bottom. Keith then shovelled the first clod onto the casket. Percy could see Toots and Queenie kick at the small mound of soil beside the hole, trying to flick some dirt onto the casket as well. It looked like an involuntary gesture. When the hole was filled a plaque was produced and Keith stuck it into the ground. It was white and already covered in mud. Pop, Percy could read, n ovin ory.

* * *

Later, Linda told Percy that no one knew where Poppy's husband was buried, or if, even, he was dead. Though she said Queenie's husband, or at least his ashes, were in the Garden of Remembrance. But she didn't think Queenie visited the spot very often.

Percy followed the limousines out of the Garden of Remembrance, the plaques now abandoned in the rain. There were fresh flowers strewn here and there. The Cavalier's windows soon steamed up. He had to wipe the windscreen with his sleeve to see the backs of the heads of Queenie and her remaining sisters in the limousine in front. They were all sitting on the back seat. Doris and Cassie were in the middle, sandwiched between their more colourful sisters. Toots's hair, remarkably he thought, was still plumed and livid, Queenie's glowing with fresh vigour. The colours glistening in the rain-drops sliding down the limousine's rear windscreen. Percy had decided to follow Queenie, to follow the sisters as best he could. He felt he couldn't just go home.

He could see in his rearview mirror Burt and Linda's vast American car. And he could see there were many, many cars behind that, winding their way through Gorleston, which was wet and deserted. No people, no dogs, no gulls, just the splash of cars coasting through puddles. The rain eased as they neared Keith's, the convoy eventually stopping by the Meadow Court housing development near the golf course. Keith's house was low, but not quite a bungalow. It sprawled around a neat forecourt, cobbled with red stones. There was a small fountain in the middle from which a wavering column of water limply rose a few inches, before collapsing in on itself. Percy managed to park just a few houses away. He climbed out and looked heavenward. The sky to the east, over the North Sea, was clearing. The air was fresher. There was a slight breeze. He noticed a young woman was looking at him abstractedly, from the front window of the house he had parked in front of. She looked as if she had been looking out of the window for some time. She did not stir.

Much noise was already coming from Keith's house. There was chatter, laughing, and Percy thought he could hear music. The heavy front door was wide open. Keith's wife Susie was standing just inside the hall talking to a cluster of old women. Percy could see she had reapplied her lipstick. Her lips were bright red. He could see she was older than Linda, and more made-up. The tight blonde curls were dyed, streaked quite white. He introduced himself, saying he was a friend of the family, and that he had been a neighbour of Poppy's.

'Ever so pleased to meet you then.' Her voice was shrill, her accent not from Gorleston, or even East Anglia. Surrey, he thought. 'Go and get stuck in.'

The house smelt of air freshener. He followed the hall until it brought him to the lounge. It was a large room and the floor had been sunk a few steps and carpeted light blue. People were standing around the edges, seemingly afraid to step down. He scanned the room. A painting of a young girl with a large tear rolling down her cheek hung above the raw-brick fireplace. A log was waiting to be lit. In the middle of the room a smoked-glass coffee table supported an array of trays overloaded with food. He couldn't see Queenie, but Cassie was helping herself to a handful of nuts from the coffee table. He was conscious of his suit. He could smell it, the dampness, the staleness, the sweetness. But he stepped down and walked over. 'Hello,' he said.

'Hello.' Her mouth was full of half-chewed peanuts. He felt a fleck of nut hit him on the cheek. 'What a lovely service. Wasn't it moving?'

Percy agreed. He didn't know why. The service had been

so quick he had barely noticed it, just the roar of the flames at the end.

'It was most considerate of you two boys to come.' Her round face beamed. John had joined them. He was holding two glasses and a bottle of Soave. He offered Percy his glass and went off to find another. 'I've had a wonderful summer,' she said, her eyes trailing John. 'Simply wonderful. And it's all thanks to you.' Percy felt himself blush. 'I am sorry,' she then said, looking over his shoulder.

Percy turned to see Queenie walk into the room with the man who had held an umbrella over her earlier. He was tall and thin and looked much younger than her. His dark hair was swept back, his hairline handsomely receding. They were both smoking. They lingered on the top step, for what Percy thought was ages, before descending in a smoky haze to the light blue plushness of the lounge proper. He suddenly felt faint.

'I am sorry we haven't seen more of you this summer. My, it seems to have gone in a flash.'

Percy was not listening to what Cassie was saying. He thought he knew what was really going on.

He didn't last much longer. Feeling faint and sick and terribly tired, he managed to speak to Queenie, once she'd stopped talking to the man. He told her he was going home to lie down. She said that that sounded like a good idea. She did say she would telephone him within the next few days to hear if he was feeling better. But he didn't know whether she would or not. He squeezed her arm and then walked away, leaving her with Doris and Cassie and Toots and Linda, Burt even, and Charlie and John. Everyone that really mattered.

A painting of a racing car hung on the hall wall. It was in an ornate, gilt frame. Percy hadn't noticed it on the way in. The racing car was bright red, the same shade as

Susie's lipstick, he thought. But it was all much of a blur. He walked to his car and saw that the young woman was still staring out of her window. He looked at her. She looked right through him. He felt sorry for her and he felt sorry for himself. As he was turning his car round Meadow Court, Keith's fat son shot past on a bicycle, swerving to miss his reversing car.

'Wanker,' the boy shouted over his shoulder as he peddled out of Meadow Court and into Warren Lane, bright and green and leafy after the storm.

14

Queenie was forever thinking about the next thing. Wanting to get on with the next thing. And it could be anything, from the next cigarette to the next trip to the High Street, the next lover even. She was never satisfied. Constantly on the move. Staving off boredom. She could not accept that nothing ever changed here. And she was right, of course. Everything was always changing in Gorleston-on-Sea, whether she had anything to do with it or not.

Percy felt the first chill airs of autumn, floating in off the sea in gentle waves. Autumn arrived here in August, though some would say it was always autumn, dank and heavy and melancholy. Elizabeth used to say so, anyway. He looked out to sea and the rising sun, faint behind a bank of cloud. Oh, how many times had he looked out to sea, trying to forget? In reality trying to remember. He was confused. But he wasn't going to give up. Not yet. He had never been one to give up. Besides, Queenie had rung, she hadn't asked him if he was feeling better, but she had asked him out to lunch. Her voice was as bright as ever. Still, he thought, she means everything. There was nothing to worry about. Nothing at all. He knew he should just calm down. Look at the sea quietly like he used to.

The beach was already busy with people, as if they too

could feel the onset of autumn, but weren't quite ready to give up the summer, now dying peacefully in a grey haze. Some people were strolling along the water's edge, zigzagging to avoid the lazy waves. Dogs lagged behind with great planks of weathered wood. Other people, the less able, were seated on deck-chairs, reading newspapers, playing in the sand with their feet, drinking tea from Thermos flasks. And there were people ambling along the pier, throwing bread to the gulls and talking to the fishermen, many of whom had been there all night. The horizon was busy too, with ships eager to enter port and unload their cargoes. Percy could discern a pilot boat, no, two pilot boats, bright and orange, tearing out of the harbour-mouth to meet the ships. He watched them go, bouncing along the dull sea, now and then lost behind a sheet of spray. He looked down and there was the Pilots hut, dark blue and sombre. He looked away, trying to convince himself it was not important. But however hard he tried not to think about it, its colour, its shape, some little detail, the heart, even, with Q loves Charlie scratched beneath it, would seep into his mind. Dark blue and confusing. And he would try to be rational about it, try to think of reasons, causes, justifications. Accidents happened. Some people wanted to die. But he thought of not just Queenie's husband's death, but also Poppy's and his wife's. Poppy, well she had suddenly struggled against the end. But he thought Elizabeth had in a way accelerated her death. He thought she had given up too easily, most uncharacteristically. He would have fought harder, he found himself thinking. There was just too much to lose. He thought about where he was now. The busy end of summer. He thought about loss.

He gazed across the grass to the houses of Marine Parade, his eyes happening to fall on Queenie's old house, the last house she had shared with her husband. The faded pink facade. A car was parked in the driveway. Percy wasn't sure but he thought it was a Rolls Royce, metallic gold perhaps. For a moment he wondered about their life together, Queenie and her husband. He just couldn't imagine Queenie married, Queenie being responsible, bringing up children. He just couldn't imagine it at all. A small child on a tricycle pedalled past, a woman trotting behind, holding reins attached to the child's back. 'Harry, Harry,' she was shouting. 'Slow down, slow down.' The little boy giggled, his legs working harder and harder. Percy stopped and watched them, the small boy pedalling madly, laughing, his mother reining him in. Protecting him. They disappeared into the distance.

Percy drove into town, parking at the lower end of Bells Road. He now always went into town after he had been to the cliff top. He liked to be surrounded by people, the bustle of shoppers, life. And he had noticed recently there was a strange sense of urgency in the High Street. People seemed to walk faster, bumping into each other more often, weighed down by heavy bags. They pushed and shoved their way in and out of the shops, the banks, the post office, the chemists. Though Yardley's Cafe was now emptier. Percy could always find a table. Condensation didn't drip down the windows and he could clearly see the people rush by outside. It was as though no one wanted to waste time drinking coffee and eating eclairs. Except himself. He would linger over two, sometimes three cups of coffee, and force down a couple of cakes. He didn't like the cakes, he never had, but Yardley's offered little else. And besides, Queenie had a sweet tooth, a penchant for the pink and creamy and puffy cakes. He somehow thought that by eating them he would be closer to her. He always kept an eye on the street. He was always on the look-out for her, and for anyone he knew, really. Sometimes he would rest his head in his hands, but never would he shut his eyes.

He strode up the High Street, trying to look purposeful.

Once he even trotted, imitating Queenie imitating Peggy, the donkey. But he felt a fool. He couldn't carry it off without her. He needed her to impress, to amuse. So he tried not to think of her or anything in particular, and he began to fill up mornings shopping again for things he didn't need. Often he would get to a cashier and decide he didn't want any of the things he had put in his basket. He would then turn round and diligently replace them on their right shelves. Cashiers and shop assistants began to recognise him. Some would even titter, while others gave him odd looks, but he didn't mind. He knew most people behaved strangely in Gorleston.

He would finish where he began, on Bells Road. He would always buy something from the butcher's, some bacon, some pork chops perhaps. In a way he thought of the butcher's as a shrine, for it was the first place he had spoken to Queenie. He had to pay homage here. He had to give a donation. And he would pop into the toy shop next door. His collection of plastic jokes, snakes, ants, dog turd, was growing daily. And like Queenie, he, too, stuffed them into a cupboard at home and forgot about them. But he didn't pretend to himself or anyone that they were for someone else. He had no grandchildren. He had no one. They were for himself. Queenie collected the cheap jokes, so why couldn't he? He knew she never sent them to her grandchildren because he had found them the morning he had been frantically searching for her. The morning he thought he had lost her.

Percy arrived early, nearly an hour early. He was far too excited to arrive any later. He parked in the Pier Hotel carpark, admiring the view it offered of Brush Quay and Yarmouth docks. It amazed him how rusty the ships seemed now. The rust, he thought, spread like a rash. He strolled around Gorleston's few amusements, peering in the windows, thick with whitewash notices announcing prices and prizes. The bingo hall was full and smoky. A man and a woman were drinking mugs of steaming tea or coffee or soup in the Seaside Cafe. They were sitting on separate tables, but it struck Percy how similar they both looked. They seemed of the same age. Both had thin white hair and both wore thick, black-framed glasses that swamped their aged, wrinkled faces. Percy watched them through the window. They would look up at each other now and then, careful not to catch the other person's eye. Neither of them were reading newspapers or anything, but playing with their spoons and packets of sugar and the tomato-shaped ketchup dispensers. They were waiting, like Percy, for a sign that everything was how it should be, how it was before.

Percy eventually made his way to the Pier Hotel and found a stool at the bar, which was empty except for himself and the barman. He drank two brandies and soda. The barman was young with untidy black hair and two earrings in one ear. He said nothing to Percy, going about his job with great weariness. Percy would have offered to buy him a drink if he had shown a little more willingness, a little more life. Music was playing in the background. Crackling quietly. Percy hadn't noticed it until Queenie appeared, trotting, perhaps in time to the music, up to him. Her smell, her presence, suddenly overwhelmed him.

'I say, this place is full of life. Really swinging.' She pecked him on the cheek. 'What's up with him?' She pointed to the barman, who was propped against the far end of the bar, his eyes shut. 'Coo-ee, wake up,' she shouted. The barman slowly made his way to their end of the bar and Queenie ordered a sherry.

They remained at the bar for a while, Queenie discussing loudly the barman's manners, and manners in general. How people didn't know how to behave any more. Percy felt uncomfortable, not because she was berating the barman, but because she was avoiding his eyes. And in a way he felt shy. He didn't know what to say. It was as though he was meeting her alone for the first time, she talking loudly in an uncommitted way. If he caught her sea green eyes in the mirror behind the bar, between a bottle of Scotch and a bottle of vodka, she would look elsewhere. He drank two more brandies and soda, quickly, nervously, feeling slightly dizzy after the fourth. She began to tap a foot on the side of her bar-stool to the crackling music, or out of impatience. Perhaps they should eat, he suggested.

'I thought you'd never ask,' she replied.

They walked to the dining room, Percy, confused, thinking it was Queenie who had asked him to lunch. The dining room was bright and large. A few couples, mostly younger than them, were scattered about the other tables. They were shown to a table by a young girl with a large bust, who walked very slowly. Percy wasn't sure whether it was because she was tired or lazy or thought she had to walk slowly for old people. He remembered her from when he had been here for lunch with Toots and Charlie, which now seemed so long ago. When everything was different. They were seated by a window, Queenie looking into the room, Percy looking out over her shoulder to the yacht pond, fluttering with small sails, and the huts, gay in the distance. But he knew there was a dark one there, somewhere.

'This is very nice, I suppose,' she said, at last looking into his eyes. She had fond memories of the place, she told him, though it had obviously seen better days. She ran her fingers along the flowery plastic table cloth and shivered. 'It's bloody draughty here, dear.' He suggested they move. But she said no, it wasn't that bad. 'It's not as if we'll be here for long.'

He turned to see the waitress disappearing out of the dining room and into the kitchen, leaving a number of people with their hands waving uselessly in the fresh air.

He wanted to order the drinks, anything to be getting on with. He felt the ice hadn't yet broken. As soon as the waitress reappeared the hands shot up around the room, all waving, all trying to get her attention. They were served at last by another waitress. This one was thin and waif-like, though as languid in her dirty uniform. Queenie ordered the gammon with pineapple and told the waitress she had a charming uniform. When the girl turned to walk back to the kitchen Queenie stuck her tongue out and waggled it about.

The wine arrived, sweet and white, the way Queenie liked it. They both started to drink frantically and she began to tell Percy about the time when the Pier Hotel dining room was once the Bongo Bongo Beach Club, or something like that. 'We all used to dress up in grass skirts, even the boys. And we'd black ourselves up, too. I loved that bit.' She stuck her lips out, opened her eyes wide, and swayed her head, as if to a jungle rhythm. She asked the waitress if the music could be turned up. If they had anything more lively, anything more tropical. The waitress scowled and sloped off through the door that led to the empty bar.

By the time they were eating pudding Percy felt quite drunk and much less shy, talkative even. 'I'm really enjoying it here,' he told Queenie. 'I always enjoy myself when I see you. I wish I could see more of you.' He gave up with his pudding, leaving the spoon sunk into the lemon meringue pie, and reached across the table for Queenie's left hand. It was warm and sticky. He enveloped its smallness, running his fingers along to her veined wrist. The top of her hand was thick with freckles or liver spots, he wasn't sure which, he couldn't focus clearly. 'I suppose that's not possible. I suppose you're too bloody busy.' He immediately regretted saying it, but he had suddenly felt very angry. She didn't say anything. She just looked at him, blankly, then around the room. She pulled her hand away and fished her bag from the floor, the cream-coloured bag he had seen so often before. The one she had been carrying when he bumped into her at the butcher's. She snapped it open and took out her cigarettes. 'I'm sorry,' he said. 'Really. Truly. Can I?' He took a Consulate from her packet. 'I just feel very emotional.' He also felt very lonely. 'I just want to be with you.' The air filled with tobacco smoke, rich and sweet. He watched the smoke rise and form a cloud above their heads. It began to drift into the middle of the room, elongating, cirrus-like. 'Boom, boom.' He tried to impersonate a fog horn, the fog horn that sounded from Gorleston Pier and out over the North Sea. 'Boom. Boom.' He liked the way his voice reverberated in the charged air.

'You men are all the same. After one thing.'

He then felt like a naughty child, out to lunch with his grandmother. 'Boom,' he went yet again. The nearest couple looked up. The waif walked over, with more vigour this time. She stood at their table, sighed, and asked if they wanted coffee. 'Filter only,' she said in her squeaky voice. 'We'll have filter only, then,' Percy replied, imitating her squeaky voice. 'Filter only.' He started to laugh at himself, exhaling smoke with gusto, blowing it everywhere. He felt quite mad.

'You can never trust them.' Queenie looked at him, her brow furrowed, deeply furrowed. She lit another cigarette and put the packet away. She started moving about in her seat, brushing the sleeves of her jacket, as if she were about to stand up.

The man from a table nearby walked over. 'Excuse me, we're trying to eat.'

Queenie stood up. 'So?'

'Your smoke is blowing onto our table.'

Percy carried on puffing furiously. The man bent down and swiped the cigarette from his mouth, dropping it into his filter coffee. The waif, who had walked over, giggled.

Percy took a long sip of his coffee and calmly stood up. He really didn't know what he was doing. As the man turned to walk back to his table Queenie swung her handbag, catching him on the face with a loud slap. He turned to look at her, so small and fragile. 'You should know better,' he growled, before returning to his seat, his right ear and cheek turning quite ruby. His companion was staring out of the window, at the model yacht pond, as though nothing had happened.

'All the same,' Queenie was saying as they walked out of the dining room, quite unaware of the other diners staring at them, 'you men never can look after yourselves. You're always needing someone to help you along. It's pathetic.' They crossed the bar. Someone had turned the music up. Percy wanted to dance, bongo bongo. He tried to dance, clasping hold of Queenie's arm for support. He wiggled his tired, arthritic hips. 'Not now,' she said soberly, pulling herself away from him.

'Another time?'

She didn't answer.

They stepped into the soft late summer afternoon. 'Let's walk,' she said, grabbing hold of him and pulling him along.

The fresh air began to clear his head. He squinted. The sun had come out and was pouring over the cliffs and onto the calm sea. He felt himself being pulled along, towards the pier. They passed the concrete shelters. They were filled with old people sitting silently. Some were smoking, others were eating sandwiches. FUCK OFF was sprayed in large red letters by the entrance to the last shelter. The K dribbled into the O. 'Mindless,' Percy muttered, his head beginning to ache. He looked at Queenie. She was staring straight ahead. Her face taut, determined. On they went, the pier eerily empty. He looked from side to side, to Yarmouth, the docks, the power station, and to

Gorleston, the cliffs, the houses of Marine Parade stretched along the top in silhouette. Dark specks of people played on the beach. They passed the harbour-master's look-out, its radar blade swirling silently in the breeze, which was stiffening as they ventured further out to sea. They reached the end. Queenie motioned him towards her. She stepped to the side, by a gap in the railings.

'I am afraid,' her voice was harsh, almost unrecognisable, 'you men just never learn.'

Percy had forgotten what she was talking about. 'What?'

'Come here.' Her hair was being blown about, the curls whipping up like flames off her forehead, her jacket lapels flapping furiously.

'What?' He found it hard to hear in the breeze. She looked angry. The air seemed to turn suddenly leaden. He realised he might never see her again. 'It's over isn't it?' He heard his voice rush off, over the wind-blown sea.

'Come here,' she said, beckoning with her hand. She was now standing in the gap in the railings, smiling. He moved closer to her, so he too was in the gap. He looked over the edge and saw some steps leading down into the swaying sea, which was in the shade here and dark grey. 'Coo-ee,' she shrieked in his ear. He jumped, backwards into the railing, which he then clung onto with all his might. 'Men,' she said, laughing. 'Men.' And she brushed past him, waved at the harbour-master, who had stepped out onto his metal platform with a pair of binoculars, and set off at a trot towards Gorleston.

There have been many attempts to stop the scouring of Gorleston beach and the erosion of Gorleston cliffs. Groynes have proved largely ineffective as there is an insufficient west-east flow of sand for them to arrest. A rip-rap wall of large granite blocks was tested in front of the model yacht pond one winter. But the blocks soon started to disintegrate and it was thought the jagged edges were a hazard to children. Vandals uprooted young fir trees planted to stabilise the slopes of Gorleston cliffs.

Many other schemes have been suggested to save the beach, to save Gorleston. There was an idea to fill barges with concrete and sink them a few hundred yards offshore. A Dutch-made plastic drift-net, designed to slow the velocity of the in-coming tide, was considered. A local company even wanted to experiment with synthetic seaweed in a bid to counteract the erosion.

No one has ever truly understood why the sand and the chalk is washed out to sea, which is perhaps why no one has come up with an effective answer. The littoral drift, the new pier, the course of the River Yare, all manner of things have been blamed. Though it seems to matter little now, for the advancement of the North Sea here, over the decades and centuries, has been quite ruthless.

Percy remained clasped to the railings, not daring to look down at the swirling, moving sea. His heart was pounding, his hands moist. He looked up and out towards Holland. A ship was close by, huge and dark, looming upon him. Gulls raced above, their terrifying calls piercing his aching head. A halyard began to rattle against a metal mast. He struggled with his breath. The ship slunk past, easing itself between the piers. A couple of deck-hands, their overalls smeared with dirt and grease, waved at him, an old man clinging to the end of the pier. For a while he was in the ship's shadow. He shivered. Slowly, slowly, he began to inch his way back through the gap and onto the safety of the pier's cracked concrete. He saw the harbour-master surveying the horizon with his binoculars, oblivious to his predicament. He started to walk, numbed, towards the Pier Hotel. Gorleston Beach stretched out to his left in a light wash.

'Coo-ee.' Queenie popped out from behind the concrete shelters. She was grinning. Her face a mass of wrinkles. He stopped and looked at her. He felt he didn't know her. 'Hello, old boy.' Even her voice sounded strange. 'Do you think you could drive me home?' She said something about not knowing where her car was. But he wasn't listening properly. The unfamiliar voice blurred in his mind with the breeze that tickled his ears. His ears felt so itchy. He knew he shouldn't drive. He could taste the alcohol in his mouth. But he didn't care. He walked to the carpark and Queenie followed, chirping away in a sing-song voice. She hummed as he drove along Marine Parade, the large houses casting long shadows across the road. And then, they were outside her bungalow. She leapt out of the car, thanking him for everything. 'It was fun,' she called and waved just before she disappeared inside. He sat looking at her front door then the front garden next door. It was alive with action. The old woman, bent double, was clipping the edges of her tiny lawn. She hadn't looked up. The red plastic sails of the windmill were whizzing round, trilling.

15

Autumn started to affect Percy's joints. He felt them stiffening, aching. A dull rheumatic pain. One afternoon he sat at the kitchen table, Sandy and Mrs Yarren playing noisily nearby outside, and he tried to compose a letter to Queenie. He couldn't telephone her. He knew he would nervously jumble up his words. He knew he would not be able to say anything he really wanted to. He was hurt and upset, and not sure where he stood. But he knew one thing, he knew how much she still meant to him. And he wanted to tell her so. How much she had changed his life, his outlook. How thankful he was to her for that.

He couldn't comprehend life in Gorleston without her now. He didn't want to let her go. He started the letter Darling Queenie, then screwed up the piece of light-blue writing paper and started again with My Dear Queenie. He looked at the clock, then outside. The sky was largely overcast but sheets of sun still somehow managed to break through in smoky bands. You don't know how much you mean to me, he wrote. He hated writing letters and put his pen down. He got up and went to the toilet. He returned, picked up the pen and, feeling stronger, continued I feel most sad I have not seen or heard from you in the last two weeks. Are you ignoring me? I need to know. He was writing quickly now, passionately. I need to know what is happening. He supposed he did know, but he just didn't want to admit it. He looked at the sky again. Winter is approaching. We could go away on holiday, to somewhere warm. Anywhere. I have some savings I can cash in. You pick the place. You have changed Gorleston forever for me. I don't think – the phone rang. He couldn't ignore the ringing. He stiffly got up again and walked through to the hall.

'Hello, hello. Is that you, you dirty old man?' It was Toots, laughing.

Percy mumbled hello. He was still composing the letter in his head, still thinking of Queenie.

'Marvellous,' she said. 'I was beginning to get worried. I've been trying you for ages. You're never at home, Percy. Where on earth do you go to now?'

He wondered what she meant by now. He wondered whether she might know something.

'Anyway, now I've got you, you're not going to wriggle out of this one. There's something I simply must talk to you about. You've got to come over for dinner next week, Tuesday. Don't worry, Charlie will be here. I can't get rid of him.' She chuckled. 'Though he goes to bed early,' she whispered.

Percy didn't protest. He was tired but pleased to hear from her. He was now also convinced she knew everything. That she knew what Queenie was up to. He thought it would be typical of her to tell him. And he thought she'd probably try it on again, when Charlie had gone to bed. But he had to find out. He just had to know what Queenie was doing, where she was, who she was with, where he stood. She plagued his mind, many things plagued his mind. He put the receiver down and walked back to the kitchen. He screwed up the second sheet of writing paper, the one which started My Dear Queenie, and threw it into the bin below the sink. He knew then he would never send the letter, any letter. He looked up and out of the kitchen window. He felt giddy. Mrs Yarren and the dog had gone in, leaving their small garden littered with chewed toys and a couple of dirty bones. He imagined them napping together in a large armchair, the dog curled on Mrs Yarren's lap, both exhausted. The cloud was breaking up. The last traces of the sun started to flood the sky. Golden slivers. It was evening. And he felt like going out, to see what was left of the world.

He set off at dusk, Bately Avenue now sunk in a deep dreamy blue. Unusually, he felt he wasn't being watched. Only the small trees lining the pavement seemed to look down on him as he slowly passed, their thin branches hanging listlessly in the twilight air. He breathed deeply. The air tasted of the coming night, soft and sweet. He felt as if he were breathing the last few lungfuls. He turned into Bridge Road in time to see the sea calmly settling itself for the night. Lights started to flicker on the merging horizon, rigs and ships proclaiming themselves in the gentle darkness. And he thought of Yarmouth's amusements, the Golden Mile, surely ablaze now, frantic with end of season abandon.

A street lamp bathed the Links Hotel forecourt in yellow, a dull, doleful yellow. He hadn't noticed this before. The forecourt was empty. There were no cars or invalid carriages. And there were no dogs tied up outside. The pub's sign was not illuminated. The pub was in darkness. He looked at his watch. It was eight-thirty. He stood in the middle of the forecourt, looking about him, looking at the emptiness. He held out his hands, palms up, in the yellow light. For a while he studied the dark creases. He wasn't sure which one was his lifeline. He couldn't hear anything except himself breathe. He walked up to the entrance. A metal bar had been placed across the door and padlocked. It reminded him of the beach huts shut up for the winter, or for good. He couldn't think of anywhere else to go. He didn't want to go anywhere else. He was suddenly afraid of what else he might find. Slowly he moved out of the artificial light and into moonlight. He drifted back, past the bungalows of Buxton Avenue, Arnott Avenue, Bately Avenue, pale and still and sad. 'Where is everybody?' he heard himself saying aloud. His voice sounding hollow in the empty night. Percy didn't want to be alone.

Days later he slowed as he passed Poppy's old bungalow, his headlights picking out the rose garden which had grown dense with weeds, wilting now in the cold. Beyond, he thought he could see bare rooms through the bungalow's small leaded panes, the car's lights chequering the dusty interior walls. The bungalow had been left empty. He pulled into Brett Avenue, the road glistening with frost. He had never wanted to be alone. He had found Queenie just in time. She had helped him to forget Elizabeth, because he had felt unable to live without her. He wasn't deceiving himself. It hadn't all been easy. Elizabeth wasn't an easy person. But simply he had grown used to a feeling of completeness with her. A feeling of fullness, life, that was taken away from him after so long. Queenie had helped him fill the gap in her noisy, boisterous way. She had inspired him to carry on. And perhaps, he thought, his mind clearing and the icy road shining, I was swamped by her, the distraction. Was she just a distraction? he wondered. Was that all? Maybe, he thought, it is best to think of Queenie as that, to not think too much of her. For now he felt he could come to terms with the past, his pain, what he had really lost. What true loss meant.

Percy reached Toots and Charlie's slightly early, as he had intended. He parked a few yards before their bungalow, so they would not be able to see his car if they happened to part their pale-green blinds and look out. He then walked past the bungalow, keeping on the far side of the road, and along the narrow path at the end of Cliff Lane, sinking into the night. Clasping hold of the railing, he stopped at the top of the wooden steps that led down the crumbling cliff to the beach. There was a slight breeze, his face stung. He noticed that since he had last stood here, nearly a year ago, much more of Toots and Charlie's garden had dropped off. The ragged cliff edge was now in places just a few feet from the patio. Shutters now blocked the French windows, as though they were hiding from view the terrible vastness of the ravaging North Sea. Not afraid but suddenly unsure of his footing, his whereabouts, he looked up and around. The green and red lights of the harbour mouth were just visible in the distance. Beyond, a great arc of orange hovered over Yarmouth. The sky above him, nothing but blackness. His eyes swept back over the North Sea, discerning the odd twinkle in the softer darkness. He thought a mist might be rolling in. To his right, towards Hopton and Lowestoft, the chalky cliffs disappeared into the night. Below, the sea broke rhythmically, beautifully.

'Elizabeth,' Percy shouted into the new night. 'Elizabeth,' he screamed. The sound pierced the emptiness, and shot across the ruffled surface of the sea. A great wail, a great release. And later, much later, he heard a bell toll in reply.

Beyond Cliff Lane, beyond the beach, lies the parish of Newton, lost to the sea. The parish is clearly marked on a 13th-century ecclesiastical map. And the bells of Newton Church can be heard from time to time. But there is no other evidence of its existence.

Maybe more of Gorleston will be remembered. For now it is Gorleston that faces the sea. Gorleston that once struggled many miles inshore, a little town, perhaps called Garleston, built around the old Roman fortress of Garianonum on the swampy marshes of the River Yare. Shortly, so like Newton, Gorleston will be buried under the sea. The bells of St James's, St John's, St Mary's, St

Paul's and St Andrew's will toll listlessly in the littoral drift. Lest we forget.

Percy walked back up the narrow path, quite dark now. He was late. But he was still here. He might not have been. He might not have been here at all. He felt different. Light-headed. Was he really here? He squeezed onto Cliff Lane through two cars that were closely parked at the entrance to the path. There were a number of other cars crowded in at the end of the lane. He didn't think they had been here before. Their windscreens calmly reflected porch lights. But there was nobody about, only the sound of waves breaking. Toots and Charlie's bungalow was dimly lit, as though it were being modest about its size. He wondered for a moment whether he had the right evening. The dimness seemed unusual. He approached the bungalow, conscious of the noise his footsteps made on the fine gravel forecourt. He was no longer full of trepidation. He no longer minded what Toots had to say to him about Queenie. Or about anything. He realised that it didn't matter. He knew what mattered now, and only he could come to terms with it.

The satellite dish clung to the chimney, black and forbidding. A fog horn sounded, far, far away. He pressed the bell. Ding-dong it chimed, but still sounding shrill compared to the distant horn. Then there was just the resonance of breaking waves again. He pressed the bell a second time. The door suddenly flung open, bright light beamed out and a great, collective cry of 'coo-ee' hit him in the chest. He couldn't see anything for some time, blinded by the brilliance. He felt someone take his arm and lead him into the noise and heat and smoke and sweet-perfumed atmosphere of Toots and Charlie's bungalow. He felt a crush of people in the hall, their shapes slowly coming into focus. He was led into the lounge, his eyes stinging. They all seemed to be there and they started to sing Happy

Birthday. It was Linda who had led him inside and she was still holding his arm. Perhaps, he thought, to stop me escaping, not that he had yet decided where to run. Toots was leading the singing, waving her arms about her head, conducting, in the centre of the hot room. Her purple bouffant swaying violently. Party streamers hung around her neck in a tangled garland of colour. The others, too, were draped with party streamers and wearing funny party hats. Burt had on a small, pointy, gold one, the elastic strap cutting into his heavy cheeks. Cassie's was pink and had half a silver moon stuck onto the front. Doris was wearing a green paper affair and she was blowing a small plastic trumpet, trying to keep in time with the others, who were now singing 'For He's A Jolly Good Fellow'. John Conway was blowing his trumpet so hard blood vessels appeared to be breaking and spreading like cobwebs across his cheeks.

Linda wrapped some streamers around Percy's neck, smiling and laughing and singing the while. 'There,' she said, 'you look quite a picture.'

Charlie, beaming, handed Percy a glass of sparkling wine and slapped him on the back. 'Happy birthday, old boy,' he shouted above the din.

Percy had difficulty swallowing the sweet, bubbly liquid. His throat was so dry he thought it would crack. He felt choked with emotion, years, decades of feelings welling up. 'What a,' he started to say. Toots came up and kissed him wetly on the lips and pinched him on the arm, hard. The others cheered. He tried to hold Toots back. 'What a wonderful surprise. I, I had no idea. No idea you all knew.' He had forgotten it was his birthday. Indeed, he wasn't sure it actually was. Birthdays hadn't seemed important for a long while. He had no idea how old he was. Cassie then came up and kissed him too, but on the cheek. A dry, muted kiss. The others cheered again but not as loudly. He looked around the room, at the smiling faces and bright, party colours. He knew Queenie wouldn't be here. And he didn't care. For he had lost something far more important. He wanted to concentrate on Elizabeth at last. His Elizabeth. Not an occasional Elizabeth, not an unreal Elizabeth. Queenie wasn't an Elizabeth. He caught Doris' eye and smiled. He walked over, not knowing what else to do.

'Happy birthday,' she said, her green hat askew. She then shuffled closer and lowered her voice. 'I'm sorry we couldn't all come, dear, but this was as much of a surprise for all of us.' She tried to straighten her hat, perhaps trying to look more serious. 'I'm not sure what to say, or whether I can be of any help.'

Percy looked over her shoulder, at the print of the horse and cart crossing a ford. The splendid blue of the stream struck him as something clear, something refreshing. He was hot and he wanted to step in it and paddle about. 'Oh, I'm sure it's for the best,' he found himself saying, almost cheerfully. 'I've learnt many things over the last year. You can't ignore the past. You can't forget what's really important.' It's always there, he thought, however hard you try to hide it. He looked at Doris, wise and old, and whispered, 'Some things last forever. Some things – places, people, memories, love.'

'Now, dear, don't you worry about things like that. We all get carried away from time to time. I was once in love, but that was a long time ago, a long, long time ago. You get over it.' She sighed.

And Percy was sure her eyes began to fill with tears. She suddenly looked so small and frail. She looked like Poppy. He looked away.

'It's not that she wants to hurt people, she doesn't know any better.'

Percy knew who she was talking about. She was talking about Queenie and he was thinking of Elizabeth. But it didn't concern him that she hadn't understood anything he was trying to say. He understood himself.

'Oh, I've tried to talk to her, countless times, as did Poppy. But I don't think it has ever done any good. After a while I think she gave up listening.' She breathed deeply.

Percy heard the smoky air fill her fragile chest, the creak of old ribs.

'She was the youngest and very pretty. When she grew up we were all jealous of her. Particularly Toots, but that's another story.'

Charlie refilled Percy's glass with great enthusiasm. The sparkling wine frothed up, reminding Percy for a moment of Cassie, and started to dribble down the sides of his glass. 'Drink up, drink up,' Charlie beamed. 'The garden's nearly all gone, it's only a matter of weeks before the bungalow breaks up and we start to go over. Drink, for there's no tomorrow.' He rolled his eyes, the way he used to, then wandered off, big and still strong. He's survived, thought Percy. He survived until the end.

'The only time I've seen her deeply upset,' Doris continued, quietly, 'was when her husband died. I know what people say about her running off afterwards with so-and-so, but it affected her deeply. She's not got over it. You must have heard the story of how he was found in the beach hut, frozen solid, with an empty bottle of Scotch, and the letter. She could have coped with the death, the manner of it, losing him, but it was the letter from Toots that really got to her. You see she had no idea. Something like that had never happened to her before. She had always had things her way. She never believed she would lose anyone, not that way. She still goes there, to the hut, I'm told, looking for I don't know what.'

At that moment Toots sprung up between them. 'It's not a wake, you two. It's a birthday party. It's Percy's night. There's plenty of food and drink. How are you both for drinks? Come on Percy, you must be ravenous.' She started to lead him away. 'Now I've got you all to myself,' she said loudly, on their way to the food tray.

Percy picked up a cheese straw. It was dry and crumbly and he wasn't in the slightest bit hungry. His lucidity was fading. He was sure the sea mist was seeping into Toots and Charlie's bungalow. He felt immensely tired. He didn't want to hear any more about Queenie, or any of the sisters. He had heard enough. He fumbled with another cheese straw, not caring what she might say. He had had enough here.

'Stop playing with that blasted thing.' She snatched the cheese straw from his hand and threw it to the floor. It crumbled into the fawn carpet. She laughed. 'Charlie does all the food, you know. He's got no imagination, look at this stuff. No imagination at all.'

He could see Charlie across the room. He had done something to his paper hat. It was purple and shaped like a plume. He was imitating Toots on his own quietly in the corner. Percy started to chuckle, then Toots grabbed his hand. She tightened her grip and he felt her hand was covered in crumbs. She bent closer.

'You don't want to listen to everything Doris says. She's getting on, you know. She confuses things. She has no sense of time. Lost it ages ago.'

He could see Charlie nodding his head from side to side in the distance. He couldn't help himself picking up another cheese straw from the tray with his spare hand. He crumbled it into his mouth.

'You're not paying attention, are you?' She started to slap him around the head playfully. 'She's losing her mind.' She pursed her lips and winked. Charlie's paper plume was collapsing. 'We all make mistakes,' she said, suddenly, seriously.

'Yes,' Percy muttered. He felt if he replied she might go away.

'I made the same mistake as your wife once. We all did, I suppose. We all fell for Christopher Mellon.' She looked at him, sweetly, innocently. 'Though of course, she stuck with him. He only had eyes for her.'

'No, no.' He turned away. He pulled his hand from Toots's grasp. He stumbled into Linda, his elbow sinking into her bosom. 'I'm sorry, I'm sorry,' he said, panicked. He looked at her, her youthful face. It seemed to distort into a grotesque mask. He looked elsewhere. But everywhere people's faces were distorting. Doris's face elongated, her mouth dropping open to reveal a blood-red tongue. Cassie's cheeks began to puff up. They grew huge and dark, and her eyes sank deeper and deeper into her skull, until they were two red dots burning in the centre of her head. The room began to pulse, shrinking and then enlarging. 'I need fresh air, I need fresh air,' he shouted. He wanted to be outside. Far away.

He tore down Cliff Lane, the Cavalier rattling and bouncing over the pot-holes and sleeping policemen, shattering the quiet of night. It wasn't late but there were few lights on now. Most bungalows and chalets had shut up for the night, some until next year, and some forever. He thought of the North Sea, deep and dark and dangerous, eating away at the cliffs, the very foundations, chasing after him. He realised that Gorleston wasn't safe and quiet. That Gorleston was never really what he had thought it was.

Queenie's bungalow was ablaze with light, glowing once more in Yallop Avenue, Gorleston-on-Sea. A couple of cars were parked outside. But Percy didn't slow as he passed, curious no longer. Instead he pressed his foot hard on the accelerator. The tires screeched as he swung into Bately Avenue, and screeched again as he skidded to a stop outside his home, pale in the fake dawn of a street lamp. He rushed inside, leaving the car unlocked and blocking Mrs Yarren's small driveway. He didn't care. He felt he had cared too much. He fumbled for his house keys, quite sober, but shaking. He smashed into the hall stool, knocking the telephone onto the floor, and smashed into his bedroom door, knocking it back with a bang against the wall.

He would never find the small indentation where the handle sank into the plaster. He didn't even notice the bang, unlike Mrs Yarren and Sandy. The dog woke with a start and began to bark. Mrs Yarren was furious as she climbed out of her bed and into the freezing, salt-laden air, cursing Percy Lanchester as she pulled on her thick, pale-pink dressing gown. Sandy wanted to go outside. Sandy wanted to know what was going on. And so did she.

Percy fell to his knees by the small cupboard that had separated his and his wife's beds. He had remembered something. He had never really forgotten. He knew where it would be. He didn't know what he would do when he found it, though. Or how he would feel. He didn't want anything to change. He didn't want to change anything. But everything had now changed. Everything was not how he had wanted it to be at all. He couldn't help himself. He opened the cupboard door and frantically began to pull the contents out onto the bedroom floor, in the gloom. In his haste he hadn't switched on the bedroom light. Only light from the hall trickled into the room. But oddly it caught the photograph of Elizabeth on the dresser. She looked down at him, the whites of her far-away brown eyes glinting. It had started to rain, in the way it only does by the sea. Drops like sand were being blown against the bedroom window. And there on the dull floor was what he knew he would find. He had known it was there all along, but he had tried to forget. He had tried to dismiss it from his troubled mind. His failed marriage.

The book was small and thin. It had lain in the cupboard undisturbed since his wife had died. On the cover was a print of an old wooden pier. He couldn't read the title in the faint light. He picked the book up, so light, fragile even, it felt in his trembling hands, and he carried it carefully, hurriedly, into the hall. *Gorleston*. The letters were big and black. *By Christopher Mellon, Honorary Freeman of the County Borough of Gorleston*. He opened the cover. *For E.L.*, it stated simply at the top of the yellowing first page. Then there were a couple of lines of verse.

> Gorleston was Gorleston ere Yarmouth begun,
> and will be Gorleston when Yarmouth is gone.
> Anon

He turned the next page and started to read, standing, shaking in the hall, the rain still softly sweeping against the window.

There is no doubt Gorleston, on the west bank of the River Yare, was begun before Great Yarmouth. Evidence suggests Gorleston, or the ground on which Gorleston was built, was populated in palaeolithic times. Yarmouth is situated on land which did not rise out of the sea until after Christ was born, and it was not populated until the 11th century.

Sadly Gorleston will not be Gorleston when Yarmouth is gone, for Gorleston will be gone first. The North Sea, which created Yarmouth, is taking Gorleston away. Gorleston is crumbling into the North Sea. Indeed, one only has to take a walk along Cliff Lane to witness the destruction already taking place.

He laughed. He shook his head. Gorleston Cliffs, the beach, the groynes, the littoral drift, the erosion. It all came flooding back. His mind was awash with history, with geology, with places, people, memories. He knew all about the shifting mouth of the River Yare, the depth of the North Sea, Joas Johnson. Of course he did. How could he forget the Gorleston Psalter, the Jew killers, Captain Manby, Maystone the ferryman? His wife's passion.

He thought of Christopher Mellon. The last time he had seen him, at his wife's funeral. He was there, yes, hanging in the background. He hadn't even offered his condolences. How could he have? He presumed Mellon often visited her in St Andrew's churchyard, next to his beloved, ruined priory. Yes, Percy said to himself, they all knew, Toots, Queenie, Poppy, Cassie, Doris. Oh, she knew all right. He remembered the time when he had told Doris his wife's name and the way the smile had dropped from her face. Then he saw in his mind's eye Elizabeth crying in the Star Hotel, trying to hide her face behind the menu. She had been there with him. It was so obvious now. He saw Elizabeth, her pale cheeks, hanging out of the train waving goodbye to him so many years ago. She was on her way to Gorleston and to Christopher Mellon. And that was just the beginning.

Reading the small book brought back so much of his life he thought he had shared with Elizabeth. So much he had blocked out. And in a way it brought Elizabeth back to life. He could smell her, taste her, the salt behind her ears. Yet he no longer felt he knew her, not what she was really like. How could he, for she had loved someone else. He no longer felt he knew himself. He felt a great gap open up inside him. A great void. The void was a grey, a greeny-grey, the colour of the sea. He felt he was being enveloped by it.

His mind began to drift, roof high, through the clipped branches and crazy chimneys of the crescents and avenues, Yallop, Bately, Brett, along the verandas and balconies of Marine Parade, by the satellite dishes and fancy aerials of the new estates, Meadow Court, the Mariner's Compass. Over the great neatness that was lazy Gorleston. And he wondered what would happen now. Now autumn was here, now everything was different, now the orderliness had been disrupted. He wondered whether it might all have been an illusion.

The day was cloaked with mist and salt. It was ethereal. People floated through the haze, out on the cliff top or in the High Street, not noticing the fine rain that slowly covered them, enshrouded them. Dogs chased seagulls, hopelessly, pointlessly. The sea was muffled, making just a slight rustle as it reached the shore, the end of land.

Percy set off at last in the Vauxhall Cavalier, reliable as ever. The air, which was part sea of course, steamed up the windows, and slowly trickled onto the dashboard leaving a salty trail. He drove with great care and attention, wiping the inside of the windscreen with the back of his hand now and then, clearing his view. He didn't want to get lost. Not yet. Though it was a short drive, a drive he had undertaken a thousand times, it was misty, so misty. He pulled into the carpark, at the end of Marine Parade, at the end of Gorleston-on-Sea. He drove to the front, manoeuvring the car into a space, his usual space, and stopped just short of the upper esplanade. He turned the engine off. He sat and stared out into the nothingness. There was no sky and there was no sea. It was late morning. It was late November. He had wanted to see the sea. He was sad it was just grey. But he was not surprised.

He opened the car door, the salt stinging his eyes, his throat, and stiffly walked over to the cliff edge. The very edge of Gorleston. He saw nothing for a while in the perfect greyness, then the beach huts, a distant smear. The colours, pinks and blues and greens, washing into each other. He stood and watched and waited. Nothing moved. Stillness. He thought of the future, of an old woman with lank white hair falling over her shoulders, still skipping along, but quite lost and forgotten. The chimney of Yarmouth Power Station suddenly broke through the overwhelming cloud.

It looked numinous. He walked back to his car, which was anonymously, neatly lined up with all the other cars, as it always was. But he didn't recognise any of the faces peering out of the other cars any more. And he didn't recognise the old woman with lank white hair who brushed past him and hurried on down the cliff. He climbed back behind the wheel. He turned the ignition and smiled as the Cavalier trembled to life. He put the car into gear. He knew he could never go back.